OXFORD STUDEN

Series Editor: Steven Croft

John Webster
The Duchess of Malfi

Edited by Jackie Moore

Oxford University Press

OXFORD
UNIVERSITY PRESS

Great Clarendon Street, Oxford OX2 6DP

Oxford University Press is a department of the University of Oxford.
It furthers the University's objective of excellence in research, scholarship,
and education by publishing worldwide in

Oxford   New York

Auckland   Cape Town   Dar es Salaam   Hong Kong   Karachi
Kuala Lumpur   Madrid   Melbourne   Mexico City   Nairobi
New Delhi   Shanghai   Taipei   Toronto

With offices in

Argentina   Austria   Brazil   Chile   Czech Republic   France   Greece
Guatemala   Hungary   Italy   Japan   South Korea   Poland   Portugal
Singapore   Switzerland   Thailand   Turkey   Ukraine   Vietnam

Oxford is a registered trade mark of Oxford University Press
in the UK and in certain other countries

British Library Cataloguing in Publication Data
Data available

ISBN 978-0-19-832574-1

7 9 10 8

Typeset in Goudy Old Style MT
by Palimpsest Book Production Limited, Grangemouth, Stirlingshire

Printed in Great Britain by Clays Ltd., Bungay

Contents

Acknowledgements

The text of the play is taken from *John Webster: The Duchess of Malfi and Other Plays*, edited by René Weis (Oxford World's Classics, 1998).

'Whispers of Immortality' by T.S. Eliot is reprinted from *Collected Poems:1909–1962* (Faber & Faber, 2001), by permission of the publisher (page 222).

Acknowledgements from Jackie Moore

I would like to thank Steven Croft for his tactful and constant guidance; I am indebted to Jan Doorly for her intuitive and sensitive editing and for her warm support. I am grateful to my friend and colleague Paul Dean for his help in the research, and for many stimulating discussions. I would also like to thank Martin Cawte for his perceptive and informed pieces about the play, and for his suggestions about practical issues of drama. I also express my gratitude to all at OUP who have helped with this text.

This book is dedicated to my brilliant mentor at the University of Manchester, Leah Scragg, who showed me how to think.

Editors

Steven Croft, the series editor, holds degrees from Leeds and Sheffield universities. He has taught at secondary and tertiary level and is currently head of the Department of English and Humanities in a tertiary college. He has 25 years' examining experience at A level and is currently a Principal Examiner for English. He has written several books on teaching English at A level, and his publications for Oxford University Press include *Literature, Criticism and Style*, *Success in AQA Language and Literature* and *Exploring Language and Literature*.

Jackie Moore read English Language and Literature at the University of Manchester with Elizabethan and Jacobean drama as a special option. She was later awarded her doctorate in English Literature with Philosophy. After lecturing in literature in higher education, she moved to the secondary sector, becoming head of an English department. She is now an educational consultant and Senior Examiner in English Literature for national and international examinations, and is the author of several books on A level literature.

Foreword

Oxford Student Texts, under the founding editorship of Victor Lee, have established a reputation for presenting literary texts to students in both a scholarly and an accessible way. The new editions aim to build on this successful approach. They have been written to help students, particularly those studying English literature for AS or A level, to develop an increased understanding of their texts. Each volume in the series, which covers a selection of key poetry and drama texts, consists of four main sections which link together to provide an integrated approach to the study of the text.

The first part provides important background information about the writer, his or her times and the factors that played an important part in shaping the work. This discussion sets the work in context and explores some key contextual factors.

This section is followed by the poetry or play itself. The text is presented without accompanying notes so that students can engage with it on their own terms without the influence of secondary ideas. To encourage this approach, the Notes are placed in the third section, immediately following the text. The Notes provide explanations of particular words, phrases, images, allusions and so forth, to help students gain a full understanding of the text. They also raise questions or highlight particular issues or ideas which are important to consider when arriving at interpretations.

The fourth section, Interpretations, goes on to discuss a range of issues in more detail. This involves an examination of the influence of contextual factors as well as looking at such aspects as language and style, and various critical views or interpretations. A range of activities for students to carry out, together with discussions as to how these might be approached, are integrated into this section.

At the end of each volume there is a selection of Essay Questions, a Further Reading list and, where appropriate, a Glossary.

We hope you enjoy reading this text and working with these supporting materials, and wish you every success in your studies.

Steven Croft *Series Editor*

John Webster in Context

The life of John Webster

In 1666 the Great Fire of London destroyed much of the capital, and valuable historical information about city life and the lives of its inhabitants was lost. Not surprisingly, therefore, relatively little is known about the life of the dramatist John Webster.

Webster was probably born between 1578 and 1580, and he was most likely the eldest son as he was given his father's Christian name. Webster's family was increasingly prosperous; his father was a member of the prestigious Guild of Merchant Taylors, but made his money out of a successful coach- and wagon-building business. He sold coaches (a 'boom' business then) and also hired them out as theatre props; records show that one was used in a production of *The Duchess of Malfi*. At about the age of nine, John Webster would have been sent to the Merchant Taylors' School, a highly regarded establishment. The First Master, the respected Richard Mulcaster, established an excellent curriculum which unusually included a grounding in English; the boys also learned the art of acting, and the school troupe was much in demand by the nobility and for court and civic pageants. Here Webster would have gained his first taste of drama. His education was interrupted by an outbreak of the plague in 1593, but probably his father engaged private tutors to complete the boy's education.

Webster went on to study at the Inns of Court. He would first have entered an Inn of Chancery, then in 1598 it is recorded that Webster entered the Middle Temple. He might well have studied law, but the Inns did not solely train lawyers; for diligent scholars they were comparable educationally to Oxford and Cambridge, and for the less academic they operated as a type of finishing school. It is thought that he did not graduate, perhaps going into the office side of his father's business; his younger brother went into the building side.

However, Webster soon became involved in playwriting. He became part of the team employed to write plays for Philip Henslowe, an important figure in the theatrical world and the man who had built the Rose in 1587, and went on to build the Fortune and Hope theatres. Henslowe also had a share in the company known as the Admiral's Men; he employed most of the playwrights of the age, except William Shakespeare, to write for him.

Fortunately, Henslowe kept a diary which offers invaluable information about the theatre of the age, and in 1602 it is recorded that Webster and three colleagues – Anthony Munday, Michael Drayton and Thomas Middleton – were paid £5 to write a play for the stage. The payment was made whether the play was produced or not. This gave these writers the opportunity to develop their professional skills, and Webster soon began to write independently, contributing an Induction and some comic scenes for John Marston's play *The Malcontent* in 1604. He then collaborated with Thomas Dekker on *Westward Ho* in 1604, followed by other plays. In 1612 the first of his two great plays, *The White Devil*, was produced, and in 1614 *The Duchess of Malfi*, which received great acclaim. The high point of his literary life was probably the publication of two of his plays in 1623.

The success of *The Duchess of Malfi* was not repeated; his next play *The Devil's Law-Case*, produced in 1618, was not of the same quality. After his successful *Monuments of Honour*, 1624, which was a pageant promoted by the Guild of Merchant Taylors (Webster had claimed his right of entry in 1615), little more is known of his life. He had married in 1606, had several children, and probably died in 1633 or 1634.

Webster's society

Elizabeth I was monarch when Webster was born, but she died in 1603, and by prior agreement James I, already James VI of Scotland, succeeded to the English throne. The rule of the House of Tudor passed to the House of Stuart, and the crowns of England and Scotland were united for the first time.

The reign of James I is considered to have been in many respects successful; he was a strong, educated and cultured king. However, there were some problems which may well be referred to in *The Duchess of Malfi*. Traditionally, Scottish kings had had to be strong to combat the ambitions of their feudal lords, and James I brought this aggressive attitude with him to his English throne. He had been criticized for his ideas about monarchy in a document written by his former tutor George Buchanan, *De Jure Regni* ('About the Rule or Justice of the King'). This had explained that the role of the king was elective – he ruled by the consent of the lords and by the agreement of the people. James I had responded in his *True Lawe of Free Monarchies*, 1598, claiming the divine right of kings – the absolute power of the monarch on earth, since the king was answerable to God alone. The English nobles were, therefore, somewhat concerned when he succeeded to the throne.

There were persistent rumours that despite his marriage James I was homosexual, causing alarm as he promoted personal favourites such as Robert Carr and George Villiers to the Privy Council, the small group of nobles who helped in policy-making. These concerns may be indirectly presented in *The Duchess of Malfi*; the taste for absolute power may be criticized in the tyrannical rule of the Aragonian brothers, and there are suggestions of possible homosexuality in Duke Ferdinand and perhaps in the rather restricted sexuality of Antonio.

Religion presented another problem; the Pope had

James VI of Scotland succeeded to the English throne as James I in 1603

excommunicated Henry VIII, declaring that English Catholics should hold their first loyalties to Rome rather than to England. Elizabeth I had consolidated the Protestant Reformation, so her Catholic subjects' conflicts of loyalties continued. However, James I had married the Catholic Anne of Denmark, and he had also appointed two Catholic sympathizers, the Earl of Northumberland and Henry Howard, to important posts, so Catholics felt more confident of tolerance when he ascended the throne. But in 1604 at the Hampton Court Conference, the king was accused of being too sympathetic to this group, and then in 1605 the Catholic-led Gunpowder Plot to blow up Parliament was exposed. Later that year James I publicly declared his 'utter detestation' of Catholicism, and he re-introduced the so-called recusancy fines for those who refused to attend the Church of England. It may be assumed that the evil traits of the Aragonian brethren of *The Duchess of Malfi* satirize Catholicism at its worst.

Webster's theatre

London was at this time alive with energetic dramatists such as Shakespeare, Ben Jonson, Marston, Dekker, Middleton, Cyril Tourneur, John Ford and of course Webster himself. There were many public theatres, such as the Globe at Southwark; the Swan and the Rose, which also stood south of the river; the Fortune, the Theatre and the Curtain, which were built at Shoreditch; the Hope at Bankside; and the Red Bull at Clerkenwell. There were two private theatres: the Cockpit-in-Court at Drury Lane, and the best of all, the Blackfriars beside the Inns of Court, the only theatre within the city walls. Between 1590 and 1620 the theatre was at a peak; writers and actors were no longer impoverished and acting companies flourished. There were several adult male companies, often attached to a particular theatre in repertory. These included the company to which Shakespeare was closely linked, the Chamberlain's Men, which became the King's Men on the accession of James I; the company who acted *The Duchess of Malfi* (Globe/Blackfriars); the Admiral's Men (Fortune); and the Queen's Men.

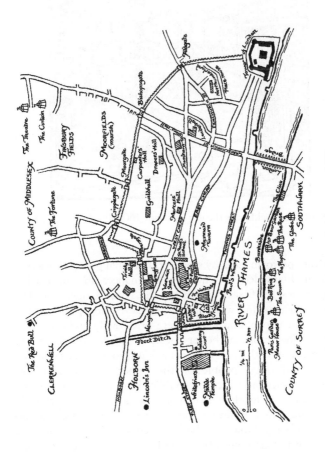

Webster's London: theatres and related venues around the city in 1600

Interior of the Blackfriar's theatre in about 1600

Private performances by small professional groups for a noble patron gradually led to public performances in purpose-built playing spaces, the first of which was the Theatre, opened in 1576. Quality varied; some were stages in bear-baiting pits, others in yards attached to public inns (where one rowdy audience rioted in 1591). The public at better theatres such as the Globe still included some of the noisy element, but also aristocrats, lawyers, courtiers and other people of the upper classes. You could compare a typical audience at a public theatre to a cross between the crowds at a football match and at a rock concert today; theatre-going was not always the decorous activity we may now regard it as being. However, the better-educated would have been familiar with stage conventions, with certain aspects of English history and international relations, would have picked up references and hints made by the dramatist, and knew how to listen. The Blackfriars Theatre had the most sophisticated audience of all; the queen herself attended a performance there.

Indirectly, Shakespeare helped Webster achieve recognition. Webster's first play, *The White Devil*, had been performed by the Queen's Men at the Red Bull and, disappointed with its reception, he called the audience 'asses' who preferred a 'new book' to a 'good book'. While Webster was finishing *The Duchess of Malfi*, Shakespeare's latest play *Henry VIII* was being staged at the Globe when cannon fire onstage caused the theatre to burn down. The King's Men, about to perform Webster's new play, had to move to the Blackfriars, ensuring the playwright a more discerning, sympathetic audience. They greatly approved of the tragedy.

Webster's tragedy and *The Duchess of Malfi*

Webster's approach to tragedy is complex and cannot readily be classified. He uses elements of several types of tragedy, rather than adopting one particular mode.

In Greek tragedy, such as that of Sophocles, man is seen to be entirely at the mercy of the gods, who determine the course of human lives. One fatal flaw (*hamartia*), usually pride (*hubris*), will send a man off on the wrong track; he will make a fatal mistake; later he will achieve the opposite of what he intended, and will then recognize the error of his ways. A hero will nobly face up to his fate. While the Duchess nobly endures her suffering, the play does not conform to a Greek model of tragedy.

Seneca, a Roman writer, adapted the work of his Greek predecessors to suggest a slightly different worldview. The finest quality one of Seneca's protagonists might display would be stoicism in the face of catastrophe – enduring calamity almost insensibly by suppressing emotion, through self-control and rationality. Characteristics of Senecan drama include violence and bloodshed (usually in the pursuit of revenge), rhetorical speeches, the display of wit, and the use of *sententiae* or moral sayings. Webster imported some of these characteristics into his drama, perhaps influenced by earlier revenge drama such as Thomas Kyd's *The Spanish Tragedy* (written in about 1589).

There are also references to medieval tragedy in the idea of the rise and inevitable fall of individuals as Fortune's wheel turns. References by several characters evoke this idea, such as the Duchess's

7

comment about blind Fortune in IV.ii.35–6. Four of the central characters may comply with the medieval theory of the humours: the four elements of which the human body was said to be composed (see Glossary, page 231). One of these elements was thought likely to be dominant, and determine an individual's character. Thus Bosola can be seen as melancholic; the Duchess as sanguine; Ferdinand as choleric; the Cardinal as phlegmatic. Throughout the play their behaviour conforms largely to these character types.

There is also evidence of Christian ideas of tragedy, which hinge on the doctrine of the Fortunate Fall – the original sin of disobedience to God being rectified by Christ's sacrifice on the cross to redeem mankind. If people were to repent of their sins, they could achieve forgiveness and joy in the life hereafter. Early criticism of *The Duchess of Malfi*, exemplified in the twentieth century by that of M.C. Bradbrook (see 'Critical Views', page 219), stressed this reading of the play through the persona of the Duchess, but nowadays it seems less prominent.

Finally, there is the influence of the genre of revenge tragedy, developed from Seneca's plays, and appearing in English drama through *The Spanish Tragedy*, for example. This genre has certain key characteristics: there will be one or more avengers; the setting will be 'exotic', for example Spain or Italy; there will be a central, discontented character who comments on the action; there will be intrigue, violence, and probably poisoning and death; there will be evidence of the use of disguise and of the supernatural. Webster's play has these characteristics, but it is not revenge that is central to Webster's concerns. His concerns seem to lie in moral and psychological issues and in assessing what he perceives to be the tragic condition of humankind.

Many in the first audiences may have held conflicting views about revenge. Although murder was against the laws of God and state, traditionally, private revenge would be tolerated in certain circumstances, such as avenging the death of a close relative, or acting on behalf of someone who would otherwise be helpless. There is evidence of many revenge killings at this period; James I became so concerned that on his accession he banned private duelling in 1603. There was a real conflict, therefore, between heart and head on this topic.

However, it is quite possible that Webster joined this debate by suggesting in his work the inappropriateness or even futility of revenge. If the brothers Ferdinand and the Cardinal are revengers, their actions are seen to be futile and they become victims in the mass slaughter of the fifth act. If Bosola is a revenger, then he may be seen to achieve little personally, dying with no hope of reward: 'Mine is another voyage' (V.v.105). It may be that Webster suggests the emptiness of the revenge act itself.

There is another aspect of the play which is centrally Jacobean: the presentation of a dark, satirical and pessimistic view of mankind presented in a combination of genres termed tragi-comedy. Jonson, in his comedy *Everyman in his Humour* (produced in 1598 with Shakespeare in the cast), offered a satirical, comic presentation of human vices, a new departure for English drama. Shortly after came Marston's play *The Malcontent*, in 1604. Marston complicated the conception of the revenger, making him more sophisticated than the one depicted by Kyd. The revenger also becomes a satirist, at times sufficiently detached from the action in which he is involved to comment on his society. Webster's Bosola clearly has his roots in Marston's Malevole.

The Duchess of Malfi is very different from Shakespearean tragedies. Here, no direct linear or narrative progression is evident on a first reading. Instead, Webster develops his ideas through an intricate web of repetition, parallelism, patterning and possibly a concentric structure. Webster uses a range of dramatic conventions including the morality play, and to distance the audience he uses rhetoric and formal *sententiae*. However, he blends these with extremely sensitive realism or naturalism, as in the private and intimate scenes between the Duchess and Antonio in Acts I–III.

The 'naturalism' or 'realism' of Webster's drama is in itself complex. Inga-Stina Ekeblad (see 'Critical Views', page 220), defines this as 'not how Webster copies life, but how he makes us accept as "real" the life he creates'. This is an extremely important definition; while the situations presented on stage would not be feasible in our open society, nevertheless they are logical and acceptable on stage as the products of the tyrannous society which engenders them.

To understand Webster's dramatic art you will need to read

the play carefully several times, working out the patterning so meticulously created. He works as a lawyer might, presenting similar evidence several times from different viewpoints. As a result of this technique there are many, extremely varied interpretations of *The Duchess of Malfi*, and you will no doubt join the ongoing discussion by making judgements of your own.

Sources for *The Duchess of Malfi*

Webster's drama is based loosely on an actual historical event: in 1510 the widowed Duchess of Amalfi wed her chief steward, Antonio Bologna. So to a limited extent *The Duchess of Malfi* is a history play; however, Webster goes far beyond a retelling of events as he offers a highly complex drama (see 'Interpretations' page 155).

Webster is not exactly non-judgemental, but he offers a compassionate and complex presentation of the universal human tragedy. There is perhaps a glimmer of hope for us all, but at the same time a warning that we have within us an essential madness, be it of love or hate, of overwhelming ambition or lust for power, which may spell disaster.

THE
TRAGEDY
OF THE DVTCHESSE
Of Malfy.

As it was Presented priuatly, at the Black-
Friers; and publiquely at the Globe, By the
Kings Maiesties Seruants.

The perfect and exact Coppy, with diuerse
things Printed, that the length of the Play would
not beare in the Presentment.

VVritten by *John Webster.*

Hora.——*Si quid*——
——*Candidus Imperti si non his vtere mecum.*

LONDON:

Printed by NICHOLAS OKES, for IOHN
WATERSON, and are to be sold at the
signe of the Crowne, in *Paules*
Church-yard, *1 6 2 3.*

Title page of the 1632 edition of the play

The Persons of the Play

The Duchess of Malfi	*R. Sharpe*
Cariola, *her waiting-woman*	*R. Pallant*
Ferdinand, Duke of Calabria, *her twin brother*	1. *R. Burbage*
	2. *J. Taylor*
The Cardinal of Aragon, *their elder brother*	1. *H. Condell*
	2. *R. Robinson*
Daniel de Bosola, *provisor of horse to the Duchess and retained as a spy by Ferdinand*	*J. Lowin*
Antonio Bologna, *steward of the household to the Duchess, later her husband*	1. *W. Ostler*
	2. *R. Benfield*
Delio, *his friend*	*J. Underwood*
Julia, *the Cardinal's mistress*	*J. Tomson*
Castruccio, *her aged husband*	
Old Lady, *a midwife*	
Marquis of Pescara, *a soldier*	*J. Rice*
Malateste, *a count*	
Silvio ⎫	*T. Pollard*
Roderigo ⎬ Lords	
Grisolan ⎭	
A Doctor	*R. Pallant*
Two Pilgrims	
Three Young Children	
Eight Madmen, an astrologer, a broker, a doctor, a farmer, a gentleman usher, a lawyer, a priest, a tailor	*N. Towley,* *J. Underwood*, etc.
Court Officers	
Executioners	
Ladies-in-waiting	
Attendants	
Servants	
Forobosco	*N. Towley*

Dedication

To the Right Honourable George Harding, Baron Berkeley of Berkeley Castle, and Knight of the Order of the Bath to the Illustrious Prince Charles.

My Noble Lord,

That I may present my excuse why, being a stranger to your 5
lordship, I offer this poem to your patronage, I plead this warrant: men who never saw the sea, yet desire to behold that regiment of waters, choose some eminent river to guide them thither, and make that, as it were, their conduct or postilion. By the like ingenious means has your fame arrived at my 10
knowledge, receiving it from some of worth who both in contemplation and practice owe to your honour their clearest service. I do not altogether look up at your title, the ancientest nobility being but a relic of time past, and the truest honour indeed being for a man to confer honour on himself, which 15
your learning strives to propagate and shall make you arrive at the dignity of a great example. I am confident this work is not unworthy your honour's perusal, for by such poems as this, poets have kissed the hands of great princes and drawn their gentle eyes to look down upon their sheets of paper when the 20
poets themselves were bound up in their winding sheets. The like courtesy from your lordship shall make you live in your grave and laurel spring out of it, when the ignorant scorners of the Muses (that like worms in libraries seem to live only to destroy learning) shall wither, neglected and forgotten. This 25
work and myself I humbly present to your approved censure, it being the utmost of my wishes to have your honourable self my weighty and perspicuous comment: which grace so done me, shall ever be acknowledged

By your Lordship's
in all duty and observance,
John Webster

Commendatory Verses

In the just worth of that well-deserver, Mr John
Webster, and upon this masterpiece of tragedy.

In this thou imitat'st one rich, and wise,
That sees his good deeds done before he dies;
As he by works, thou by this work of fame,   5
Hast well provided for thy living name.
To trust to others' honourings is worth's crime –
Thy monument is raised in thy life-time;
And 'tis most just; for every worthy man
Is his own marble, and his merit can   10
Cut him to any figure and express
More art than Death's cathedral palaces,
Where royal ashes keep their court. Thy note
Be ever plainness, 'tis the richest coat,
Thy epitaph only the title be –   15
Write, 'Duchess', that will fetch a tear for thee,
For who e'er saw this duchess live, and die,
That could get off under a bleeding eye?
                    In Tragediam.
Ut lux ex tenebris ictu percussa Tonantis,   20
Illa, ruina malis, claris fit vita poetis.
                              Thomas Middletonus,
                                    Poeta & Chron. Londinensis

To his friend, Mr John Webster, upon his
    Duchess of Malfi.   25

I never saw thy duchess till the day
That she was lively bodied in thy play;
Howe'er she answered her low-rated love,
Her brothers' anger did so fatal prove,

Yet my opinion is, she might speak more,   30
But never, in her life, so well before.
Wil. Rowley

To the reader of the author, and his *Duchess of Malfi.*

Crown him a poet, whom nor Rome, nor Greece,
Transcend in all theirs, for a masterpiece: 35
In which, whiles words and matter change, and men
Act one another, he, from whose clear pen
They all took life, to memory hath lent
A lasting fame, to raise his monument.
John Ford

Act I Scene I

[Enter Antonio and Delio]

DELIO You are welcome to your country, dear Antonio.
  You have been long in France, and you return
  A very formal Frenchman in your habit.
  How do you like the French court?

ANTONIO   I admire it;
  In seeking to reduce both state and people   5
  To a fixed order, their judicious king
  Begins at home: quits first his royal palace
  Of flattering sycophants, of dissolute
  And infamous persons, which he sweetly terms
  His Master's masterpiece, the work of heaven,   10
  Considering duly that a prince's court
  Is like a common fountain, whence should flow
  Pure silver drops in general; but if't chance
  Some cursed example poison 't near the head,
  Death, and diseases through the whole land spread.   15
  And what is't makes this blessèd government,
  But a most provident Council, who dare freely
  Inform him the corruption of the times?
  Though some o'th' court hold it presumption
  To instruct princes what they ought to do,   20
  It is a noble duty to inform them
  What they ought to foresee.
    [Enter Bosola]
                              Here comes Bosola,
  The only court-gall; yet I observe his railing
  Is not for simple love of piety;
  Indeed he rails at those things which he wants,   25
  Would be as lecherous, covetous, or proud,
  Bloody, or envious, as any man,

17

If he had means to be so.
    [*Enter Cardinal*]
                    Here's the Cardinal.
BOSOLA I do haunt you still.
CARDINAL   So.
BOSOLA   I have done you
   Better service than to be slighted thus.   30
   Miserable age, where only the reward,
   Of doing well, is the doing of it.
CARDINAL You enforce your merit too much.
BOSOLA I fell into the galleys in your service, where, for
   two years together, I wore two towels instead of a   35
   shirt, with a knot on the shoulder, after the fashion
   of a Roman mantle. Slighted thus? I will thrive some
   way: blackbirds fatten best in hard weather; why not
   I, in these dog-days?
CARDINAL Would you could become honest.   40
BOSOLA With all your divinity, do but direct me the way
   to it.
    [*Exit Cardinal*]
   I have known many travel far for it, and yet return as
   arrant knaves as they went forth, because they carried
   themselves always along with them. Are you gone?   45
   [*To Antonio and Delio*] Some fellows, they say, are
   possessed with the devil, but this great fellow were
   able to possess the greatest devil, and make him worse.
ANTONIO He hath denied thee some suit?
BOSOLA He and his brother are like plum-trees that grow   50
   crooked over standing pools; they are rich, and o'er-
   laden with fruit, but none but crows, pies, and caterpillars feed on them. Could I be one of their flattering
   panders, I would hang on their ears like a horse-leech
   till I were full, and then drop off. I pray leave me.   55
   Who would rely upon these miserable dependences,

in expectation to be advanced tomorrow? What creature ever fed worse than hoping Tantalus? Nor ever
died any man more fearfully than he that hoped for
a pardon. There are rewards for hawks, and dogs, and   60
(. . .), when they have done us service; but for a soldier,
that hazards his limbs in a battle, nothing but a kind
of geometry is his last supportation.
DELIO Geometry?
BOSOLA Ay, to hang in a fair pair of slings, take his latter   65
   swing in the world upon an honourable pair of
   crutches, from hospital to hospital; fare ye well, sir.
   And yet do not you scorn us, for places in the court
   are but like beds in the hospital, where this man's
   head lies at that man's foot, and so lower, and lower.   70
      [*Exit Bosola*]
DELIO I knew this fellow seven years in the galleys
   For a notorious murder, and 'twas thought
   The Cardinal suborned it; he was released
   By the French general, Gaston de Foix,
   When he recovered Naples.
ANTONIO   'Tis great pity   75
   He should be thus neglected. I have heard
   He's very valiant. This foul melancholy
   Will poison all his goodness, for, I'll tell you,
   If too immoderate sleep be truly said
   To be an inward rust unto the soul,   80
   It then doth follow want of action
   Breeds all black malcontents, and their close rearing,
   Like moths in cloth, do hurt for want of wearing.
      [*Enter Silvio, Castruccio, Roderigo, and Grisolan*]
DELIO The presence 'gins to fill. You promised me
   To make me the partaker of the natures   85
   Of some of your great courtiers.
ANTONIO   The Lord Cardinal's

And other strangers', that are now in court?
I shall.
    [*Enter Ferdinand*]
    Here comes the great Calabrian Duke.
FERDINAND Who took the ring oftenest?
SILVIO Antonio Bologna, my lord.   90
FERDINAND Our sister Duchess' great master of her
  household?
  Give him the jewel.
    [*Antonio receives the jewel*]
  When shall we leave this sportive action, and fall to
  action indeed?   95
CASTRUCCIO Methinks, my lord, you should not desire
  to go to war in person.
FERDINAND Now for some gravity. Why, my lord?
CASTRUCCIO It is fitting a soldier arise to be a prince,
  but not necessary a prince descend to be a captain.   100
FERDINAND No?
CASTRUCCIO No, my lord, he were far better do it by a
  deputy.
FERDINAND Why should he not as well sleep, or eat, by
  a deputy? This might take idle, offensive, and base   105
  office from him, whereas the other deprives him of
  honour.
CASTRUCCIO Believe my experience: that realm is never
  long in quiet, where the ruler is a soldier.
FERDINAND Thou told'st me thy wife could not endure   110
  fighting.
CASTRUCCIO True, my lord.
FERDINAND And of a jest she broke of a captain she
  met full of wounds: I have forgot it.
CASTRUCCIO She told him, my lord, he was a pitiful   115
  fellow, to lie, like the children of Israel, all in tents.
FERDINAND Why, there's a wit were able to undo all the

chirurgeons o' the city, for although gallants should
quarrel, and had drawn their weapons, and were ready
to go to it, yet her persuasions would make them put 120
up.

CASTRUCCIO That she would, my lord.

FERDINAND How do you like my Spanish jennet?

RODERIGO He is all fire.

FERDINAND I am of Pliny's opinion, I think he was 125
begot by the wind; he runs as if he were ballasted
with quicksilver.

SILVIO True, my lord, he reels from the tilt often.

RODERIGO *and* GRISOLAN Ha, ha, ha!

FERDINAND Why do you laugh? Methinks you that are 130
courtiers should be my touchwood, take fire, when I
give fire; that is, laugh when I laugh, were the subject
never so witty.

CASTRUCCIO True, my lord, I myself have heard a very
good jest, and have scorned to seem to have so silly 135
a wit as to understand it.

FERDINAND But I can laugh at your fool, my lord.

CASTRUCCIO He cannot speak, you know, but he makes
faces: my lady cannot abide him.

FERDINAND No? 140

CASTRUCCIO Nor endure to be in merry company, for
she says too much laughing, and too much company,
fills her too full of the wrinkle.

FERDINAND I would then have a mathematical instrument made for her face, that she might not laugh out 145
of compass. I shall shortly visit you at Milan, Lord
Silvio.

SILVIO Your grace shall arrive most welcome.

FERDINAND You are a good horseman, Antonio; you
have excellent riders in France; what do you think of 150
good horsemanship?

ANTONIO Nobly, my lord. As out of the Grecian horse
  issued many famous princes, so out of brave horse-
  manship arise the first sparks of growing resolution,
  that raise the mind to noble action.   155
FERDINAND You have bespoke it worthily.
    [*Enter Cardinal, Julia, Duchess, Cariola, with
    Attendants*]
SILVIO Your brother, the Lord Cardinal, and sister
  Duchess.
CARDINAL Are the galleys come about?
GRISOLAN They are, my lord.   160
FERDINAND Here's the Lord Silvio, is come to take his
  leave.
DELIO (*to Antonio*) Now, sir, your promise: what's that
    cardinal?
  I mean his temper? They say he's a brave fellow,
  Will play his five thousand crowns at tennis, dance,   165
  Court ladies, and one that hath fought single combats.
ANTONIO Some such flashes superficially hang on him,
  for form; but observe his inward character: he is a
  melancholy churchman. The spring in his face is
  nothing but the engendering of toads; where he is   170
  jealous of any man, he lays worse plots for them than
  ever was imposed on Hercules, for he strews in his way
  flatterers, panders, intelligencers, atheists, and a thousand such political monsters. He should have been
  Pope; but instead of coming to it by the primitive   175
  decency of the church, he did bestow bribes so largely,
  and so impudently, as if he would have carried it away
  without heaven's knowledge. Some good he hath done.
DELIO You have given too much of him. What's his
  brother?   180
ANTONIO The Duke there? A most perverse, and turbulent nature:

What appears in him mirth, is merely outside –
If he laugh heartily, it is to laugh
All honesty out of fashion.
DELIO   Twins?
ANTONIO   In quality:
He speaks with others' tongues, and hears men's suits   185
With others' ears; will seem to sleep o'th' bench
Only to entrap offenders in their answers;
Dooms men to death by information,
Rewards by hearsay.
DELIO   Then the law to him
Is like a foul black cobweb to a spider: 190
He makes it his dwelling, and a prison
To entangle those shall feed him.
ANTONIO   Most true.
He ne'er pays debts, unless they be shrewd turns,
And those he will confess that he doth owe.
Last: for his brother, there, the Cardinal,   195
They that do flatter him most say oracles
Hang at his lips; and verily I believe them,
For the devil speaks in them.
But for their sister, the right noble Duchess,
You never fixed your eye on three fair medals,   200
Cast in one figure, of so different temper.
For her discourse, it is so full of rapture,
You only will begin then to be sorry
When she doth end her speech; and wish, in wonder,
She held it less vainglory to talk much,   205
Than your penance to hear her. Whilst she speaks,
She throws upon a man so sweet a look,
That it were able raise one to a galliard
That lay in a dead palsy, and to dote
On that sweet countenance; but in that look   210
There speaketh so divine a continence

As cuts off all lascivious and vain hope.
Her days are practised in such noble virtue
That sure her nights, nay more, her very sleeps,
Are more in heaven than other ladies' shrifts.   215
Let all sweet ladies break their flatt'ring glasses,
And dress themselves in her.
DELIO   Fie, Antonio,
You play the wire-drawer with her commendations.
ANTONIO I'll case the picture up: only thus much –
All her particular worth grows to this sum: 220
She stains the time past, lights the time to come.
       [*Cariola joins Antonio and Delio*]
CARIOLA You must attend my lady, in the gallery,
Some half an hour hence.
ANTONIO I shall.
FERDINAND Sister, I have a suit to you.
DUCHESS   To me, sir?   225
FERDINAND A gentleman here, Daniel de Bosola:
One that was in the galleys.
DUCHESS   Yes, I know him.
FERDINAND A worthy fellow he's. Pray let me entreat for
The provisorship of your horse.
DUCHESS   Your knowledge of him
Commends him, and prefers him.
FERDINAND   Call him hither.   230
       [*Exit Attendant*]
We are now upon parting. Good Lord Silvio,
Do us commend to all our noble friends
At the leaguer.
SILVIO   Sir, I shall.
DUCHESS   You are for Milan?
SILVIO I am.
DUCHESS Bring the caroches; we'll bring you down to
       the haven.   235

[*Exeunt all except Cardinal and Ferdinand.*]
CARDINAL Be sure you entertain that Bosola
  For your intelligence. I would not be seen in't;
  And therefore many times I have slighted him
  When he did court our furtherance, as this morning.
FERDINAND Antonio, the great master of her house
      hold,   240
  Had been far fitter.
CARDINAL   You are deceived in him,
  His nature is too honest for such business.
     [*Enter Bosola.*]
  He comes: I'll leave you.
     [*Exit Cardinal*]
BOSOLA   I was lured to you.
FERDINAND My brother here, the Cardinal, could never
  Abide you.
BOSOLA   Never since he was in my debt.   245
FERDINAND Maybe some oblique character in your face
  Made him suspect you?
BOSOLA   Doth he study physiognomy?
  There's no more credit to be given to th'face
  Than to a sick man's urine, which some call
  The physician's whore, because she cozens him. 250
  He did suspect me wrongfully.
FERDINAND   For that
  You must give great men leave to take their times.
  Distrust doth cause us seldom be deceived;
  You see, the oft shaking of the cedar-tree
  Fastens it more at root.
BOSOLA   Yet take heed: 255
  For to suspect a friend unworthily
  Instructs him the next way to suspect you,
  And prompts him to deceive you.
FERDINAND   There's gold.

BOSOLA   So:
What follows? Never rained such show'rs as these
Without thunderbolts in the tail of them.   260
Whose throat must I cut?
FERDINAND Your inclination to shed blood rides post
Before my occasion to use you. I give you that
To live i'th' court, here, and observe the Duchess:
To note all the particulars of her 'haviour,   265
What suitors do solicit her for marriage
And whom she best affects: she's a young widow,
I would not have her marry again.
BOSOLA   No, sir?
FERDINAND Do not you ask the reason, but be satisfied
I say I would not.
BOSOLA   It seems you would create me   270
One of your familiars.
FERDINAND   Familiar! What's that?
BOSOLA Why, a very quaint invisible devil, in flesh:
An intelligencer.
FERDINAND   Such a kind of thriving thing
I would wish thee, and ere long thou may'st arrive
At a higher place by't.
BOSOLA   Take your devils   275
Which hell calls angels. These cursed gifts would make
You a corrupter, me an impudent traitor,
And should I take these they'd take me to hell.
FERDINAND Sir, I'll take nothing from you that I have
    given.
There is a place that I procured for you   280
This morning, the provisorship o'th' horse;
Have you heard on't?
BOSOLA   No.
FERDINAND   'Tis yours. Is't not worth
    thanks?

BOSOLA I would have you curse yourself now, that your
    bounty,
  Which makes men truly noble, e'er should make
  Me a villain. O, that to avoid ingratitude   285
  For the good deed you have done me, I must do
  All the ill man can invent. Thus the devil
  Candies all sins o'er; and what heaven terms vile,
  That names he complimental.
FERDINAND   Be yourself:
  Keep your old garb of melancholy; 'twill express   290
  You envy those that stand above your reach,
  Yet strive not to come near 'em. This will gain
  Access to private lodgings, where yourself
  May, like a politic dormouse –
BOSOLA   As I have seen some
  Feed in a lord's dish, half asleep, not seeming   295
  To listen to any talk; and yet these rogues
  Have cut his throat in a dream. What's my place?
  The provisorship o'th' horse? Say then my corruption
  Grew out of horse-dung. I am your creature.
FERDINAND Away.   300
BOSOLA Let good men, for good deeds, covet good fame,
  Since place and riches oft are bribes of shame;
  Sometimes the devil doth preach.
      Exit Bosola. [Enter Duchess and Cardinal]
CARDINAL We are to part from you; and your own
    discretion
  Must now be your director.
FERDINAND   You are a widow: 305
  You know already what man is, and therefore
  Let not youth, high promotion, eloquence –
CARDINAL No, nor anything without the addition,
    honour,
  Sway your high blood.

FERDINAND   Marry? They are most luxurious
  Will wed twice.
CARDINAL   O fie!
FERDINAND   Their livers are more spotted   310
  Than Laban's sheep.
DUCHESS   Diamonds are of most value,
  They say, that have passed through most jewellers'
    hands.
FERDINAND Whores, by that rule, are precious.
DUCHESS   Will you hear me?
  I'll never marry:
CARDINAL   So most widows say,
  But commonly that motion lasts no longer   315
  Than the turning of an hour-glass; the funeral sermon
  And it, end both together.
FERDINAND   Now hear me:
  You live in a rank pasture here, i'th' court;
  There is a kind of honey-dew that's deadly:
  'Twill poison your fame; look to't; be not cunning,   320
  For they whose faces do belie their hearts
  Are witches, ere they arrive at twenty years;
  Ay, and give the devil suck.
DUCHESS This is terrible good counsel.
FERDINAND Hypocrisy is woven of a fine small thread,   325
  Subtler than Vulcan's engine; yet, believe't,
  Your darkest actions, nay, your privat'st thoughts,
  Will come to light.
CARDINAL   You may flatter yourself,
  And take your own choice: privately be married
  Under the eaves of night.
FERDINAND   Think't the best voyage   330
  That e'er you made like the irregular crab,
  Which, though't goes backward, thinks that it goes
    right,

Because it goes its own way. But observe,
Such weddings may more properly be said
To be executed, than celebrated.   335
CARDINAL The marriage night
  Is the entrance into some prison.
FERDINAND   And those joys,
  Those lustful pleasures, are like heavy sleeps
  Which do fore-run man's mischief.
CARDINAL   Fare you well.
  Wisdom begins at the end: remember it.   340
        [*Exit Cardinal*]
DUCHESS I think this speech between you both was
        studied,
  It came so roundly off.
FERDINAND   You are my sister,
  This was my father's poniard: do you see?
  I'd be loth to see't look rusty, 'cause 'twas his.
  I would have you to give o'er these chargeable revels; 345
  A visor and a mask are whispering-rooms
  That were ne'er built for goodness: fare ye well:
  And women like that part which, like the lamprey,
  Hath ne'er a bone in't.
DUCHESS   Fie, sir!
FERDINAND   Nay,
  I mean the tongue: variety of courtship.   350
  What cannot a neat knave with a smooth tale
  Make a woman believe? Farewell, lusty widow.
        [*Exit Ferdinand*]
DUCHESS Shall this move me? If all my royal kindred
  Lay in my way unto this marriage,
  I'd make them my low footsteps; and even now,   355
  Even in this hate, as men in some great battles,
  By apprehending danger, have achieved
  Almost impossible actions (I have heard soldiers say so)

So I, through frights, and threatenings, will assay
This dangerous venture. Let old wives report   360
I winked and chose a husband. Cariola,
   [*Enter Cariola*]
To thy known secrecy I have given up
More than my life, my fame.
CARIOLA   Both shall be safe:
  For I'll conceal this secret from the world
  As warily as those that trade in poison   365
  Keep poison from their children.
DUCHESS   Thy protestation
  Is ingenious and hearty: I believe it.
  Is Antonio come?
CARIOLA   He attends you.
DUCHESS   Good dear soul,
  Leave me, but place thyself behind the arras,
  Where thou may'st overhear us. Wish me good speed   370
  For I am going into a wilderness,
  Where I shall find nor path, nor friendly clew
  To be my guide.
    [*Cariola withdraws behind the arras. Enter Antonio*]
            I sent for you: sit down,
  Take pen and ink, and write. Are you ready?
ANTONIO   Yes.
DUCHESS What did I say?
ANTONIO   That I should write somewhat.   375
DUCHESS O, I remember.
  After these triumphs, and this large expense,
  It's fit, like thrifty husbands, we inquire
  What's laid up for tomorrow.
ANTONIO So please your beauteous excellence.
DUCHESS   Beauteous?   380
  Indeed I thank you: I look young for your sake.
  You have ta'en my cares upon you.

ANTONIO   I'll fetch your grace
  The particulars of your revenue and expense.
DUCHESS O, you are an upright treasure; but you mistook,
  For when I said I meant to make inquiry   385
  What's laid up for tomorrow, I did mean
  What's laid up yonder for me.
ANTONIO   Where?
DUCHESS   In heaven.
  I am making my will, as 'tis fit princes should
  In perfect memory; and I pray, sir, tell me
  Were not one better make it smiling, thus,   390
  Than in deep groans, and terrible ghastly looks,
  As if the gifts we parted with procured
  That violent distraction?
ANTONIO   O, much better.
DUCHESS If I had a husband now, this care were quit;
  But I intend to make you overseer.   395
  What good deed shall we first remember? Say.
ANTONIO Begin with that first good deed began i'th' world
  After man's creation, the sacrament of marriage;
  I'd have you first provide for a good husband,
  Give him all.
DUCHESS   All?
ANTONIO   Yes, your excellent self.   400
DUCHESS In a winding sheet?
ANTONIO   In a couple.
DUCHESS Saint Winifred, that were a strange will!
ANTONIO 'Twere strange if there were no will in you To
  marry again.
DUCHESS   What do you think of marriage?
ANTONIO I take't, as those that deny purgatory: 405
  It locally contains or heaven or hell;
  There's no third place in't.
DUCHESS   How do you affect it?

ANTONIO My banishment, feeding my melancholy,
  Would often reason thus: –
DUCHESS   Pray let's hear it.
ANTONIO Say a man never marry, nor have children,   410
  What takes that from him? Only the bare name
  Of being a father, or the weak delight
  To see the little wanton ride a-cock-horse
  Upon a painted stick, or hear him chatter
  Like a taught starling.
DUCHESS   Fie, fie, what's all this?   415
  One of your eyes is bloodshot; use my ring to't,
  They say 'tis very sovereign: 'twas my wedding ring,
  And I did vow never to part with it,
  But to my second husband.
ANTONIO You have parted with it now.   420
DUCHESS Yes, to help your eyesight.
ANTONIO   You have made me
    stark blind.
DUCHESS How?
ANTONIO There is a saucy and ambitious devil
  Is dancing in this circle.
DUCHESS   Remove him.
ANTONIO   How?
DUCHESS There needs small conjuration, when your
    finger   425
  May do it: thus, is it fit?
    [*She puts her ring upon his finger*]. *He kneels*
ANTONIO   What said you?
DUCHESS   Sir,
  This goodly roof of yours is too low built;
  I cannot stand upright in't, nor discourse,
  Without I raise it higher: raise yourself,
  Or if you please, my hand to help you: so.   430
    [*Raises him*]

ANTONIO Ambition, madam, is a great man's madness,
   That is not kept in chains, and close-pent rooms,
   But in fair lightsome lodgings, and is girt
   With the wild noise of prattling visitants,
   Which makes it lunatic, beyond all cure.   435
   Conceive not I am so stupid but I aim
   Whereto your favours tend; but he's a fool
   That, being a-cold, would thrust his hands i'th' fire
   To warm them.
DUCHESS   So, now the ground's broke,
   You may discover what a wealthy mine   440
   I make you lord of.
ANTONIO   O, my unworthiness.
DUCHESS You were ill to sell yourself;
   This darkning of your worth is not like that
   Which tradesmen use i'th' city: their false lights
   Are to rid bad wares off; and I must tell you,   445
   If you will know where breathes a complete man
   (I speak it without flattery) turn your eyes
   And progress through yourself.
ANTONIO Were there nor heaven nor hell,
   I should be honest, I have long served virtue,   450
   And ne'er ta'en wages of her.
DUCHESS   Now she pays it.
   The misery of us that are born great:
   We are forced to woo, because none dare woo us;
   And as a tyrant doubles with his words,
   And fearfully equivocates, so we   455
   Are forced to express our violent passions
   In riddles, and in dreams, and leave the path
   Of simple virtue, which was never made
   To seem the thing it is not. Go, go brag
   You have left me heartless: mine is in your bosom,   460
   I hope 'twill multiply love there. You do tremble:

Make not your heart so dead a piece of flesh
To fear more than to love me. Sir, be confident;
What is't distracts you? This is flesh, and blood, sir;
'Tis not the figure cut in alabaster   465
Kneels at my husband's tomb. Awake, awake, man.
I do here put off all vain ceremony,
And only do appear to you a young widow
That claims you for her husband, and like a widow
I use but half a blush in't.
ANTONIO   Truth speak for me: 470
  I will remain the constant sanctuary
  Of your good name.
DUCHESS   I thank you, gentle love,
  And 'cause you shall not come to me in debt,
  Being now my steward, here upon your lips
  I sign your *Quietus est.*   475
      [*Kisses him*]
  This you should have begged now.
  I have seen children oft eat sweetmeats thus,
  As fearful to devour them too soon.
ANTONIO But for your brothers?
DUCHESS   Do not think of them.
  All discord, without this circumference,   480
  Is only to be pitied, and not feared;
  Yet, should they know it, time will easily
  Scatter the tempest.
ANTONIO   These words should be mine,
  And all the parts you have spoke, if some part of it
  Would not have savoured flattery.   485
DUCHESS Kneel.
      [*They kneel. Cariola comes from behind the arras*]
ANTONIO Hah?
DUCHESS Be not amazed, this woman's of my counsel.
  I have heard lawyers say, a contract in a chamber

Per verba de presenti is absolute marriage. 490
Bless, heaven, this sacred Gordian, which let violence
Never untwine.
ANTONIO And may our sweet affections, like the spheres,
Be still in motion.
DUCHESS   Quickening, and make
The like soft music. 495
ANTONIO That we may imitate the loving palms,
Best emblem of a peaceful marriage,
That ne'er bore fruit divided.
DUCHESS What can the church force more?
ANTONIO That Fortune may not know an accident, 500
Either of joy or sorrow, to divide
Our fixèd wishes.
DUCHESS   How can the church build faster?
We now are man and wife, and 'tis the church
That must but echo this. – Maid, stand apart –
I now am blind.
ANTONIO   What's your conceit in this? 505
DUCHESS I would have you lead your fortune by the hand,
Unto your marriage bed
(You speak in me this, for we now are one):
We'll only lie, and talk together, and plot
T'appease my humorous kindred; and if you please, 510
Like the old tale, in 'Alexander and Lodovic',
Lay a naked sword between us, keep us chaste.
O, let me shroud my blushes in your bosom,
Since 'tis the treasury of all my secrets.
    [*Exeunt Duchess and Antonio*]
CARIOLA Whether the spirit of greatness or of woman 515
Reign most in her, I know not, but it shows
A fearful madness; I owe her much of pity.
    [*Exit*]

Act II Scene I

[*Enter Bosola and Castruccio*]

BOSOLA You say you would fain be taken for an eminent courtier?

CASTRUCCIO 'Tis the very main of my ambition.

BOSOLA Let me see, you have a reasonable good face for't already, and your night-cap expresses your ears sufficient largely; I would have you learn to twirl the strings of your band with a good grace; and in a set speech, at th'end of every sentence, to hum, three or four times, or blow your nose, till it smart again, to recover your memory. When you come to be a president in criminal causes, if you smile upon a prisoner, hang him, but if you frown upon him and threaten him, let him be sure to 'scape the gallows.

CASTRUCCIO I would be a very merry president.

BOSOLA Do not sup o' nights, 'twill beget you an admirable wit.

CASTRUCCIO Rather it would make me have a good stomach to quarrel, for they say your roaring boys eat meat seldom, and that makes them so valiant. But how shall I know whether the people take me for an eminent fellow?

BOSOLA I will teach a trick to know it: give out you lie a-dying, and if you hear the common people curse you, be sure you are taken for one of the prime night-caps.

[*Enter an Old Lady*]

You come from painting now?

OLD LADY From what?

BOSOLA Why, from your scurvy face-physic. To behold thee not painted inclines somewhat near a miracle.

These, in thy face here, were deep ruts and foul sloughs   30
the last progress. There was a lady in France that,
having had the smallpox, flayed the skin off her face,
to make it more level; and whereas before she looked
like a nutmeg-grater, after she resembled an abortive
hedgehog.   35

OLD LADY Do you call this painting?

BOSOLA No, no, but careening of an old morphewed
lady, to make her disembogue again. There's rough-
cast phrase to your plastic.

OLD LADY It seems you are well acquainted with my   40
closet.

BOSOLA One would suspect it for a shop of witchcraft,
to find in it the fat of serpents, spawn of snakes, Jews'
spittle, and their young children's ordures, and all
these for the face. I would sooner eat a dead pigeon,   45
taken from the soles of the feet of one sick of the
plague, than kiss one of you fasting. Here are two of
you, whose sin of your youth is the very patrimony
of the physician, makes him renew his footcloth with
the spring and change his high-prized courtezan with   50
the fall of the leaf: I do wonder you do not loathe
yourselves. Observe my meditation now:
What thing is in this outward form of man
To be beloved? We account it ominous
If nature do produce a colt, or lamb,   55
A fawn, or goat, in any limb resembling
A man; and fly from't as a prodigy.
Man stands amazed to see his deformity
In any other creature but himself.
But in our own flesh, though we bear diseases   60
Which have their true names only ta'en from beasts,
As the most ulcerous wolf, and swinish measle;
Though we are eaten up of lice and worms,

37

And though continually we bear about us
A rotten and dead body, we delight   65
To hide it in rich tissue. All our fear,
Nay, all our terror, is lest our physician
Should put us in the ground, to be made sweet.
Your wife's gone to Rome: you two couple, and get you
To the wells at Lucca, to recover your aches.   70
      [*Exeunt Castruccio and Old Lady*]
I have other work on foot. I observe our Duchess
Is sick o' days, she pukes, her stomach seethes,
The fins of her eyelids look most teeming blue,
She wanes i'th' cheek, and waxes fat i'th' flank;
And, contrary to our Italian fashion,   75
Wears a loose-bodied gown: there's somewhat in't!
I have a trick may chance discover it,
A pretty one; I have bought some apricots,
The first our spring yields.
      [*Enter Antonio and Delio in conversation apart*]
DELIO   And so long since married?
      You amaze me.
ANTONIO   Let me seal your lips for ever,   80
      For did I think that anything but th'air
      Could carry these words from you, I should wish
      You had no breath at all.
[*To Bosola*] Now, sir, in your contemplation? You are
      studying to become a great wise fellow?   85
BOSOLA O sir, the opinion of wisdom is a foul tetter
      that runs all over a man's body: if simplicity direct
      us to have no evil, it directs us to a happy being, for
      the subtlest folly proceeds from the subtlest wisdom.
      Let me be simply honest.   90
ANTONIO I do understand your inside.
BOSOLA Do you so?
ANTONIO Because you would not seem to appear to th'

world puffed up with your preferment, you continue
this out-of-fashion melancholy. Leave it, leave it.   95
BOSOLA Give me leave to be honest in any phrase, in
any compliment whatsoever. Shall I confess myself to
you? I look no higher than I can reach. They are the
gods that must ride on winged horses; a lawyer's mule
of a slow pace will both suit my disposition and busi-   100
ness; for mark me, when a man's mind rides faster
than his horse can gallop, they quickly both tire.
ANTONIO You would look up to heaven, but I think
The devil, that rules i'th' air, stands in your light.
BOSOLA O sir, you are lord of the ascendant, chief man 105
with the Duchess, a Duke was your cousin-german
removed. Say you were lineally descended from King
Pepin, or he himself, what of this? Search the heads
of the greatest rivers in the world, you shall find them
but bubbles of water. Some would think the souls of   110
princes were brought forth by some more weighty
cause than those of meaner persons. They are
deceived; there's the same hand to them, the like
passions sway them: the same reason that makes a
vicar go to law for a tithe-pig and undo his neigh-   115
bours, makes them spoil a whole province, and batter
down goodly cities with the cannon.
    [*Enter Duchess with Cariola and Old Lady*]
DUCHESS Your arm, Antonio: do I not grow fat?
I am exceeding short-winded. Bosola,
I would have you, sir, provide for me a litter,   120
Such a one as the Duchess of Florence rode in.
BOSOLA The Duchess used one when she was great with
child.
DUCHESS I think she did. [*To Old Lady*] Come hither,
mend my ruff.
Here, when? Thou art such a tedious lady, and   125

39

Thy breath smells of lemon pills. Would thou hadst
    done!
Shall I swoon under thy fingers? I am
So troubled with the mother.
BOSOLA [*aside*]   I fear too much.
DUCHESS I have heard you say that the French courtiers
    Wear their hats on 'fore the King.
ANTONIO   I have seen it.   130
DUCHESS In the presence?
ANTONIO Yes.
DUCHESS   Why should not we bring up that fashion?
    'Tis ceremony more than duty, that consists
    In the removing of a piece of felt.
    Be you the example to the rest o'th' court,   135
    Put on your hat first.
ANTONIO   You must pardon me:
    I have seen, in colder countries than in France,
    Nobles stand bare to th'Prince; and the distinction
    Methought showed reverently.
BOSOLA I have a present for your grace.
DUCHESS   For me, sir?   140
BOSOLA Apricots, madam.
DUCHESS   O sir, where are they?
    I have heard of none to-year.
BOSOLA [*aside*]   Good, her colour rises.
DUCHESS Indeed I thank you; they are wondrous fair
    ones.
    What an unskilful fellow is our gardener!
    We shall have none this month.   145
BOSOLA Will not your grace pare them?
DUCHESS No, they taste of musk, methinks; indeed they
    do.
BOSOLA I know not; yet I wish your grace had pared 'em.
DUCHESS Why?

BOSOLA   I forgot to tell you the knave gardener
  Only to raise his profit by them the sooner,   150
  Did ripen them in horse-dung.
DUCHESS   O you jest.
  [*To Antonio*] You shall judge: pray taste one.
ANTONIO   Indeed, madam,
  I do not love the fruit.
DUCHESS   Sir, you are loth
  To rob us of our dainties: 'tis a delicate fruit,
  They say they are restorative.
BOSOLA   'Tis a pretty art,   155
  This grafting.
DUCHESS   'Tis so: a bettering of nature.
BOSOLA To make a pippin grow upon a crab,
  A damson on a blackthorn. [*Aside*] How greedily she
      eats them!
  A whirlwind strike off these bawd farthingales,
  For, but for that, and the loose-bodied gown,   160
  I should have discovered apparently
  The young springal cutting a caper in her belly.
DUCHESS I thank you, Bosola, they were right good
      ones –
  If they do not make me sick.
ANTONIO   How now, madam?
DUCHESS This green fruit and my stomach are not
      friends.   165
  How they swell me!
BOSOLA [*aside*]   Nay, you are too much swelled already.
DUCHESS O, I am in an extreme cold sweat!
BOSOLA I am very sorry.
DUCHESS Lights to my chamber. O good Antonio,
  I fear I am undone.
        Exit [*Duchess*]
DELIO   Lights there, lights!   170

[*Exeunt all except Antonio and Delio*]

ANTONIO O my most trusty Delio, we are lost.
I fear she's fallen in labour, and there's left
No time for her remove.

DELIO   Have you prepared
Those ladies to attend her? and procured
That politic safe conveyance for the midwife 175
Your Duchess plotted?

ANTONIO I have.

DELIO   Make use then of this forced occasion.
Give out that Bosola hath poisoned her
With these apricots: that will give some colour
For her keeping close.

ANTONIO   Fie, fie, the physicians 180
Will then flock to her.

DELIO   For that you may pretend
She'll use some prepared antidote of her own,
Lest the physicians should repoison her.

ANTONIO I am lost in amazement, I know not what to
think on't. 185
    Exeunt

Act II Scene II

[*Enter Bosola*]

BOSOLA So, so: there's no question but her tetchiness
and most vulturous eating of the apricots are apparent
signs of breeding.

[*Enter Old Lady. Bosola intercepts her*]

OLD LADY Now? I am in haste, sir.

BOSOLA There was a young waiting-woman had a 5
monstrous desire to see the glass-house.

OLD LADY Nay, pray let me go.

BOSOLA And it was only to know what strange instrument it was should swell up a glass to the fashion of a woman's belly.   10

OLD LADY I will hear no more of the glass-house; you are still abusing women!

BOSOLA Who I? No, only, by the way now and then, mention your frailties. The orange tree bears ripe and green fruit, and blossoms all together, and some of   15
you give entertainment for pure love, but more, for more precious reward. The lusty spring smells well; but drooping autumn tastes well. If we have the same golden showers that rained in the time of Jupiter the Thunderer, you have the same Danäes still, to hold   20
up their laps to receive them. Didst thou never study the mathematics?

OLD LADY What's that, sir?

BOSOLA Why, to know the trick how to make a many lines meet in one centre. Go, go: give your foster-   25
daughters good counsel: tell them that the devil takes delight to hang at a woman's girdle, like a false rusty watch, that she cannot discern how the time passes.

[*Exit Old Lady. Enter Antonio, Delio, Roderigo, Grisolan*]

ANTONIO Shut up the court gates.

RODERIGO   Why, sir? What's the danger?

ANTONIO Shut up the posterns presently, and call   30
All the officers o'th' court.

GRISOLAN   I shall instantly.

[*Exit Grisolan*]

ANTONIO Who keeps the key o'th' park gate?

RODERIGO   Forobosco.

ANTONIO Let him bring't presently.

[*Exit Roderigo. Enter Grisolan with Officers.*]

FIRST OFFICER O, gentlemen o'th' court, the foulest
   treason!   35
BOSOLA [*aside*] If that these apricots should be poisoned
      now,
   Without my knowledge!
FIRST OFFICER There was taken even now a Switzer in
   the Duchess' bedchamber.
SECOND OFFICER A Switzer?   40
FIRST OFFICER With a pistol in his great cod-piece.
BOSOLA Ha, ha, ha!
FIRST OFFICER The cod-piece was the case for't.
SECOND OFFICER There was a cunning traitor. Who
   would have searched his cod-piece?   45
FIRST OFFICER True, if he had kept out of the ladies'
   chambers: and all the moulds of his buttons were
   leaden bullets.
SECOND OFFICER O, wicked cannibal – a fire-lock in's
   cod-piece!   50
FIRST OFFICER 'Twas a French plot, upon my life.
SECOND OFFICER To see what the devil can do!
ANTONIO All the officers here?
OFFICERS We are.
ANTONIO Gentlemen,   55
   We have lost much plate you know; and but this
      evening
   Jewels, to the value of four thousand ducats,
   Are missing in the Duchess' cabinet.
   Are the gates shut?
OFFICERS   Yes.
ANTONIO   'Tis the Duchess' pleasure
   Each officer be locked into his chamber   60
   Till the sun-rising; and to send the keys
   Of all their chests, and of their outward doors,
   Into her bedchamber. She is very sick.

RODERIGO At her pleasure.

ANTONIO She entreats you take 't not ill; the innocent   65
    Shall be the more approved by it.

BOSOLA [*to the Officer*] Gentleman o'th' wood-yard,
    where's your Switzer now?

FIRST OFFICER By this hand, 'twas credibly reported by
    one o' the blackguard.   70
        [*Exeunt all except Antonio and Delio*]

DELIO How fares it with the Duchess?

ANTONIO   She's exposed
    Unto the worst of torture, pain, and fear.

DELIO Speak to her all happy comfort.

ANTONIO How I do play the fool with mine own danger!
    You are this night, dear friend, to post to Rome;   75
    My life lies in your service.

DELIO   Do not doubt me.

ANTONIO O, 'tis far from me, and yet fear presents me
    Somewhat that looks like danger.

DELIO   Believe it,
    'Tis but the shadow of your fear, no more.
    How superstitiously we mind our evils!   80
    The throwing down salt, or crossing of a hare,
    Bleeding at nose, the stumbling of a horse,
    Or singing of a cricket, are of power
    To daunt whole man in us. Sir, fare you well.
    I wish you all the joys of a blessed father;   85
    And, for my faith, lay this unto your breast:
    Old friends, like old swords, still are trusted best.
        [*Exit Delio. Enter Cariola*]

CARIOLA Sir, you are the happy father of a son;
    Your wife commends him to you.

ANTONIO   Blessed comfort!
    For heaven' sake tend her well; I'll presently   90
    Go set a figure for's nativity.
        Exeunt

Act II Scene III

[*Enter Bosola with a dark lantern*]

BOSOLA Sure I did hear a woman shriek: list, ha?
And the sound came, if I received it right,
From the Duchess' lodgings. There's some stratagem
In the confining all our courtiers
To their several wards. I must have part of it,   5
My intelligence will freeze else. List again!
It may be 'twas the melancholy bird,
Best friend of silence and of solitariness,
The owl, that screamed so.
        [*Enter Antonio*]
                                    Ha, Antonio!

ANTONIO I heard some noise. Who's there? What art
        thou? Speak.   10

BOSOLA Antonio? Put not your face nor body
To such a forced expression of fear:
I am Bosola, your friend.

ANTONIO   Bosola!
    [*Aside*] This mole does undermine me. [*To him*] Heard
        you not
    A noise even now?

BOSOLA   From whence?

ANTONIO   From the Duchess' lodging.   15

BOSOLA Not I. Did you?

ANTONIO   I did: or else I dreamed.

BOSOLA Let's walk towards it.

ANTONIO   No: it may be 'twas
    But the rising of the wind.

BOSOLA   Very likely.
    Methinks 'tis very cold, and yet you sweat.
    You look wildly.

ANTONIO   I have been setting a figure   20
  For the Duchess' jewels.
BOSOLA   Ah, and how falls your question?
  Do you find it radical?
ANTONIO   What's that to you?
  'Tis rather to be questioned what design,
  When all men were commanded to their lodgings,
  Makes you a night-walker.
BOSOLA   In sooth I'll tell you: 25
  Now all the court's asleep, I thought the devil
  Had least to do here; I came to say my prayers.
  And if it do offend you I do so,
  You are a fine courtier.
ANTONIO [*aside*]   This fellow will undo me.
  [*To him*] You gave the Duchess apricots today;   30
  Pray heaven they were not poisoned!
BOSOLA   Poisoned! A Spanish fig
  For the imputation.
ANTONIO   Traitors are ever confident,
  Till they are discovered. There were jewels stol'n too;
  In my conceit, none are to be suspected
  More than yourself.
BOSOLA   You are a false steward.   35
ANTONIO Saucy slave! I'll pull thee up by the roots.
BOSOLA Maybe the ruin will crush you to pieces.
ANTONIO You are an impudent snake indeed, sir;
  Are you scarce warm, and do you show your sting?
[BOSOLA] . . .   40
ANTONIO You libel well, sir.
BOSOLA   No, sir, copy it out,
  And I will set my hand to't.
ANTONIO [*aside*]   My nose bleeds.
    [*He draws an initialled handkerchief*]
  One that were superstitious would count

This ominous, when it merely comes by chance:
Two letters, that are wrought here for my name,   45
Are drowned in blood!
Mere accident. [*To him*] For you, sir, I'll take order:
I'th'morn you shall be safe. [*Aside*] 'Tis that must colour
Her lying-in. [*To him*] Sir, this door you pass not:
I do not hold it fit that you come near   50
The Duchess' lodgings, till you have quit yourself.
[*Aside*] The great are like the base, nay, they are the same,
When they seek shameful ways to avoid shame.
    Exit [Antonio]
BOSOLA Antonio hereabout did drop a paper;
Some of your help, false friend. O, here it is: 55
What's here? A child's nativity calculated!
[*Reads*] 'The Duchess was delivered of a son, 'tween
the hours twelve and one, in the night: Anno Dom.
1504' – that's this year – 'decimo nono Decembris' –
that's this night – 'taken according to the meridian of   60
Malfi' – that's our Duchess: happy discovery! – 'The
lord of the first house, being combust in the ascendant,
signifies short life; and Mars being in a human sign,
joined to the tail of the Dragon, in the eighth house,
doth threaten a violent death; caetera non scrutantur.'   65
Why now 'tis most apparent. This precise fellow
Is the Duchess' bawd. I have it to my wish.
This is a parcel of intelligency
Our courtiers were cased up for! It needs must follow
That I must be committed on pretence   70
Of poisoning her; which I'll endure, and laugh at.
If one could find the father now; but that
Time will discover. Old Castruccio
I'th' morning posts to Rome; by him I'll send
A letter, that shall make her brothers' galls   75
O'erflow their livers. This was a thrifty way.

Though lust do mask in ne'er so strange disguise,
She's oft found witty, but is never wise.
　　[*Exit*]

Act II Scene IV

　　[*Enter Cardinal and Julia*]
CARDINAL　Sit, thou art my best of wishes. Prithee tell
　　me
What trick didst thou invent to come to Rome
Without thy husband.
JULIA　　　　　　　Why, my lord, I told him
I came to visit an old anchorite
Here, for devotion.
CARDINAL　　　　Thou art a witty false one:　　　5
I mean to him.
JULIA　　　　You have prevailed with me
Beyond my strongest thoughts; I would not now
Find you inconstant.
CARDINAL　　　　Do not put thyself
To such a voluntary torture, which proceeds
Out of your own guilt.
JULIA　　　　　　How, my lord?
CARDINAL　　　　　　　　You fear　　　10
My constancy, because you have approved
Those giddy and wild turnings in yourself.
JULIA　Did you e'er find them?
CARDINAL　　　　　Sooth, generally for women.
A man might strive to make glass malleable,
Ere he should make them fixèd.
JULIA　　　　　　　So, my lord.　　　15
CARDINAL　We had need go borrow that fantastic glass

Invented by Galileo the Florentine,
To view another spacious world i'th' moon,
And look to find a constant woman there.
JULIA This is very well, my lord.
CARDINAL   Why do you weep?   20
Are tears your justification? The self-same tears
Will fall into your husband's bosom, lady,
With a loud protestation that you love him
Above the world. Come, I'll love you wisely,
That's jealously, since I am very certain   25
You cannot me make cuckold.
JULIA   I'll go home
To my husband.
CARDINAL   You may thank me, lady,
I have taken you off your melancholy perch,
Bore you upon my fist, and showed you game,
And let you fly at it. I pray thee, kiss me.   30
When thou wast with thy husband, thou wast watched
Like a tame elephant: still you are to thank me.
Thou hadst only kisses from him, and high feeding,
But what delight was that? 'Twas just like one
That hath a little fingering on the lute,   35
Yet cannot tune it: still you are to thank me.
JULIA You told me of a piteous wound i'th' heart,
And a sick liver, when you wooed me first,
And spake like one in physic.
CARDINAL [*calling off-stage*]   Who's that?
Rest firm: for my affection to thee,   40
Lightning moves slow to't.
     [*Enter Servant*]
SERVANT   Madam, a gentleman,
That's come post from Malfi, desires to see you.
CARDINAL Let him enter, I'll withdraw.
     Exit [*Cardinal*]

SERVANT   He says,
  Your husband, old Castruccio, is come to Rome,
  Most pitifully tired with riding post.   45
        [*Exit Servant. Enter Delio*]
JULIA Signor Delio! [*Aside*] 'Tis one of my old suitors.
DELIO I was bold to come and see you.
JULIA   Sir, you are welcome.
DELIO Do you lie here?
JULIA   Sure, your own experience
  Will satisfy you, no: our Roman prelates
  Do not keep lodging for ladies.
DELIO   Very well.   50
  I have brought you no commendations from your
        husband,
  For I know none by him.
JULIA   I hear he's come to Rome?
DELIO I never knew man and beast, of a horse and a
        knight,
  So weary of each other. If he had had a good back,
  He would have undertook to have borne his horse,   55
  His breech was so pitifully sore.
JULIA   Your laughter
  Is my pity.
DELIO   Lady, I know not whether
  You want money, but I have brought you some.
JULIA From my husband?
DELIO   No, from mine own allowance.
JULIA I must hear the condition, ere I be bound to take
        it.   60
DELIO Look on't, 'tis gold: hath it not a fine colour?
JULIA I have a bird more beautiful.
DELIO Try the sound on't.
JULIA   A lute-string far exceeds it.
  It hath no smell, like cassia or civet,

Nor is it physical, though some fond doctors   65
Persuade us seethe 't in cullises. I'll tell you,
This is a creature bred by –
   [Enter Servant]
SERVANT   Your husband's come,
Hath delivered a letter to the Duke of Calabria,
That, to my thinking, hath put him out of his wits.
   [Exit Servant]
JULIA Sir, you hear: 70
Pray let me know your business and your suit,
As briefly as can be.
DELIO   With good speed. I would wish you,
At such time as you are non-resident
With your husband, my mistress.
JULIA Sir, I'll go ask my husband if I shall,   75
And straight return your answer.
   Exit [Julia]
DELIO   Very fine.
Is this her wit or honesty that speaks thus?
I heard one say the Duke was highly moved
With a letter sent from Malfi: I do fear
Antonio is betrayed. How fearfully   80
Shows his ambition now! Unfortunate fortune!
They pass through whirlpools and deep woes do shun,
Who the event weigh, ere the action's done.
   Exit

Act II Scene V

   [Enter] Cardinal, and Ferdinand with a letter
FERDINAND I have this night digged up a mandrake.
CARDINAL   Say you?

FERDINAND And I am grown mad with't.
CARDINAL   What's the prodigy?
FERDINAND Read there, a sister damned; she's loose i'th'
    hilts,
  Grown a notorious strumpet.
CARDINAL   Speak lower.
FERDINAND   Lower?
  Rogues do not whisper 't now, but seek to publish 't,   5
  As servants do the bounty of their lords,
  Aloud; and with a covetous searching eye
  To mark who note them. O confusion seize her!
  She hath had most cunning bawds to serve her turn,
  And more secure conveyances for lust   10
  Than towns of garrison for service.
CARDINAL   Is't possible?
  Can this be certain?
FERDINAND   Rhubarb, O for rhubarb
  To purge this choler! Here's the cursèd day
  To prompt my memory, and here 't shall stick
  Till of her bleeding heart I make a sponge   15
  To wipe it out.
CARDINAL   Why do you make yourself
  So wild a tempest?
FERDINAND   Would I could be one,
  That I might toss her palace 'bout her ears,
  Root up her goodly forests, blast her meads,
  And lay her general territory as waste   20
  As she hath done her honours.
CARDINAL   Shall our blood,
  The royal blood of Aragon and Castile,
  Be thus attainted?
FERDINAND   Apply desperate physic –
  We must not now use balsamum, but fire,
  The smarting cupping-glass, for that's the mean   25

To purge infected blood, such blood as hers.
There is a kind of pity in mine eye,
I'll give it to my handkercher; and now 'tis here,
I'll bequeath this to her bastard.

CARDINAL   What to do?

FERDINAND Why, to make soft lint for his mother's
    wounds,   30
When I have hewed her to pieces.

CARDINAL   Cursed creature!
Unequal nature, to place women's hearts
So far upon the left side!

FERDINAND   Foolish men,
That e'er will trust their honour in a bark
Made of so slight, weak bulrush as is woman,   35
Apt every minute to sink it!

CARDINAL Thus ignorance, when it hath purchased
    honour,
It cannot wield it.

FERDINAND   Methinks I see her laughing,
Excellent hyena! Talk to me somewhat, quickly,
Or my imagination will carry me   40
To see her in the shameful act of sin.

CARDINAL With whom?

FERDINAND   Haply with some strong thighed
    bargeman,
Or one o'th' wood-yard, that can quoit the sledge,
Or toss the bar, or else some lovely squire
That carries coals up to her privy lodgings.   45

CARDINAL You fly beyond your reason.

FERDINAND   Go to, mistress!
'Tis not your whore's milk that shall quench my wild-
    fire,
But your whore's blood.

CARDINAL How idly shows this rage! which carries you,

54

As men conveyed by witches, through the air   50
On violent whirlwinds. This intemperate noise
Fitly resembles deaf men's shrill discourse,
Who talk aloud, thinking all other men
To have their imperfection.
FERDINAND   Have not you
  My palsy?
CARDINAL   Yes, I can be angry   55
Without this rupture. There is not in nature
A thing that makes man so deformed, so beastly,
As doth intemperate anger. Chide yourself.
You have divers men who never yet expressed
Their strong desire of rest, but by unrest,   60
By vexing of themselves. Come, put yourself
In tune.
FERDINAND So, I will only study to seem
The thing I am not. I could kill her now,
In you, or in myself, for I do think   65
It is some sin in us heaven doth revenge
By her.
CARDINAL Are you stark mad?
FERDINAND   I would have their bodies
Burnt in a coal-pit, with the ventage stopped,
That their cursed smoke might not ascend to heaven;   70
Or dip the sheets they lie in, in pitch or sulphur,
Wrap them in't, and then light them like a match;
Or else to boil their bastard to a cullis,
And give 't his lecherous father, to renew
The sin of his back.
CARDINAL   I'll leave you.   75
FERDINAND Nay, I have done.
I am confident, had I been damned in hell
And should have heard of this, it would have put me
Into a cold sweat. In, in, I'll go sleep.

Till I know who leaps my sister, I'll not stir: 80
That known, I'll find scorpions to string my whips,
And fix her in a general eclipse.
    Exeunt

Act III Scene I

[*Enter Antonio and Delio*]

ANTONIO Our noble friend, my most beloved Delio,
O, you have been a stranger long at court.
Came you along with the Lord Ferdinand?

DELIO I did, sir; and how fares your noble Duchess?

ANTONIO Right fortunately well. She's an excellent   5
Feeder of pedigrees: since you last saw her,
She hath had two children more, a son and daughter.

DELIO Methinks 'twas yesterday. Let me but wink,
And not behold your face, which to mine eye
Is somewhat leaner, verily I should dream   10
It were within this half-hour.

ANTONIO You have not been in law, friend Delio,
Nor in prison, nor a suitor at the court,
Nor begged the reversion of some great man's place,
Nor troubled with an old wife, which doth make   15
Your time so insensibly hasten.

DELIO   Pray, sir, tell me,
Hath not this news arrived yet to the ear
Of the Lord Cardinal?

ANTONIO   I fear it hath.
The Lord Ferdinand, that's newly come to court,
Doth bear himself right dangerously.

DELIO   Pray why?   20

ANTONIO He is so quiet, that he seems to sleep
The tempest out, as dormice do in winter.
Those houses that are haunted are most still,
Till the devil be up.

DELIO   What say the common people?

ANTONIO The common rabble do directly say   25
She is a strumpet.

DELIO   And your graver heads,
  Which would be politic, what censure they?
ANTONIO They do observe I grow to infinite purchase
  The left-hand way, and all suppose the Duchess
  Would amend it, if she could. For, say they,   30
  Great princes, though they grudge their officers
  Should have such large and unconfinèd means
  To get wealth under them, will not complain
  Lest thereby they should make them odious
  Unto the people; for other obligation   35
  Of love, or marriage, between her and me,
  They never dream of.
        [*Enter Ferdinand and Duchess*]
DELIO   The Lord Ferdinand
  Is going to bed.
FERDINAND   I'll instantly to bed,
  For I am weary. [*To the Duchess*] I am to bespeak
  A husband for you.
DUCHESS   For me, sir! Pray who is't?   40
FERDINAND The great Count Malateste.
DUCHESS   Fie upon him,
  A count! He's a mere stick of sugar-candy,
  You may look quite thorough him. When I choose
  A husband, I will marry for your honour.
FERDINAND You shall do well in't. How is't, worthy
     Antonio?   45
DUCHESS But, sir, I am to have private conference with
     you
  About a scandalous report is spread
  Touching mine honour.
FERDINAND   Let me be ever deaf to't:
  One of Pasquil's paper bullets, court-calumny,
  A pestilent air which princes' palaces   50
  Are seldom purg'd of. Yet, say that it were true,

I pour it in your bosom, my fixed love
Would strongly excuse, extenuate, nay, deny
Faults, were they apparent in you. Go, be safe
In your own innocency.
DUCHESS   O blessed comfort!   55
This deadly air is purg'd.
        Exeunt [all except Ferdinand]
FERDINAND   Her guilt treads on
Hot-burning coulters.
        [Enter Bosola]
                    Now, Bosola,
How thrives our intelligence?
BOSOLA   Sir, uncertainly.
'Tis rumoured she hath had three bastards, but
By whom, we may go read i'th' stars.
FERDINAND   Why, some   60
Hold opinion all things are written there.
BOSOLA Yes, if we could find spectacles to read them.
I do suspect there hath been some sorcery
Used on the Duchess.
FERDINAND   Sorcery, to what purpose?
BOSOLA To make her dote on some desertless fellow   65
She shames to acknowledge.
FERDINAND   Can your faith give way
To think there's power in potions, or in charms,
To make us love, whether we will or no?
BOSOLA Most certainly.
FERDINAND Away, these are mere gulleries, horrid things   70
Invented by some cheating mountebanks
To abuse us. Do you think that herbs or charms
Can force the will? Some trials have been made
In this foolish practice; but the ingredients
Were lenitive poisons, such as are of force   75
To make the patient mad; and straight the witch

Swears, by equivocation, they are in love.
The witchcraft lies in her rank blood. This night
I will force confession from her. You told me
You had got, within these two days, a false key   80
Into her bedchamber.
BOSOLA   I have.
FERDINAND   As I would wish.
BOSOLA What do you intend to do?
FERDINAND   Can you guess?
BOSOLA   No.
FERDINAND Do not ask then.
He that can compass me, and know my drifts,
May say he hath put a girdle 'bout the world   85
And sounded all her quicksands.
BOSOLA   I do not
Think so.
FERDINAND What do you think then, pray?
BOSOLA   That you
Are your own chronicle too much, and grossly
Flatter yourself.
FERDINAND   Give me thy hand; I thank thee.
I never gave pension but to flatterers,   90
Till I entertained thee. Farewell;
That friend a great man's ruin strongly checks,
Who rails into his belief all his defects.
    Exeunt

Act III Scene II

[*Enter Duchess, Antonio and Cariola*]
DUCHESS [*to Cariola*] Bring me the casket hither, and the
    glass;

You get no lodging here tonight, my lord.
ANTONIO Indeed, I must persuade one.
DUCHESS   Very good.
  I hope in time 'twill grow into a custom
  That noblemen shall come with cap and knee,   5
  To purchase a night's lodging of their wives.
ANTONIO I must lie here.
DUCHESS   Must? You are a lord of misrule.
ANTONIO Indeed, my rule is only in the night.
DUCHESS To what use will you put me?
ANTONIO   We'll sleep together.
DUCHESS Alas, what pleasure can two lovers find in
    sleep?   10
    [*Cariola gives the Duchess the casket and a mirror*]
CARIOLA My lord, I lie with her often, and I know
  She'll much disquiet you.
ANTONIO   See, you are complained of.
CARIOLA For she's the sprawling'st bedfellow.
ANTONIO I shall like her the better for that.
CARIOLA Sir, shall I ask you a question?   15
ANTONIO I pray thee, Cariola.
CARIOLA Wherefore still when you lie with my lady
  Do you rise so early?
ANTONIO   Labouring men
  Count the clock oftenest Cariola,
  Are glad when their task's ended.
DUCHESS   I'll stop your mouth.   20
    [*Kisses him*]
ANTONIO Nay, that's but one: Venus had two soft doves
  To draw her chariot – I must have another.
    [*Kisses her*]
  When wilt thou marry, Cariola?
CARIOLA   Never, my lord.
ANTONIO O fie upon this single life. Forgo it.

We read how Daphne, for her peevish flight,   25
Became a fruitless bay-tree; Syrinx turned
To the pale empty reed; Anaxarete
Was frozen into marble: whereas those
Which married, or proved kind unto their friends,
Were, by a gracious influence, transshaped   30
Into the olive, pomegranate, mulberry:
Became flowers, precious stones, or eminent stars.

CARIOLA This is a vain poetry. But I pray you tell me,
  If there were proposed me wisdom, riches, and beauty,
  In three several young men, which should I choose?   35

ANTONIO 'Tis a hard question. This was Paris' case
  And he was blind in't, and there was great cause:
  For how was't possible he could judge right,
  Having three amorous goddesses in view,
  And they stark naked? 'Twas a motion   40
  Were able to benight the apprehension
  Of the severest counsellor of Europe.
  Now I look on both your faces, so well formed,
  It puts me in mind of a question I would ask.

CARIOLA What is't?

ANTONIO   I do wonder why hard-favoured ladies,   45
  For the most part, keep worse-favoured waiting-women
  To attend them, and cannot endure fair ones.

DUCHESS O, that's soon answered.
  Did you ever in your life know an ill painter
  Desire to have his dwelling next door to the shop   50
  Of an excellent picture-maker? 'Twould disgrace
  His face-making, and undo him. I prithee,
  When were we so merry? My hair tangles.

ANTONIO [*aside to Cariola*] Pray thee, Cariola, let's steal
    forth the room
  And let her talk to herself. I have divers times   55
  Served her the like, when she hath chafed extremely.

I love to see her angry. Softly, Cariola.
   Exeunt [Antonio and Cariola]
DUCHESS Doth not the colour of my hair 'gin to change?
   When I wax gray, I shall have all the court
   Powder their hair with orris, to be like me.   60
   You have cause to love me: I entered you into my
      heart
     [Enter Ferdinand behind]
   Before you would vouchsafe to call for the keys.
   We shall one day have my brothers take you napping.
   Methinks his presence, being now in court,
   Should make you keep your own bed; but you'll say   65
   Love mixed with fear is sweetest. I'll assure you
   You shall get no more children till my brothers
   Consent to be your gossips: have you lost your tongue?
     [Sees Ferdinand who holds a poniard]
   'Tis welcome:
   For know, whether I am doomed to live or die,   70
   I can do both like a prince.
     Ferdinand gives her a poniard
FERDINAND   Die then, quickly.
   Virtue, where art thou hid? What hideous thing
   Is it that doth eclipse thee?
DUCHESS   Pray, sir, hear me.
FERDINAND Or is it true, thou art but a bare name,
   And no essential thing?
DUCHESS   Sir –
FERDINAND   Do not speak.
DUCHESS   No, sir.   75
   I will plant my soul in mine ears to hear you.
FERDINAND O most imperfect light of human reason,
   That mak'st us so unhappy, to foresee
   What we can least prevent. Pursue thy wishes,
   And glory in them: there's in shame no comfort   80

63

But to be past all bounds, and sense of shame.
DUCHESS I pray, sir, hear me: I am married.
FERDINAND   So.
DUCHESS Haply, not to your liking; but for that,
    Alas, your shears do come untimely now
    To clip the bird's wings that's already flown.   85
    Will you see my husband?
FERDINAND   Yes, if I could change
    Eyes with a basilisk.
DUCHESS   Sure you came hither
    By his confederacy.
FERDINAND   The howling of a wolf
    Is music to thee, screech-owl; prithee peace.
    Whate'er thou art, that hast enjoyed my sister   90
    (For I am sure thou hear'st me), for thine own sake
    Let me not know thee. I came hither prepared
    To work thy discovery, yet am now persuaded
    It would beget such violent effects
    As would damn us both. I would not for ten millions   95
    I had beheld thee; therefore use all means
    I never may have knowledge of thy name.
    Enjoy thy lust still, and a wretched life,
    On that condition. And for thee, vile woman,
    If thou do wish thy lecher may grow old   100
    In thy embracements, I would have thee build
    Such a room for him as our anchorites
    To holier use inhabit. Let not the sun
    Shine on him, till he's dead. Let dogs and monkeys
    Only converse with him, and such dumb things   105
    To whom nature denies use to sound his name.
    Do not keep a paraquito, lest she learn it.
    If thou do love him, cut out thine own tongue
    Lest it bewray him.
DUCHESS   Why might not I marry?

I have not gone about, in this, to create   110
Any new world, or custom.
FERDINAND   Thou art undone;
And thou hast ta'en that massy sheet of lead
That hid thy husband's bones, and folded it
About my heart.
DUCHESS   Mine bleeds for't.
FERDINAND   Thine? Thy heart?
What should I name't, unless a hollow bullet   115
Filled with unquenchable wild-fire?
DUCHESS   You are, in this,
Too strict; and were you not my princely brother
I would say too wilful. My reputation
Is safe.
FERDINAND Dost thou know what reputation is?   120
I'll tell thee, to small purpose, since th' instruction
Comes now too late:
Upon a time, Reputation, Love, and Death
Would travel o'er the world; and it was concluded
That they should part, and take three several ways.   125
Death told them, they should find him in great battles,
Or cities plagued with plagues. Love gives them counsel
To inquire for him 'mongst unambitious shepherds,
Where dowries were not talked of, and sometimes
'Mongst quiet kindred that had nothing left   130
By their dead parents. 'Stay', quoth Reputation,
'Do not forsake me; for it is my nature,
If once I part from any man I meet,
I am never found again.' And so, for you:
You have shook hands with Reputation,   135
And made him invisible. So fare you well.
I will never see you more.
DUCHESS Why should only I,
Of all the other princes of the world,

65

Be cased up, like a holy relic? I have youth,   140
And a little beauty.
FERDINAND   So you have some virgins
  That are witches. I will never see thee more.
      Exit [Ferdinand. Enter Antonio with a Pistol, and
      Cariola]
DUCHESS You saw this apparition?
ANTONIO   Yes: we are
  Betrayed. How came he hither? [*To Cariola*] I should turn
  This to thee, for that.
CARIOLA   Pray, sir, do; and when   145
  That you have cleft my heart, you shall read there
  Mine innocence.
DUCHESS   That gallery gave him entrance.
ANTONIO I would this terrible thing would come again,
  That, standing on my guard, I might relate
  My warrantable love.
      [*The Duchess*] *shows the poniard*
                      Ha, what means this?   150
DUCHESS He left this with me.
ANTONIO   And it seems did wish
  You would use it on yourself?
DUCHESS   His action seemed
  To intend so much.
ANTONIO   This hath a handle to't
  As well as a point. Turn it towards him,
  And so fasten the keen edge in his rank gall: –   155
      [*Knocking within*]
  How now! Who knocks? More earthquakes?
DUCHESS   I stand
  As if a mine beneath my feet were ready
  To be blown up.
CARIOLA   'Tis Bosola.

DUCHESS   Away!
  O misery, methinks unjust actions
  Should wear these masks and curtains, and not we.   160
  You must instantly part hence; I have fashioned it
    already.
    Exit Antonio. Enter Bosola
BOSOLA The Duke your brother is ta'en up in a whirl-
    wind,
  Hath took horse, and's rid post to Rome.
DUCHESS   So late?
BOSOLA He told me, as he mounted into th' saddle,
  You were undone.
DUCHESS   Indeed, I am very near it.   165
BOSOLA What's the matter?
DUCHESS Antonio, the master of our household,
  Hath dealt so falsely with me, in's accounts.
  My brother stood engaged with me for money
  Ta'en up of certain Neapolitan Jews,   170
  And Antonio lets the bonds be forfeit.
BOSOLA Strange! [*Aside*] This is cunning.
DUCHESS   And hereupon
  My brother's bills at Naples are protested
  Against. Call up our officers.
BOSOLA   I shall.
    Exit [Bosola. Enter Antonio]
DUCHESS The place that you must fly to is Ancona.   175
  Hire a house there. I'll send after you
  My treasure and my jewels. Our weak safety
  Runs upon enginous wheels; short syllables
  Must stand for periods. I must now accuse you
  Of such a feignèd crime as Tasso calls   180
  Magnanima menzogna: a noble lie,
  'Cause it must shield our honours. Hark!, they are
    coming.

[*Enter Bosola and Officers*]

ANTONIO Will your grace hear me?

DUCHESS I have got well by you: you have yielded me
A million of loss. I am like to inherit   185
The people's curses for your stewardship.
You had the trick in audit-time to be sick,
Till I had signed your *quietus*; and that cured you
Without help of a doctor. Gentlemen,
I would have this man be an example to you all: 190
So shall you hold my favour. I pray let him;
For he's done that, alas, you would not think of,
And, because I intend to be rid of him,
I mean not to publish. [*To Antonio*] Use your fortune
    elsewhere.

ANTONIO I am strongly armed to brook my overthrow, 195
As commonly men bear with a hard year.
I will not blame the cause on't, but do think
The necessity of my malevolent star
Procures this, not her humour. O the inconstant
And rotten ground of service! You may see.   200
'Tis even like him that, in a winter night,
Takes a long slumber o'er a dying fire,
As loth to part from't, yet parts thence as cold
As when he first sat down.

DUCHESS   We do confiscate,
Towards the satisfying of your accounts,   205
All that you have.

ANTONIO I am all yours, and 'tis very fit
All mine should be so.

DUCHESS   So, sir; you have your pass.

ANTONIO You may see, gentlemen, what 'tis to serve
A prince with body and soul.   210
        Exit [*Antonio*]

BOSOLA Here's an example for extortion: what moisture

is drawn out of the sea, when foul weather comes,
pours down and runs into the sea again.
DUCHESS I would know what are your opinions of this
  Antonio.   215
SECOND OFFICER He could not abide to see a pig's head
  gaping; I thought your grace would find him a Jew.
THIRD OFFICER I would you had been his officer, for
  your own sake.
FOURTH OFFICER You would have had more money.   220
FIRST OFFICER He stopped his ears with black wool; and
  to those came to him for money, said he was thick of
  hearing.
SECOND OFFICER Some said he was an hermaphrodite,
  for he could not abide a woman.   225
FOURTH OFFICER How scurvy proud he would look,
  when the treasury was full! Well, let him go.
FIRST OFFICER Yes, and the chippings of the buttery fly
  after him, to scour his gold chain.
DUCHESS Leave us.   230
    Exeunt [Officers]
  What do you think of these?
BOSOLA That these are rogues, that in's prosperity,
  But to have waited on his fortune, could have wished
  His dirty stirrup riveted through their noses,
  And followed after's mule, like a bear in a ring;   235
  Would have prostituted their daughters to his lust;
  Made their first-born intelligencers; thought none
    happy
  But such as were born under his blessed planet,
  And wore his livery: and do these lice drop off now?
  Well, never look to have the like again.   240
  He hath left a sort of flattering rogues behind him;
  Their doom must follow. Princes pay flatterers
  In their own money. Flatterers dissemble their vices,

And they dissemble their lies: that's justice.
Alas, poor gentleman!   245
DUCHESS Poor? He hath amply filled his coffers.
BOSOLA   Sure
He was too honest. Pluto, the god of riches,
When he's sent by Jupiter to any man
He goes limping, to signify that wealth
That comes on God's name comes slowly; but when
      he's sent   250
On the devil's errand, he rides post and comes in by
      scuttles.
Let me show you what a most unvalued jewel
You have, in a wanton humour, thrown away,
To bless the man shall find him. He was an excellent
Courtier, and most faithful, a soldier that thought it   255
As beastly to know his own value too little
As devilish to acknowledge it too much.
Both his virtue and form deserved a far better fortune.
His discourse rather delighted to judge itself, than
      show itself.
His breast was filled with all perfection,   260
And yet it seemed a private whisp'ring-room,
It made so little noise of't.
DUCHESS   But he was basely descended.
BOSOLA Will you make yourself a mercenary herald,
Rather to examine men's pedigrees than virtues?
You shall want him,   265
For know an honest statesman to a prince
Is like a cedar, planted by a spring:
The spring bathes the tree's root, the grateful tree
Rewards it with his shadow. You have not done so.
I would sooner swim to the Bermudes on   270
Two politicians' rotten bladders, tied
Together with an intelligencer's heart-string,

Than depend on so changeable a prince's favour.
Fare thee well, Antonio; since the malice of the world
Would needs down with thee, it cannot be said yet   275
That any ill happened unto thee,
Considering thy fall was accompanied with virtue.
DUCHESS O, you render me excellent music.
BOSOLA   Say you?
DUCHESS This good one that you speak of, is my husband.
BOSOLA Do I not dream? Can this ambitious age   280
Have so much goodness in't, as to prefer
A man merely for worth, without these shadows
Of wealth, and painted honours? Possible?
DUCHESS I have had three children by him.
BOSOLA   Fortunate lady,
For you have made your private nuptial bed   285
The humble and fair seminary of peace.
No question but many an unbeneficed scholar
Shall pray for you for this deed, and rejoice
That some preferment in the world can yet
Arise from merit. The virgins of your land,   290
That have no dowries, shall hope your example
Will raise them to rich husbands. Should you want
Soldiers, 'twould make the very Turks and Moors
Turn Christians, and serve you for this act.
Last, the neglected poets of your time,   295
In honour of this trophy of a man,
Raised by that curious engine, your white hand,
Shall thank you, in your grave, for't, and make that
More reverend than all the cabinets
Of living princes. For Antonio,   300
His fame shall likewise flow from many a pen,
When heralds shall want coats to sell to men.
DUCHESS As I taste comfort in this friendly speech,
So would I find concealment.

BOSOLA O, the secret of my Prince,   305
    Which I will wear on th' inside of my heart.
DUCHESS You shall take charge of all my coin and jewels,
    And follow him, for he retires himself
    To Ancona.
BOSOLA   So.
DUCHESS   Whither, within few days,
    I mean to follow thee.
BOSOLA   Let me think: 310
    I would wish your grace to feign a pilgrimage
    To our Lady of Loreto, scarce seven leagues
    From fair Ancona; so may you depart
    Your country with more honour, and your flight
    Will seem a princely progress, retaining   315
    Your usual train about you.
DUCHESS   Sir, your direction
    Shall lead me by the hand.
CARIOLA   In my opinion,
    She were better progress to the baths
    At Lucca, or go visit the Spa
    In Germany, for, if you will believe me,   320
    I do not like this jesting with religion,
    This feignèd pilgrimage.
DUCHESS Thou art a superstitious fool.
    Prepare us instantly for our departure.
    Past sorrows, let us moderately lament them,   325
    For those to come, seek wisely to prevent them.
        Exit [*Duchess with Cariola*]
BOSOLA A politician is the devil's quilted anvil:
    He fashions all sins on him, and the blows
    Are never heard; he may work in a lady's chamber,
    As here for proof. What rests, but I reveal   330
    All to my lord? O, this base quality
    Of intelligencer! Why, every quality i'th' world

Prefers but gain or commendation.
Now, for this act I am certain to be raised,
And men that paint weeds to the life are praised.   335
  Exit

Act III Scene III

  [*Enter*] *Cardinal, Malateste; Ferdinand with Delio,*
  Silvio, [*and*] *Pescara,* [*apart*]
CARDINAL Must we turn soldier then?
MALATESTE   The Emperor,
  Hearing your worth that way, ere you attained
  This reverend garment, joins you in commission
  With the right fortunate soldier, the Marquis of Pescara,
  And the famous Lannoy.
CARDINAL   He that had the honour   5
  Of taking French King prisoner?
MALATESTE   The same.
  Here's a plot drawn for a new fortification
  At Naples.
      [*Malateste unfolds a map*]
FERDINAND This great Count Malateste, I perceive,
  Hath got employment?
DELIO   No employment, my lord;   10
  A marginal note in the muster-book, that he is
  A voluntary lord.
FERDINAND   He's no soldier?
DELIO He has worn gunpowder in's hollow tooth,
  For the toothache.
SILVIO He comes to the leaguer with a full intent   15
  To eat fresh beef and garlic, means to stay
  Till the scent be gone, and straight return to court.

DELIO He hath read all the late service
　As the City Chronicle relates it,
　And keeps two painters going, only to express　20
　Battles in model.
SILVIO　　　　　　Then he'll fight by the book?
DELIO By the almanac, I think,
　To choose good days, and shun the critical.
　That's his mistress' scarf.
SILVIO　　　　　　　Yes, he protests
　He would do much for that taffeta.　25
DELIO I think he would run away from a battle
　To save it from taking prisoner.
SILVIO　　　　　　　　He is horribly afraid
　Gunpowder will spoil the perfume on't.
DELIO I saw a Dutchman break his pate once
　For calling him pot-gun; he made his head　30
　Have a bore in't, like a musket.
SILVIO I would he had made a touch-hole to't.
　He is indeed a guarded sumpter-cloth,
　Only for the remove of the court.
　　　[*Enter Bosola, who speaks to Ferdinand and the*
　　　Cardinal aside]
PESCARA Bosola arrived! What should be the business?　35
　Some falling out amongst the cardinals.
　These factions amongst great men, they are like
　Foxes: when their heads are divided
　They carry fire in their tails, and all the country
　About them goes to wrack for't.
SILVIO　　　　　　　What's that Bosola?　40
DELIO I knew him in Padua: a fantastical scholar, like
　such who study to know how many knots was in
　Hercules' club, of what colour Achilles' beard was,
　or whether Hector were not troubled with the
　toothache. He hath studied himself half blear-eyed to　45

know the true symmetry of Caesar's nose by a
shoeing-horn; and this he did to gain the name of a
speculative man.

PESCARA Mark Prince Ferdinand,
    A very salamander lives in's eye,   50
    To mock the eager violence of fire.

SILVIO That Cardinal hath made more bad faces with his
    oppression than ever Michelangelo made good ones;
    he lifts up's nose, like a foul porpoise before a storm.

PESCARA The Lord Ferdinand laughs.

DELIO   Like a deadly cannon 55
    That lightens ere it smokes.

PESCARA These are your true pangs of death,
    The pangs of life that struggle with great statesmen.

DELIO In such a deformèd silence, witches whisper
    Their charms.   60
       [*The Cardinal, Ferdinand and Bosola come forward*]

CARDINAL Doth she make religion her riding hood
    To keep her from the sun and tempest?

FERDINAND   That.
    That damns her. Methinks her fault and beauty,
    Blended together, show like leprosy,
    The whiter, the fouler. I make it a question   65
    Whether her beggarly brats were ever christened.

CARDINAL I will instantly solicit the state of Ancona
    To have them banished.

FERDINAND   You are for Loreto?
    I shall not be at your ceremony; fare you well.
    Write to the Duke of Malfi, my young nephew   70
    She had by her first husband, and acquaint him
    With's mother's honesty.

BOSOLA   I will.

FERDINAND   Antonio:
    A slave, that only smelled of ink and counters,

75

And ne'er in's life looked like a gentleman,
But in the audit-time. Go, go presently,   75
Draw me out an hundred and fifty of our horse,
And meet me at the fort-bridge.
    Exeunt

Act III Scene IV

[*Enter*] *Two Pilgrims to the Shrine of Our Lady of Loreto*

FIRST PILGRIM I have not seen a goodlier shrine than this,
Yet I have visited many.
SECOND PILGRIM The Cardinal of Aragon
Is this day to resign his cardinal's hat.
His sister Duchess likewise is arrived   5
To pay her vow of pilgrimage. I expect
A noble ceremony.
FIRST PILGRIM   No question. They come.
Here the ceremony of the Cardinal's instalment in the habit of a soldier, performed in delivering up his cross, hat, robes and ring at the shrine, and investing him with sword, helmet, shield and spurs. Then Antonio, the Duchess and their Children, having presented themselves at the shrine, are (by a form of banishment in dumb show expressed towards them by the Cardinal and the state of Ancona) banished. During all which ceremony, this ditty is sung to very solemn music, by divers Churchmen; and then exeunt [all, except the Two Pilgrims].
CHURCHMEN *Arms and honours deck thy story*
        To thy fame's eternal glory;
        Adverse fortune ever fly thee,   10
        No disastrous fate come nigh thee.

I alone will sing thy praises,
Whom to honour virtue raises;
And thy study that divine is,
Bent to martial discipline is.   15
Lay aside all those robes lie by thee,
Crown thy arts with arms, they'll beautify thee.

O worthy of worthiest name, adorned in this
    manner,
Lead bravely thy forces on under war's warlike
    banner.
O, may'st thou prove fortunate in all martial
    courses,   20
Guide thou still by skill, in arts and forces.
Victory attend thee nigh whilst Fame sings
    loud thy powers,
Triumphant conquest crown thy head, and
    blessings pour down showers.

FIRST PILGRIM Here's a strange turn of state: who would
   have thought
  So great a lady would have matched herself   25
  Unto so mean a person? Yet the Cardinal
  Bears himself much too cruel.
SECOND PILGRIM   They are banished.
FIRST PILGRIM But I would ask what power hath this state
  Of Ancona to determine of a free prince?
SECOND PILGRIM They are a free state, sir, and her
   brother showed   30
  How that the Pope, forehearing of her looseness,
  Hath seized into th' protection of the church
  The dukedom which she held as dowager.
FIRST PILGRIM But by what justice?
SECOND PILGRIM   Sure I think by none,

77

Only her brother's instigation. 35

FIRST PILGRIM What was it with such violence he took
Off from her finger?

SECOND PILGRIM   'Twas her wedding ring,
Which he vowed shortly he would sacrifice
To his revenge.

FIRST PILGRIM   Alas, Antonio!
If that a man be thrust into a well, 40
No matter who sets hand to't, his own weight
Will bring him sooner to th' bottom. Come, let's
    hence.
Fortune makes this conclusion general:
All things do help th' unhappy man to fall.
    Exeunt

Act III Scene V

[*Enter*] *Antonio, Duchess, Children, Cariola,
Servants*

DUCHESS Banished Ancona!

ANTONIO   Yes, you see what power
Lightens in great men's breath.

DUCHESS   Is all our train
Shrunk to this poor remainder?

ANTONIO   These poor men,
Which have got little in your service, vow
To take your fortune; but your wiser buntings, 5
Now they are fledged, are gone.

DUCHESS   They have done wisely.
This puts me in mind of death: physicians thus,
With their hands full of money, use to give o'er
Their patients.

ANTONIO   Right the fashion of the world:
  From decayed fortunes every flatterer shrinks,   10
  Men cease to build where the foundation sinks.
DUCHESS I had a very strange dream tonight.
ANTONIO   What was't?
DUCHESS Methought I wore my coronet of state,
  And on a sudden all the diamonds
  Were changed to pearls.
ANTONIO   My interpretation   15
  Is, you'll weep shortly, for to me, the pearls
  Do signify your tears.
DUCHESS The birds that live i'th' field
  On the wild benefit of nature, live
  Happier than we; for they may choose their mates,   20
  And carol their sweet pleasures to the spring.
     [*Enter Bosola with a letter*]
BOSOLA You are happily o'erta'en.
DUCHESS   From my brother?
BOSOLA Yes, from the Lord Ferdinand, your brother,
  All love and safety.
DUCHESS   Thou dost blanch mischief,
  Wouldst make it white. See, see, like to calm weather   25
  At sea, before a tempest, false hearts speak fair
  To those they intend most mischief.
     [*She reads the*] letter
  'Send Antonio to me; I want his head in a business:'
  A politic equivocation!
  He doth not want your counsel, but your head;   30
  That is, he cannot sleep till you be dead.
  And here's another pitfall that's strewed o'er
  With roses; mark it, 'tis a cunning one:
  'I stand engaged for your husband, for several debts
  at Naples; let not that trouble him: I had rather have   35
  his heart than his money.'

And I believe so too.

BOSOLA   What do you believe?

DUCHESS That he so much distrusts my husband's love,
He will by no means believe his heart is with him
Until he see it. The devil is not cunning enough   40
To circumvent us in riddles.

BOSOLA Will you reject that noble and free league
Of amity and love which I present you?

DUCHESS Their league is like that of some politic kings:
Only to make themselves of strength and pow'r   45
To be our after-ruin. Tell them so.

BOSOLA And what from you?

ANTONIO   Thus tell him: I will not come.

BOSOLA And what of this?

ANTONIO   My brothers have dispersed
Bloodhounds abroad; which till I hear are muzzled,
No truce, though hatched with ne'er such politic skill,   50
Is safe, that hangs upon our enemies' will.
I'll not come at them.

BOSOLA   This proclaims your breeding.
Every small thing draws a base mind to fear,
As the adamant draws iron. Fare you well, sir,
You shall shortly hear from's.   55
        Exit [Bosola]

DUCHESS I suspect some ambush:
Therefore, by all my love, I do conjure you
To take your eldest son, and fly towards Milan.
Let us not venture all this poor remainder
In one unlucky bottom.

ANTONIO   You counsel safely.   60
Best of my life, farewell. Since we must part
Heaven hath a hand in't; but no otherwise
Than as some curious artist takes in sunder
A clock or watch when it is out of frame,

To bring 't in better order.   65
DUCHESS I know not which is best,
    To see you dead, or part with you. [*To her son*] Farewell,
        boy,
    Thou art happy, that thou hast not understanding
    To know thy misery, for all our wit
    And reading brings us to a truer sense   70
    Of sorrow. [*To Antonio*] In the eternal church, sir,
    I do hope we shall not part thus.
ANTONIO   O, be of comfort!
    Make patience a noble fortitude,
    And think not how unkindly we are used:
    Man, like to cassia, is proved best, being bruised.   75
DUCHESS Must I, like to a slave-born Russian,
    Account it praise to suffer tyranny?
    And yet, O Heaven, thy heavy hand is in't.
    I have seen my little boy oft scourge his top
    And compared myself to't: nought made me e'er   80
    Go right but heaven's scourge-stick.
ANTONIO   Do not weep:
    Heaven fashioned us of nothing, and we strive
    To bring ourselves to nothing. Farewell, Cariola,
    And thy sweet armful. [*To the Duchess*] If I do never
        see thee more,
    Be a good mother to your little ones,   85
    And save them from the tiger: fare you well.
DUCHESS Let me look upon you once more, for that
        speech
    Came from a dying father. Your kiss is colder
    Than that I have seen an holy anchorite
    Give to a dead man's skull.   90
ANTONIO My heart is turned to a heavy lump of lead,
    With which I sound my danger: fare you well.
        Exit [*Antonio with his elder Son*]

The Duchess of Malfi

DUCHESS My laurel is all withered.
CARIOLA Look, madam, what a troop of armèd men
    Make toward us.

      Enter Bosola with a guard of soldiers, [all wearing]
      vizards.

DUCHESS   O, they are very welcome.   95
    When Fortune's wheel is overcharged with princes,
    The weight makes it move swift. I would have my ruin
    Be sudden. I am your adventure, am I not?
BOSOLA You are: you must see your husband no more.
DUCHESS What devil art thou, that counterfeits heaven's
    thunder?   100
BOSOLA Is that terrible? I would have you tell me
    Whether is that note worse that frights the silly birds
    Out of the corn, or that which doth allure them
    To the nets? You have hearkened to the last too much.
DUCHESS O misery! Like to a rusty o'ercharged cannon,   105
    Shall I never fly in pieces? Come: to what prison?
BOSOLA To none.
DUCHESS   Whither then?
BOSOLA   To your palace.
DUCHESS   I have heard
    That Charon's boat serves to convey all o'er
    The dismal lake, but brings none back again.
BOSOLA Your brothers mean you safety and pity.
DUCHESS   Pity?   110
    With such a pity men preserve alive
    Pheasants and quails, when they are not fat enough
    To be eaten.
BOSOLA These are your children?
DUCHESS   Yes.
BOSOLA   Can they prattle?
DUCHESS   No:
    But I intend, since they were born accursed,   115

82

Curses shall be their first language.
BOSOLA   Fie, madam,
   Forget this base, low fellow.
DUCHESS   Were I a man
   I'd beat that counterfeit face into thy other.
BOSOLA One of no birth.
DUCHESS   Say that he was born mean:
   Man is most happy when's own actions   120
   Be arguments and examples of his virtue.
BOSOLA A barren, beggarly virtue.
DUCHESS I prithee, who is greatest? Can you tell?
   Sad tales befit my woe: I'll tell you one.
   A salmon, as she swam unto the sea,   125
   Met with a dog-fish, who encounters her
   With this rough language: 'Why art thou so bold
   To mix thyself with our high state of floods,
   Being no eminent courtier, but one
   That for the calmest and fresh time o'th' year   130
   Dost live in shallow rivers, rank'st thyself
   With silly smelts and shrimps? And darest thou
   Pass by our dog-ship, without reverence?'
   'O', quoth the salmon, 'sister, be at peace;
   Thank Jupiter we both have passed the net.   135
   Our value never can be truly known
   Till in the fisher's basket we be shown;
   I'th' market then my price may be the higher,
   Even when I am nearest to the cook and fire.'
   So, to great men, the moral may be stretched: 140
   Men oft are valued high, when th'are most wretch'd.
   But come: whither you please; I am armed 'gainst
          misery,
   Bent to all sways of the oppressor's will.
   There's no deep valley, but near some great hill.
          Exeunt

Act IV Scene I

[*Enter Ferdinand and Bosola*]

FERDINAND How doth our sister Duchess bear herself
  In her imprisonment?

BOSOLA   Nobly. I'll describe her:
  She's sad, as one long used to't, and she seems
  Rather to welcome the end of misery
  Than shun it; a behaviour so noble
  As gives a majesty to adversity.   5
  You may discern the shape of loveliness
  More perfect in her tears than in her smiles;
  She will muse four hours together, and her silence,
  Methinks, expresseth more than if she spake.   10

FERDINAND Her melancholy seems to be fortified
  With a strange disdain.

BOSOLA   'Tis so; and this restraint,
  Like English mastiffs, that grow fierce with tying,
  Makes her too passionately apprehend
  Those pleasures she's kept from.

FERDINAND   Curse upon her!   15
  I will no longer study in the book
  Of another's heart. Inform her what I told you.
     Exit [*Ferdinand. Enter Duchess*]

BOSOLA All comfort to your grace.

DUCHESS   I will have none.
  Pray thee, why dost thou wrap thy poisoned pills
  In gold and sugar?   20

BOSOLA Your elder brother, the Lord Ferdinand,
  Is come to visit you, and sends you word,
  'Cause once he rashly made a solemn vow
  Never to see you more, he comes i'th' night;
  And prays you, gently, neither torch nor taper   25

Shine in your chamber. He will kiss your hand,
And reconcile himself; but, for his vow,
He dares not see you.
DUCHESS   At his pleasure.
  Take hence the lights;
      [*Bosola removes the lights and walks apart. Enter
      Ferdinand*]
                  he's come.
FERDINAND   Where are you?
DUCHESS   Here, sir.
FERDINAND This darkness suits you well. *symptomatic of Ferdinand's incest*
DUCHESS   I would ask you pardon. *Misguided response to his sister*
FERDINAND You have it;
  For I account it the honourabl'st revenge,
  Where I may kill, to pardon. Where are your cubs? *animalisation*
DUCHESS Whom?
FERDINAND Call them your children,   35
  For though our national law distinguish bastards
  From true legitimate issue, compassionate nature
  Makes them all equal.
DUCHESS   Do you visit me for this?
  You violate a sacrament o'th' church
  Shall make you howl in hell for't.
FERDINAND   It had been well,   40
  Could you have lived thus always; for indeed
  You were too much i'th' light. But no more,
  I come to seal my peace with you: here's a hand,
      Gives her a dead man's hand
  To which you have vowed much love; the ring upon't
  You gave.
DUCHESS   I affectionately kiss it.   45
FERDINAND Pray do, and bury the print of it in your
      heart.
  I will leave this ring with you for a love-token;

And the hand, as sure as the ring; and do not doubt
But you shall have the heart too. When you need a
    friend
Send it to him that owed it; you shall see   50
Whether he can aid you.

DUCHESS   You are very cold.
    I fear you are not well after your travel.
    Ha! Lights!
        [*Bosola brings up lights*]
                O horrible!

FERDINAND   Let her have lights enough.
        Exit [Ferdinand]

DUCHESS What witchcraft doth he practise that he hath
    left
    A dead man's hand here?   55
        [*A curtain opens*]. *Here is discovered, behind a
        traverse, the figures of Antonio and his children,
        appearing as if they were dead*

BOSOLA Look you: here's the piece from which 'twas
    ta'en.
    He doth present you this sad spectacle
    That, now you know directly they are dead,
    Hereafter you may wisely cease to grieve
    For that which cannot be recoverèd.   60

DUCHESS There is not between heaven and earth one
    wish
    I stay for after this. It wastes me more
    Than were't my picture, fashioned out of wax,
    Stuck with a magical needle, and then buried
    In some foul dunghill; and yon's an excellent property   65
    For a tyrant, which I would account mercy.

BOSOLA What's that?

DUCHESS If they would bind me to that lifeless trunk,
    And let me freeze to death.

Stoicism

86
1 → he wants to mould her   [coincidentally relates to the merchants
2 → figures made of wax   tale.

BOSOLA   Come, you must live.
DUCHESS That's the greatest torture souls feel in hell,   70
   In hell: that they must live, and cannot die.
   Portia, I'll new-kindle thy coals again,
   And revive the rare and almost dead example
   Of a loving wife.
BOSOLA   O fie! Despair? Remember
   You are a Christian.
DUCHESS   The church enjoins fasting: 75
   I'll starve myself to death.
BOSOLA   Leave this vain sorrow.
   Things being at the worst begin to mend.
   The bee when he hath shot his sting into your hand
   May then play with your eyelid.
DUCHESS Good comfortable fellow,   80
   Persuade a wretch that's broke upon the wheel
   To have all his bones new set; entreat him live
   To be executed again. Who must despatch me?
   I account this world a tedious theatre,
   For I do play a part in't 'gainst my will.   85
BOSOLA Come, be of comfort, I will save your life.
DUCHESS Indeed I have not leisure to tend so small a
      business.
BOSOLA Now, by my life, I pity you.
DUCHESS   Thou art a fool then,
   To waste thy pity on a thing so wretch'd
   As cannot pity itself. I am full of daggers.   90
   Puff! Let me blow these vipers from me.
      [*Enter Servant*]
   What are you?
SERVANT   One that wishes you long life.
DUCHESS I would thou wert hanged for the horrible curse
   Thou hast given me:
      [*Exit Servant*]

                                              87

                    I shall shortly grow one
Of the miracles of pity. I'll go pray; no,   95
I'll go curse.
BOSOLA   O fie!
DUCHESS   I could curse the stars. *pute.*
BOSOLA   O fearful!
DUCHESS And those three smiling seasons of the year
    Into a Russian winter, nay the world *hope.*
    To its first chaos.
BOSOLA Look you, the stars shine still.
DUCHESS   O, but you must   100
    Remember, my curse hath a great way to go.
    Plagues, that make lanes through largest families,
    Consume them!
BOSOLA   Fie, lady!
DUCHESS   Let them, like tyrants,
    Never be remembered, but for the ill they have done;
    Let all the zealous prayers of mortified   105
    Churchmen forget them!
BOSOLA   O uncharitable!
DUCHESS Let heaven, a little while, cease crowning
        martyrs,   *sententiae.*
    To punish them!
    Go, howl them this, and say I long to bleed:
    It is some mercy, when men kill with speed.   110
        Exit [Duchess. Enter Ferdinand]
FERDINAND Excellent; as I would wish; she's plagued in
        art.
    These presentations are but framed in wax,
    By the curious master in that quality,
    Vincentio Lauriola, and she takes them
    For true substantial bodies.   115
BOSOLA Why do you do this?
FERDINAND   To bring her to despair.

[handwritten annotation: literal re-enactment of the fall of mankind from heaven to hell]

BOSOLA Faith, end here,
 And go no farther in your cruelty.
 Send her a penitential garment to put on
 Next to her delicate skin, and furnish her   120
 With beads and prayer-books. *[handwritten: Juxtaposition of prayer with damnation]*
FERDINAND   Damn her! That body of hers,
 While that my blood ran pure in't, was more worth *[handwritten: INCEST!]*
 Than that which thou wouldst comfort, called a soul.
 I will send her masques of common courtesans,
 Have her meat served up by bawds and ruffians,   125
 And, 'cause she'll needs be mad, I am resolved
 To remove forth the common hospital *[handwritten: Ferdinand's ultimate motivation is]*
 All the mad-folk, and place them near her lodging; *[handwritten: a deep incestuous]*
 There let them practise together, sing, and dance, *[handwritten: desire for his]*
 And act their gambols to the full o'th' moon: *[handwritten: sister!]* 130
 If she can sleep the better for it, let her.
 Your work is almost ended.
BOSOLA Must I see her again?
FERDINAND   Yes.
BOSOLA   Never.
FERDINAND   You must.
BOSOLA Never in mine own shape;
 That's forfeited by my intelligence,   135
 And this last cruel lie. When you send me next,
 The business shall be comfort.
FERDINAND   Very likely.
 Thy pity is nothing of kin to thee. Antonio
 Lurks about Milan; thou shalt shortly thither
 To feed a fire, as great as my revenge,   140
 Which ne'er will slack, till it have spent his fuel:
 Intemperate agues make physicians cruel.
      Exeunt

Act IV Scene II

[*Enter Duchess and Cariola*]

DUCHESS What hideous noise was that?

CARIOLA   'Tis the wild consort
Of madmen, lady, which your tyrant brother
Hath placed about your lodging. This tyranny,
I think, was never practised till this hour.

DUCHESS Indeed I thank him: nothing but noise and folly 5
Can keep me in my right wits, whereas reason
And silence make me stark mad. Sit down,
Discourse to me some dismal tragedy.

CARIOLA O, 'twill increase your melancholy.

DUCHESS   Thou art deceived;
To hear of greater grief would lessen mine. 10
This is a prison?

CARIOLA   Yes, but you shall live
To shake this durance off.

DUCHESS   Thou art a fool;
The robin redbreast, and the nightingale,
Never live long in cages.

CARIOLA   Pray dry your eyes.
What think you of, madam?

DUCHESS   Of nothing: 15
When I muse thus, I sleep.

CARIOLA Like a madman, with your eyes open?

DUCHESS Dost thou think we shall know one another,
In th'other world?

CARIOLA   Yes, out of question.

DUCHESS O that it were possible we might 20
But hold some two days' conference with the dead,
From them I should learn somewhat, I am sure
I never shall know here. I'll tell thee a miracle:

I am not mad yet, to my cause of sorrow.
Th' heaven o'er my head seems made of molten brass,   25
The earth of flaming sulphur, yet I am not mad.
I am acquainted with sad misery,
As the tanned galley-slave is with his oar.
Necessity makes me suffer constantly,
And custom makes it easy. Who do I look like now?   30
CARIOLA Like to your picture in the gallery,
    A deal of life in show, but none in practice;
    Or rather like some reverend monument
    Whose ruins are even pitied.
DUCHESS   Very proper;
    And Fortune seems only to have her eyesight   35
    To behold my tragedy. How now!
    What noise is that?
        [*Enter Servant*]
SERVANT   I am come to tell you
    Your brother hath intended you some sport.
    A great physician, when the Pope was sick
    Of a deep melancholy, presented him   40
    With several sorts of madmen, which wild object,
    Being full of change and sport, forced him to laugh,
    And so th' imposthume broke. The self-same cure
    The duke intends on you.
DUCHESS   Let them come in.
SERVANT There's a mad lawyer, and a secular priest,   45
    A doctor that hath forfeited his wits
    By jealousy; an astrologian
    That in his works said such a day o'th' month
    Should be the day of doom, and failing of't,
    Ran mad; an English tailor, crazed i'th' brain   50
    With the study of new fashion; a gentleman usher
    Quite beside himself, with care to keep in mind
    The number of his lady's salutations,

Or 'How do you', she employed him in each morning;
A farmer too, an excellent knave in grain,   55
Mad 'cause he was hindered transportation;
And let one broker that's mad loose to these,
You'd think the devil were among them.
DUCHESS Sit, Cariola. – Let them loose when you please,
For I am chained to endure all your tyranny.   60
    [*Enter Madmen*]
Here, by a Madman, this song is sung to a dismal kind of
    music.
MADMAN (*sings*) *O, let us howl some heavy note,*
            Some deadly dogged howl,
        Sounding as from the threatening throat
            Of beasts, and fatal fowl.   65
        As ravens, screech-owls, bulls, and bears,
            We'll bill and bawl our parts,
        Till irksome noise have cloyed your ears
            And corrosived your hearts.
        At last when as our choir wants breath,   70
            Our bodies being blest,
        We'll sing like swans, to welcome death,
            And die in love and rest.
MAD ASTROLOGER Doomsday not come yet? I'll draw it
    nearer by a perspective, or make a glass that shall   75
    set all the world on fire upon an instant. I cannot
    sleep, my pillow is stuffed with a litter of porcu-
    pines.
MAD LAWYER Hell is a mere glass-house, where the devils
    are continually blowing up women's souls, on hollow   80
    irons, and the fire never goes out.
MAD PRIEST I will lie with every woman in my parish
    the tenth night; I will tithe them over, like haycocks.
MAD DOCTOR Shall my pothecary outgo me, because I
    am a cuckold? I have found out his roguery: he makes   85

alum of his wife's urine, and sells it to puritans that
have sore throats with over-straining.

MAD ASTROLOGER I have skill in heraldry.

MAD LAWYER Hast?

MAD ASTROLOGER You do give for your crest a wood- 90
cock's head, with the brains picked out on't. You are
a very ancient gentleman.

MAD PRIEST Greek is turned Turk; we are only to be
saved by the Helvetian translation.

MAD ASTROLOGER [*to the mad lawyer*] Come on sir, I will 95
lay the law to you.

MAD LAWYER O, rather lay a corrosive; the law will eat
to the bone.

MAD PRIEST He that drinks but to satisfy nature is
damned. 100

MAD DOCTOR If I had my glass here, I would show a
sight should make all the women here call me mad
doctor.

MAD ASTROLOGER [*pointing at the mad priest*] What's he,
a rope-maker? 105

MAD LAWYER No, no, no, a snuffling knave, that while
he shows the tombs, will have his hand in a wench's
placket.

MAD PRIEST Woe to the caroche that brought home my
wife from the masque, at three o'clock in the morning; 110
it had a large featherbed in it.

MAD DOCTOR I have pared the devil's nails forty times,
roasted them in raven's eggs, and cured agues with
them.

MAD PRIEST Get me three hundred milch-bats to make 115
possets to procure sleep.

MAD DOCTOR All the college may throw their caps at
me, I have made a soap-boiler costive. It was my
master-piece.

*Here the dance, consisting of eight Madmen, with
music answerable thereunto; after which Bosola,
like an old man, enters [and the madmen leave]*

DUCHESS Is he mad too?

SERVANT   Pray question him; I'll leave you.   120
[*Exit Servant*]

BOSOLA I am come to make thy tomb.

DUCHESS   Ha, my tomb!
Thou speak'st as if I lay upon my death-bed,
Gasping for breath. Dost thou perceive me sick?

BOSOLA Yes, and the more dangerously, since thy sick-
ness is insensible.   125

DUCHESS Thou art not mad, sure; dost know me?

BOSOLA Yes.

DUCHESS Who am I?

BOSOLA Thou art a box of worm seed, at best, but a
salvatory of green mummy. What's this flesh? A little   130
curded milk, fantastical puff-paste; our bodies are
weaker than those paper prisons boys use to keep flies
in; more contemptible, since ours is to preserve earth-
worms. Didst thou ever see a lark in a cage? Such is
the soul in the body: this world is like her little turf   135
of grass, and the heaven o'er our heads, like her
looking-glass, only gives us a miserable knowledge of
the small compass of our prison.

DUCHESS Am not I thy Duchess?

BOSOLA Thou art some great woman, sure, for riot   140
begins to sit on thy forehead, clad in gray hairs, twenty
years sooner than on a merry milkmaid's. Thou
sleep'st worse than if a mouse should be forced to
take up her lodging in a cat's ear; a little infant that
breeds its teeth, should it lie with thee, would cry out,   145
as if thou wert the more unquiet bedfellow.

DUCHESS I am Duchess of Malfi still.

BOSOLA That makes thy sleeps so broken:
    Glories, like glow-worms, afar off shine bright,
    But looked to near, have neither heat, nor light.   150
DUCHESS Thou art very plain.
BOSOLA My trade is to flatter the dead, not the living;
    I am a tomb-maker.
DUCHESS And thou com'st to make my tomb?
BOSOLA Yes.   155
DUCHESS Let me be a little merry:
    Of what stuff wilt thou make it?
BOSOLA Nay, resolve me first, of what fashion?
DUCHESS Why, do we grow fantastical in our death-bed?
    Do we affect fashion in the grave?   160
BOSOLA Most ambitiously. Princes' images on their
    tombs do not lie, as they were wont, seeming to pray
    up to heaven, but with their hands under their cheeks,
    as if they died of the tooth-ache. They are not carved
    with their eyes fixed upon the stars, but as their minds 165
    were wholly bent upon the world, the selfsame way
    they seem to turn their faces.
DUCHESS Let me know fully therefore the effect
    Of this thy dismal preparation,
    This talk fit for a charnel.
BOSOLA   Now I shall.   170
      [*Enter Executioners with*] *a coffin, cords and a bell.*
    Here is a present from your princely brothers,
    And may it arrive welcome, for it brings
    Last benefit, last sorrow.
DUCHESS   Let me see it.
    I have so much obedience in my blood,
    I wish it in their veins, to do them good.   175
BOSOLA This is your last presence-chamber.
CARIOLA O my sweet lady!
DUCHESS   Peace, it affrights not me.

BOSOLA I am the common bellman
  That usually is sent to condemned persons
  The night before they suffer.
DUCHESS   Even now thou said'st   180
  Thou wast a tomb-maker.
BOSOLA   'Twas to bring you
  By degrees to mortification. Listen:
    [Bosola rings the bell]
      Hark, now everything is still,
      The screech-owl and the whistler shrill
      Call upon our dame, aloud,   185
      And bid her quickly don her shroud.
      Much you had of land and rent,
      Your length in clay's now competent.
      A long war disturbed your mind,
      Here your perfect peace is signed.   190
      Of what is't fools make such vain keeping?
      Sin their conception, their birth weeping;
      Their life a general mist of error,
      Their death a hideous storm of terror.
      Strew your hair with powders sweet,   195
      Don clean linen, bathe your feet,
      And, the foul fiend more to check,
      A crucifix let bless your neck.
      Tis now full tide 'tween night and day:
      End your groan, and come away.   200
    [Executioners approach]
CARIOLA Hence villains, tyrants, murderers! Alas,
  What will you do with my lady? – Call for help.
DUCHESS To whom? To our next neighbours? They are
  mad-folks.
BOSOLA Remove that noise.
    [Executioners seize Cariola]
DUCHESS   Farewell, Cariola.   205

In my last will I have not much to give;
A many hungry guests have fed upon me,
Thine will be a poor reversion.

CARIOLA   I will die with her.

DUCHESS I pray thee look thou giv'st my little boy
  Some syrup for his cold, and let the girl   210
  Say her prayers, ere she sleep.
    [*Executioners force Cariola off*]
                        Now what you please:
  What death?

BOSOLA   Strangling: here are your executioners.

DUCHESS I forgive them:
  The apoplexy, catarrh, or cough o'th' lungs
  Would do as much as they do.   215

BOSOLA Doth not death fright you?

DUCHESS   Who would be afraid on't,
  Knowing to meet such excellent company
  In th'other world?

BOSOLA Yet, methinks,
  The manner of your death should much afflict you,   220
  This cord should terrify you?

DUCHESS   Not a whit.
  What would it pleasure me to have my throat cut
  With diamonds? or to be smothered
  With cassia? or to be shot to death with pearls?
  I know death hath ten thousand several doors   225
  For men to take their exits; and 'tis found
  They go on such strange geometrical hinges,
  You may open them both ways. Any way, for heaven'
    sake,
  So I were out of your whispering. Tell my brothers
  That I perceive death, now I am well awake,   230
  Best gift is they can give, or I can take.
  I would fain put off my last woman's fault,

I'd not be tedious to you.

EXECUTIONER   We are ready.

DUCHESS Dispose my breath how please you, but my
    body
Bestow upon my women, will you?

EXECUTIONER   Yes.   235

DUCHESS Pull, and pull strongly, for your able strength
    Must pull down heaven upon me.
    Yet stay; heaven' gates are not so highly arched
    As princes' palaces; they that enter there
    Must go upon their knees. [*Kneels*] Come, violent
    death,   240
    Serve for mandragora to make me sleep.
    Go tell my brothers, when I am laid out,
    They then may feed in quiet.
        They strangle her

BOSOLA Where's the waiting-woman?
    Fetch her. Some other strangle the children.   245
    [*Executioners bring Cariola, and some go to
    strangle the children.*]
    Look you, there sleeps your mistress.

CARIOLA   O, you are damned
    Perpetually for this. My turn is next,
    Is't not so ordered?

BOSOLA   Yes, and I am glad
    You are so well prepared for't.

CARIOLA   You are deceived sir,
    I am not prepared for't, I will not die;   250
    I will first come to my answer, and know
    How I have offended.

BOSOLA   Come, despatch her.
    You kept her counsel, now you shall keep ours.

CARIOLA I will not die, I must not, I am contracted
    To a young gentleman.

EXECUTIONER [*showing the noose*] Here's your wedding
    ring.   255
CARIOLA Let me but speak with the Duke. I'll discover
  Treason to his person.
BOSOLA   Delays: throttle her.
EXECUTIONER She bites, and scratches.
CARIOLA   If you kill me now
  I am damned: I have not been at confession
  This two years.
BOSOLA   When!
CARIOLA   I am quick with child.
BOSOLA   Why then, 260
  Your credit's saved.
    [*The Executioners strangle Cariola*]
                 Bear her into th'next room;
  Let this lie still.
    [*Exeunt Executioners with the body of Cariola.*
    Enter Ferdinand]
FERDINAND   Is she dead?
BOSOLA   She is what
  You'd have her. But here begin your pity:
    [*Bosola draws a traverse and*] *shows the children*
     strangled
  Alas, how have these offended?
FERDINAND   The death
  Of young wolves is never to be pitied.   265
BOSOLA Fix your eye here.
FERDINAND   Constantly.
BOSOLA   Do you not weep?
  Other sins only speak; murder shrieks out.
  The element of water moistens the earth,
  But blood flies upwards, and bedews the heavens.
FERDINAND Cover her face: mine eyes dazzle: she died
    young.   270

BOSOLA I think not so; her infelicity
  Seemed to have years too many.
FERDINAND She and I were twins;
  And should I die this instant, I had lived
  Her time to a minute.
BOSOLA   It seems she was born first.   275
  You have bloodily approved the ancient truth,
  That kindred commonly do worse agree
  Than remote strangers.
FERDINAND   Let me see her face again.
  Why didst not thou pity her? What an excellent
  Honest man might'st thou have been   280
  If thou hadst borne her to some sanctuary!
  Or, bold in a good cause, opposed thyself
  With thy advancèd sword above thy head,
  Between her innocence and my revenge!
  I bade thee, when I was distracted of my wits,   285
  Go kill my dearest friend, and thou hast done't.
  For let me but examine well the cause:
  What was the meanness of her match to me?
  Only I must confess, I had a hope,
  Had she continued widow, to have gained   290
  An infinite mass of treasure by her death;
  And that was the main cause. Her marriage,
  That drew a stream of gall quite through my heart.
  For thee (as we observe in tragedies
  That a good actor many times is cursed   295
  For playing a villain's part), I hate thee for't:
  And for my sake say thou hast done much ill well.
BOSOLA Let me quicken your memory; for I perceive
  You are falling into ingratitude. I challenge
  The reward due to my service.
FERDINAND   I'll tell thee   300
  What I'll give thee.

BOSOLA   Do.

FERDINAND   I'll give thee a pardon
  For this murder.

BOSOLA   Ha?

FERDINAND   Yes: and 'tis
  The largest bounty I can study to do thee.
  By what authority didst thou execute
  This bloody sentence?

BOSOLA   By yours.

FERDINAND   Mine? Was I her judge? 305
  Did any ceremonial form of law
  Doom her to not-being? Did a complete jury
  Deliver her conviction up i'th' court?
  Where shalt thou find this judgement registered
  Unless in hell? See: like a bloody fool   310
  Thou'st forfeited thy life, and thou shalt die for't.

BOSOLA The office of justice is perverted quite
  When one thief hangs another. Who shall dare
  To reveal this?

FERDINAND   O, I'll tell thee:
  The wolf shall find her grave, and scrape it up;   315
  Not to devour the corpse, but to discover
  The horrid murder.

BOSOLA   You, not I, shall quake for't.

FERDINAND Leave me.

BOSOLA   I will first receive my pension.

FERDINAND You are a villain.

BOSOLA   When your ingratitude
  Is judge, I am so.

FERDINAND   O horror!   320
  That not the fear of him which binds the devils
  Can prescribe man obedience.
  Never look upon me more.

BOSOLA   Why, fare thee well.

Your brother and yourself are worthy men;
You have a pair of hearts are hollow graves,   325
Rotten, and rotting others; and your vengeance,
Like two chained bullets, still goes arm in arm,
You may be brothers; for treason, like the plague,
Doth take much in a blood. I stand like one
That long hath ta'en a sweet and golden dream: 330
I am angry with myself, now that I wake.
FERDINAND Get thee into some unknown part o'th'
    world
That I may never see thee.
BOSOLA   Let me know
Wherefore I should be thus neglected. Sir,
I served your tyranny, and rather strove   335
To satisfy yourself, than all the world;
And though I loathed the evil, yet I loved
You that did counsel it, and rather sought
To appear a true servant than an honest man.
FERDINAND I'll go hunt the badger by owl-light: 340
'Tis a deed of darkness.
    Exit [Ferdinand]
BOSOLA He's much distracted. Off my painted honour!
While with vain hopes our faculties we tire,
We seem to sweat in ice, and freeze in fire.
What would I do, were this to do again?   345
I would not change my peace of conscience
For all the wealth of Europe. She stirs; here's life.
Return, fair soul, from darkness, and lead mine
Out of this sensible hell. She's warm, she breathes.
Upon thy pale lips I will melt my heart   350
To store them with fresh colour. Who's there?
Some cordial drink! Alas, I dare not call:
So pity would destroy pity; her eye opes,
And heaven in it seems to ope, that late was shut,

To take me up to mercy.   355
DUCHESS Antonio.
BOSOLA   Yes, madam, he is living;
  The dead bodies you saw were but feigned statues;
  He's reconciled to your brothers; the Pope hath
      wrought
  The atonement.
DUCHESS   Mercy.
      She dies
BOSOLA O, she's gone again; there the cords of life
      broke.   360
  O sacred innocence, that sweetly sleeps
  On turtles' feathers, whilst a guilty conscience
  Is a black register, wherein is writ
  All our good deeds, and bad, a perspective
  That shows us hell. That we cannot be suffered   365
  To do good when we have a mind to it!
  [*He weeps*] This is manly sorrow:
  These tears, I am very certain, never grew
  In my mother's milk. My estate is sunk
  Below the degree of fear; where were   370
  These penitent fountains while she was living?
  O, they were frozen up. Here is a sight
  As direful to my soul as is the sword
  Unto a wretch hath slain his father. Come,
  I'll bear thee hence,   375
  And execute thy last will; that's deliver
  Thy body to the reverent dispose
  Of some good women; that the cruel tyrant
  Shall not deny me. Then I'll post to Milan
  Where somewhat I will speedily enact   380
  Worth my dejection.
      Exit [*with the body*]

Act V Scene I

[*Enter Antonio and Delio*]

ANTONIO What think you of my hope of reconcilement
  To the Aragonian brethren?

DELIO   I misdoubt it,
  For though they have sent their letters of safe conduct
  For your repair to Milan, they appear
  But nets to entrap you. The Marquis of Pescara,   5
  Under whom you hold certain land in cheat,
  Much 'gainst his noble nature, hath been moved
  To seise those lands, and some of his dependants
  Are at this instant making it their suit
  To be invested in your revenues.   10
  I cannot think they mean well to your life
  That do deprive you of your means of life,
  Your living.

ANTONIO   You are still an heretic
  To any safety I can shape myself.
      [*Enter Pescara*]

DELIO Here comes the Marquis. I will make myself   15
  Petitioner for some part of your land,
  To know whither it is flying.

ANTONIO   I pray do.
      [*Antonio retires*]

DELIO Sir, I have a suit to you.

PESCARA   To me?

DELIO   An easy one.
  There is the Citadel of Saint Benet,
  With some demesnes, of late in the possession   20
  Of Antonio Bologna; please you bestow them on me?

PESCARA You are my friend; but this is such a suit,
  Nor fit for me to give, nor you to take.

DELIO No, sir?
PESCARA   I will give you ample reason for't
  Soon in private.
      [*Enter Julia*]
                    Here's the Cardinal's mistress.   25
JULIA My lord, I am grown your poor petitioner,
  And should be an ill beggar, had I not
  A great man's letter here, the Cardinal's,
  To court you in my favour.
      [*Gives Pescara a letter which he reads*]
PESCARA   He entreats for you
  The Citadel of Saint Bennet, that belonged   30
  To the banished Bologna.
JULIA   Yes.
PESCARA I could not have thought of a friend I could
  Rather pleasure with it: 'tis yours.
JULIA   Sir, I thank you;
  And he shall know how doubly I am engaged
  Both in your gift, and speediness of giving,   35
  Which makes your grant the greater.
      Exit [*Julia*]
ANTONIO [*aside*]   How they fortify
  Themselves with my ruin!
DELIO   Sir, I am
  Little bound to you.
PESCARA   Why?
DELIO Because you denied this suit to me, and gave't
  To such a creature.
PESCARA   Do you know what it was?   40
  It was Antonio's land; not forfeited
  By course of law, but ravished from his throat
  By the Cardinal's entreaty. It were not fit
  I should bestow so main a piece of wrong
  Upon my friend; 'tis a gratification   45

Only due to a strumpet, for it is injustice.
Shall I sprinkle the pure blood of innocents
To make those followers I call my friends
Look ruddier upon me? I am glad
This land, ta'en from the owner by such wrong,   50
Returns again unto so foul an use
As salary for his lust. Learn, good Delio,
To ask noble things of me, and you shall find
I'll be a noble giver.
DELIO   You instruct me well.
ANTONIO [*aside*] Why, here's a man now, would fright
     impudence   55
     From sauciest beggars.
PESCARA Prince Ferdinand's come to Milan
     Sick, as they give out, of an apoplexy;
     But some say 'tis a frenzy; I am going
     To visit him.
           Exit [*Pescara*]
ANTONIO [*advancing*] 'Tis a noble old fellow.   60
DELIO What course do you mean to take, Antonio?
ANTONIO This night I mean to venture all my fortune,
     Which is no more than a poor lingering life,
     To the Cardinal's worst of malice. I have got
     Private access to his chamber, and intend   65
     To visit him, about the mid of night,
     As once his brother did our noble Duchess.
     It may be that the sudden apprehension
     Of danger (for I'll go in mine own shape),
     When he shall see it fraught with love and duty,   70
     May draw the poison out of him, and work
     A friendly reconcilement; if it fail,
     Yet it shall rid me of this infamous calling,
     For better fall once, than be ever falling.
DELIO I'll second you in all danger; and howe'er,   75

My life keeps rank with yours.
ANTONIO You are still my loved and best friend.
    Exeunt

Act V Scene II

    [*Enter Pescara and a Doctor*]
PESCARA Now, doctor, may I visit your patient?
DOCTOR If't please your lordship; but he's instantly
  To take the air here in the gallery,
  By my direction.   Pray thee, what's his disease?
DOCTOR A very pestilent disease, my lord,   5
  They call lycanthropia.
PESCARA   What's that?
  I need a dictionary to't.
DOCTOR   I'll tell you:
  In those that are possessed with't there o'erflows
  Such melancholy humour, they imagine
  Themselves to be transformèd into wolves,   10
  Steal forth to churchyards in the dead of night,
  And dig dead bodies up; as two nights since
  One met the Duke, 'bout midnight in a lane
  Behind Saint Mark's church, with the leg of a man
  Upon his shoulder; and he howled fearfully;   15
  Said he was a wolf, only the difference
  Was a wolf's skin was hairy on the outside,
  His on the inside; bade them take their swords,
  Rip up his flesh, and try. Straight I was sent for,
  And having ministered to him, found his grace   20
  Very well recoverèd.
PESCARA   I am glad on't.

DOCTOR Yet not without some fear
  Of a relapse. If he grow to his fit again
  I'll go a nearer way to work with him
  Than ever Paracelsus dreamed of. If   25
  They'll give me leave, I'll buffet his madness out of
    him.
    [*Enter Ferdinand, Malateste, and Cardinal;*
    Bosola apart]
  Stand aside, he comes.
FERDINAND Leave me.
MALATESTE Why doth your lordship love this solitari-
  ness?   30
FERDINAND Eagles commonly fly alone. They are crows,
  daws, and starlings that flock together. Look, what's
  that follows me?
MALATESTE Nothing, my lord.
FERDINAND Yes.   35
MALATESTE 'Tis your shadow.
FERDINAND Stay it, let it not haunt me.
MALATESTE Impossible, if you move, and the sun
  shine.
FERDINAND I will throttle it.   40
    [*Throws himself upon his shadow*]
MALATESTE O, my lord, you are angry with nothing.
FERDINAND You are a fool. How is't possible I should
  catch my shadow unless I fall upon't? When I go to
  hell, I mean to carry a bribe; for look you, good gifts
  evermore make way for the worst persons.   45
PESCARA Rise, good my lord.
FERDINAND I am studying the art of patience.
PESCARA 'Tis a noble virtue.
FERDINAND To drive six snails before me, from this
  town to Moscow; neither use goad nor whip to them,   50
  but let them take their own time (the patient'st man

i'th' world match me for an experiment), and I'll crawl
after like a sheep-biter.

CARDINAL Force him up.

    [*They raise him*]

FERDINAND Use me well, you were best. What I have   55
done, I have done; I'll confess nothing.

DOCTOR Now let me come to him. Are you mad, my
lord? Are you out of your princely wits?

FERDINAND What's he?

PESCARA Your doctor.   60

FERDINAND Let me have his beard sawed off, and his
eyebrows filed more civil.

DOCTOR I must do mad tricks with him, for that's the
only way on't. I have brought your grace a salamander's skin, to keep you from sun-burning.   65

FERDINAND I have cruel sore eyes.

DOCTOR The white of a cockatrice's egg is present remedy.

FERDINAND Let it be a new-laid one, you were best.
Hide me from him. Physicians are like kings,
They brook no contradiction.   70

DOCTOR Now he begins to fear me, now let me alone
with him.

    [*Ferdinand tries to undress; the Cardinal restrains
    him*]

CARDINAL How now, put off your gown?

DOCTOR Let me have some forty urinals filled with rose-
water: he and I'll go pelt one another with them, now   75
he begins to fear me. Can you fetch a frisk, sir? Let
him go, let him go upon my peril. I find by his eye,
he stands in awe of me; I'll make him as tame as a
dormouse.

    [*Cardinal releases Ferdinand*]

FERDINAND Can you fetch your frisks, sir? I will stamp   80
him into a cullis, flay off his skin, to cover one of the

anatomies this rogue hath set i'th' cold yonder, in
Barber-Chirurgeons' Hall. Hence, hence, you are all
of you like beasts for sacrifice; there's nothing left of
you, but tongue and belly, flattery and lechery.   85
    [*Exit Ferdinand*]
PESCARA Doctor, he did not fear you throughly.
DOCTOR True, I was somewhat too forward.
    [*Exit Doctor*]
BOSOLA [*aside*] Mercy upon me, what a fatal judgement
  Hath fallen upon this Ferdinand!
PESCARA   Knows your grace
  What accident hath brought unto the Prince   90
  This strange distraction?
CARDINAL [*aside*] I must feign somewhat. [*To them*] Thus
    they say it grew:
  You have heard it rumoured for these many years,
  None of our family dies, but there is seen
  The shape of an old woman, which is given   95
  By tradition to us to have been murdered
  By her nephews, for her riches. Such a figure
  One night, as the Prince sat up late at's book,
  Appeared to him when, crying out for help,
  The gentlemen of's chamber found his grace   100
  All on a cold sweat, alter'd much in face
  And language. Since which apparition,
  He hath grown worse and worse, and I much fear
  He cannot live.
BOSOLA [*to the Cardinal*] Sir, I would speak with you.
PESCARA   We'll leave your grace, 105
  Wishing to the sick Prince, our noble lord,
  All health of mind and body.
CARDINAL   You are most welcome.
    [*Exeunt all except Cardinal and Bosola*]
  Are you come? So; [*aside*] this fellow must not know

By any means I had intelligence
In our Duchess' death; for, though I counselled it,   110
The full of all th'engagement seemed to grow
From Ferdinand. [*To him*] Now, sir, how fares our
          sister?
I do not think but sorrow makes her look
Like to an oft-dyed garment. She shall now
Taste comfort from me. Why do you look so wildly?   115
O, the fortune of your master here, the Prince,
Dejects you, but be you of happy comfort:
If you'll do one thing for me I'll entreat,
Though he had a cold tombstone o'er his bones,
I'd make you what you would be.
BOSOLA   Anything;   120
Give it me in a breath, and let me fly to 't.
They that think long, small expedition win,
For musing much o'th' end, cannot begin.
          [*Enter Julia*]
JULIA Sir, will you come in to supper?
CARDINAL   I am busy, leave me.
JULIA [*aside*] What an excellent shape hath that fellow!   125
          [*Exit Julia*]
CARDINAL 'Tis thus: Antonio lurks here in Milan;
Inquire him out, and kill him. While he lives
Our sister cannot marry, and I have thought
Of an excellent match for her. Do this, and style me
Thy advancement.
BOSOLA   But by what means shall I find him out?   130
CARDINAL There is a gentleman, called Delio,
Here in the camp, that hath been long approved
His loyal friend. Set eye upon that fellow,
Follow him to mass; maybe Antonio,
Although he do account religion   135
But a school-name, for fashion of the world

May accompany him; or else go inquire out
Delio's confessor, and see if you can bribe
Him to reveal it. There are a thousand ways
A man might find to trace him; as to know   140
What fellows haunt the Jews for taking up
Great sums of money, for sure he's in want;
Or else to go to th' picture-makers, and learn
Who brought her picture lately: some of these
Happily may take.

BOSOLA   Well, I'll not freeze i'th' business; 145
I would see that wretched thing, Antonio,
Above all sights i'th' world.

CARDINAL   Do, and be happy.
    Exit [Cardinal]

BOSOLA This fellow doth breed basilisks in's eyes.
He's nothing else but murder; yet he seems
Not to have notice of the Duchess' death.   150
'Tis his cunning. I must follow his example;
There cannot be a surer way to trace
Than that of an old fox.
    [Enter Julia holding a pistol]

JULIA   So, sir, you are well met.

BOSOLA How now?

JULIA   Nay, the doors are fast enough.
Now, sir, I will make you confess your treachery. 155

BOSOLA Treachery?

JULIA   Yes, confess to me
Which of my women 'twas you hired, to put
Love-powder into my drink?

BOSOLA   Love-powder!

JULIA   Yes,
When I was at Malfi.
Why should I fall in love with such a face else? 160
I have already suffered for thee so much pain,

The only remedy to do me good
Is to kill my longing.
BOSOLA   Sure your pistol holds
   Nothing but perfumes, or kissing-comfits.
   Excellent lady,   165
   You have a pretty way on't to discover
   Your longing. Come, come, I'll disarm you,
   And arm you thus [*embraces her*]; yet this is wondrous
        strange.
JULIA Compare thy form and my eyes together,
   You'll find my love no such great miracle.   170
   Now you'll say
   I am wanton. This nice modesty in ladies
   Is but a troublesome familiar
   That haunts them.
BOSOLA Know you me, I am a blunt soldier.
JULIA   The better;   175
   Sure there wants fire where there are no lively sparks
   Of roughness.
BOSOLA   And I want compliment.
JULIA   Why, ignorance
   In courtship cannot make you do amiss,
   If you have a heart to do well.
BOSOLA   You are very fair.
JULIA Nay, if you lay beauty to my charge,   180
   I must plead unguilty.
BOSOLA   Your bright eyes
   Carry a quiver of darts in them, sharper
   Than sunbeams.
JULIA   You will mar me with commendation,
   Put yourself to the charge of courting me,
   Whereas now I woo you.   185
BOSOLA [*aside*] I have it, I will work upon this creature.
   [*To her*] Let us grow most amorously familiar.

If the great Cardinal now should see me thus,
Would he not count me a villain?
JULIA   No, he might count me a wanton,   190
   Not lay a scruple of offence on you;
   For if I see and steal a diamond,
   The fault is not i'th' stone, but in me the thief
   That purloins it. I am sudden with you;
   We that are great women of pleasure use to cut off   195
   These uncertain wishes, and unquiet longings,
   And in an instant join the sweet delight
   And the pretty excuse together; had you been i'th'
      street,
   Under my chamber window, even there
   I should have courted you.
BOSOLA   O, you are an excellent lady.   200
JULIA Bid me do somewhat for you presently
   To express I love you.
BOSOLA   I will, and if you love me,
   Fail not to effect it.
   The Cardinal is grown wondrous melancholy;
   Demand the cause; let him not put you off   205
   With feigned excuse, discover the main ground on't.
JULIA Why would you know this?
BOSOLA   I have depended on him,
   And I hear that he is fallen in some disgrace
   With the Emperor. If he be, like the mice
   That forsake falling houses, I would shift   210
   To other dependance.
JULIA You shall not need follow the wars;
   I'll be your maintenance.
BOSOLA   And I your loyal servant;
   But I cannot leave my calling.
JULIA   Not leave
   An ungrateful general for the love of a sweet lady?

You are like some, cannot sleep in feather-beds,
But must have blocks for their pillows.
BOSOLA   Will you do this?
JULIA Cunningly.
BOSOLA   Tomorrow I'll expect th'intelligence.
JULIA Tomorrow? Get you into my cabinet,
   You shall have it with you; do not delay me,   220
   No more than I do you. I am like one
   That is condemned: I have my pardon promised,
   But I would see it sealed. Go, get you in,
   You shall see me wind my tongue about his heart,
   Like a skein of silk.   225
      [*Bosola withdraws. Enter Cardinal, attended by
      Servants*]
CARDINAL Where are you?
SERVANTS   Here.
CARDINAL   Let none upon your lives
   Have conference with the Prince Ferdinand,
   Unless I know it.
      [*Exeunt Servants*]
                   [*Aside*] In this distraction
   He may reveal the murder.
   Yon's my lingering consumption: 230
   I am weary of her, and by any means
   Would be quit of.
JULIA   How now, my lord?
   What ails you?
CARDINAL   Nothing.
JULIA   O, you are much altered:
   Come, I must be your secretary, and remove
   This lead from off your bosom: what's the matter?   235
CARDINAL I may not tell you.
JULIA Are you so far in love with sorrow,
   You cannot part with part of it? Or think you

I cannot love your grace when you are sad,
As well as merry? Or do you suspect   240
I, that have been a secret to your heart
These many winters, cannot be the same
Unto your tongue?
CARDINAL   Satisfy thy longing,
The only way to make thee keep my counsel
Is not to tell thee.
JULIA   Tell your echo this,   245
Or flatterers that, like echoes, still report
What they hear (though most imperfect), and not me;
For, if that you be true unto yourself,
I'll know.
CARDINAL Will you rack me?
JULIA   No, judgement shall
Draw it from you. It is an equal fault   250
To tell one's secrets unto all, or none.
CARDINAL The first argues folly.
JULIA   But the last tyranny.
CARDINAL Very well. Why, imagine I have committed
Some secret deed, which I desire the world
May never hear of.
JULIA   Therefore may not I know it?   255
You have concealed for me as great a sin
As adultery. Sir, never was occasion
For perfect trial of my constancy
Till now. Sir, I beseech you.
CARDINAL   You'll repent it.
JULIA   Never.
CARDINAL It hurries thee to ruin. I'll not tell thee.   260
Be well advised, and think what danger 'tis
To receive a prince's secrets; they that do,
Had need have their breasts hooped with adamant
To contain them. I pray thee yet be satisfied,

Examine thine own frailty; 'tis more easy   265
To tie knots, than unloose them; 'tis a secret
That, like a ling'ring poison, may chance lie
Spread in thy veins, and kill thee seven year hence.

JULIA Now you dally with me.

CARDINAL   No more, thou shalt know it.
By my appointment the great Duchess of Malfi,   270
And two of her young children, four nights since,
Were strangled.

JULIA   O heaven! Sir, what have you done?

CARDINAL How now? How settles this? Think you your
    bosom
Will be a grave dark and obscure enough
For such a secret?

JULIA   You have undone yourself, sir.   275

CARDINAL Why?

JULIA   It lies not in me to conceal it.

CARDINAL   No?
Come, I will swear you to't upon this book.
    [*He holds out a bible*]

JULIA Most religiously.

CARDINAL   Kiss it.
    [*She kisses it*]
Now you shall never utter it; thy curiosity
Hath undone thee: thou'rt poisoned with that book; 280
Because I knew thou couldst not keep my counsel,
I have bound thee to't by death.
    [*Enter Bosola*]

BOSOLA For pity' sake, hold!

CARDINAL   Ha, Bosola!

JULIA   I forgive you
This equal piece of justice you have done,
For I betrayed your counsel to that fellow;   285
He overheard it; that was the cause I said

It lay not in me to conceal it.
BOSOLA O foolish woman,
  Couldst not thou have poisoned him?
JULIA   'Tis weakness
  Too much to think what should have been done. I go, 290
  I know not whither.
        [*Julia dies*]
CARDINAL   Wherefore com'st thou hither?
BOSOLA That I might find a great man, like yourself,
  Not out of his wits, as the Lord Ferdinand,
  To remember my service.
CARDINAL   I'll have thee hewed in pieces.
BOSOLA Make not yourself such a promise of that life 295
  Which is not yours to dispose of.
CARDINAL   Who placed thee here?
BOSOLA Her lust, as she intended.
CARDINAL   Very well;
  Now you know me for your fellow murderer.
BOSOLA And wherefore should you lay fair marble
        colours
  Upon your rotten purposes to me?   300
  Unless you imitate some that do plot great treasons,
  And when they have done, go hide themselves i'th'
        graves
  Of those were actors in't?
CARDINAL No more, there is a fortune attends thee.
BOSOLA Shall I go sue to Fortune any longer?   305
  'Tis the fool's pilgrimage.
CARDINAL   I have honours in store for thee.
BOSOLA There are a many ways that conduct to seeming
  Honour, and some of them very dirty ones.
CARDINAL Throw to the devil
  Thy melancholy. The fire burns well,   310
  What need we keep a-stirring of't, and make

A greater smother? Thou wilt kill Antonio?
BOSOLA Yes.
CARDINAL   Take up that body.
BOSOLA   I think I shall
  Shortly grow the common bier for churchyards.
CARDINAL I will allow thee some dozen of attendants   315
  To aid thee in the murder.
BOSOLA O, by no means: Physicians that apply horse-
  leeches to any rank swelling use to cut off their tails,
  that the blood may run through them the faster. Let
  me have no train when I go to shed blood, lest it make   320
  me have a greater when I ride to the gallows.
CARDINAL Come to me after midnight, to help to
      remove that body
  To her own lodging; I'll give out she died o'th' plague;
  'Twill breed the less inquiry after her death.
BOSOLA Where's Castruccio, her husband?   325
CARDINAL He's rode to Naples to take possession
  Of Antonio's citadel.
BOSOLA Believe me, you have done a very happy turn.
CARDINAL Fail not to come. There is the master-key
  Of our lodgings; and by that you may conceive   330
  What trust I plant in you.
BOSOLA   You shall find me ready.
      Exit [Cardinal]
  O poor Antonio, though nothing be so needful
  To thy estate as pity, yet I find
  Nothing so dangerous. I must look to my footing.
  In such slippery ice-pavements, men had need   335
  To be frost-nailed well: they may break their necks
      else.
  The precedent's here afore me: how this man
  Bears up in blood! seems fearless! Why, 'tis well:
  Security some men call the suburbs of hell,

Only a dead wall between. Well, good Antonio,   340
I'll seek thee out, and all my care shall be
To put thee into safety from the reach
Of these most cruel biters, that have got
Some of thy blood already. It may be
I'll join with thee in a most just revenge.   345
The weakest arm is strong enough, that strikes
With the sword of justice. Still methinks the Duchess
Haunts me; there, there:
'Tis nothing but my melancholy.
O penitence, let me truly taste thy cup,   350
That throws men down, only to raise them up.
    Exit [with the body]

Act V Scene III

    [*Enter Antonio and Delio]. There is an echo from
    the Duchess' grave*

DELIO Yon's the Cardinal's window. This fortification
  Grew from the ruins of an ancient abbey,
  And to yond side o'th' river lies a wall,
  Piece of a cloister, which in my opinion
  Gives the best echo that you ever heard: 5
  So hollow, and so dismal, and withal
  So plain in the distinction of our words,
  That many have supposed it is a spirit
  That answers.
ANTONIO   I do love these ancient ruins:
  We never tread upon them but we set   10
  Our foot upon some reverend history.
  And questionless, here in this open court,
  Which now lies naked to the injuries

Of stormy weather, some men lie interred
Loved the church so well, and gave so largely to't,   15
They thought it should have canopied their bones
Till doomsday. But all things have their end:
Churches and cities, which have diseases like to men,
Must have like death that we have.

ECHO   Like death that we have.

DELIO Now the echo hath caught you.

ANTONIO   It groaned, methought, and gave   20
A very deadly accent.

ECHO   Deadly accent.

DELIO I told you 'twas a pretty one. You may make it
A huntsman, or a falconer, a musician,
Or a thing of sorrow.

ECHO   A thing of sorrow.

ANTONIO Ay, sure: that suits it best.

ECHO   That suits it best.   25

ANTONIO 'Tis very like my wife's voice.

ECHO   Ay, wife's voice.

DELIO Come, let's us walk farther from't.
I would not have you go to th' Cardinal's tonight:
Do not.

ECHO   Do not.

DELIO Wisdom doth not more moderate wasting sorrow   30
Than time: take time for't; be mindful of thy safety.

ECHO Be mindful of thy safety.

ANTONIO   Necessity compels me:
Make scrutiny throughout the passes
Of your own life, you'll find it impossible
To fly your fate.

ECHO   O, fly your fate.   35

DELIO Hark, the dead stones seem to have pity on you
And give you good counsel.

ANTONIO Echo, I will not talk with thee,

For thou art a dead thing.
ECHO   Thou art a dead thing.
ANTONIO My Duchess is asleep now,   40
  And her little ones, I hope, sweetly. O heaven,
  Shall I never see her more?
ECHO   Never see her more.
ANTONIO I marked not one repetition of the echo
  But that; and on the sudden, a clear light
  Presented me a face folded in sorrow.   45
DELIO Your fancy, merely.
ANTONIO Come, I'll be out of this ague;
  For to live thus is not indeed to live:
  It is a mockery, and abuse of life.
  I will not henceforth save myself by halves;   50
  Lose all, or nothing.
DELIO   Your own virtue save you.
  I'll fetch your eldest son, and second you;
  It may be that the sight of his own blood,
  Spread in so sweet a figure, may beget
  The more compassion.
ANTONIO   However, fare you well.   55
  Though in our miseries Fortune have a part,
  Yet in our noble suff'rings she hath none:
  Contempt of pain, that we may call our own.
      Exeunt

Act V Scene IV

[*Enter*] *Cardinal, Pescara, Malateste, Roderigo, Grisolan*
CARDINAL You shall not watch tonight by the sick
  Prince,

His grace is very well recovered.
MALATESTE Good my lord, suffer us.
CARDINAL   O, by no means;
  The noise and change of object in his eye
  Doth more distract him. I pray, all to bed,   5
  And though you hear him in his violent fit,
  Do not rise, I entreat you.
PESCARA So sir, we shall not.
CARDINAL   Nay, I must have you promise
  Upon your honours, for I was enjoined to't
  By himself; and he seemed to urge it sensibly.   10
PESCARA Let our honours bind this trifle.
CARDINAL Nor any of your followers.
MALATESTE   Neither.
CARDINAL It may be, to make trial of your promise
  When he's asleep, myself will rise and feign
  Some of his mad tricks, and cry out for help,   15
  And feign myself in danger.
MALATESTE   If your throat were cutting,
  I'd not come at you, now I have protested against it.
CARDINAL Why, I thank you.
    [*Cardinal withdraws*]
GRISOLAN   'Twas a foul storm tonight.
RODERIGO The Lord Ferdinand's chamber shook like an
  osier.
MALATESTE 'Twas nothing but pure kindness in the
  devil   20
  To rock his own child.
    Exeunt [*all except the Cardinal*]
CARDINAL The reason why I would not suffer these
  About my brother, is because at midnight
  I may with better privacy convey
  Julia's body to her own lodging. O, my conscience!   25
  I would pray now, but the devil takes away my heart

123

For having any confidence in prayer.
About this hour I appointed Bosola
To fetch the body. When he hath served my turn,
He dies.   30
          Exit [Cardinal. Enter Bosola]
BOSOLA Ha? 'Twas the Cardinal's voice. I heard him name
    Bosola, and my death. Listen, I hear one's footing.
          [Enter Ferdinand]
FERDINAND Strangling is a very quiet death.
BOSOLA *[aside]* Nay then, I see I must stand upon my
          guard.
FERDINAND What say' to that? Whisper, softly: do you
          agree to't?   35
    So it must be done i'th' dark: the Cardinal
    Would not for a thousand pounds the doctor should
          see it.
          Exit [Ferdinand]
BOSOLA My death is plotted; here's the consequence of
          murder:
    We value not desert, nor Christian breath,
    When we know black deeds must be cured with death.   40
          [Enter Antonio and Servant]
SERVANT Here stay, sir, and be confident, I pray.
    I'll fetch you a dark lantern.
          Exit [Servant]
ANTONIO   Could I take him
    At his prayers, there were hope of pardon.
BOSOLA Fall right my sword!
          [Stabs Antonio]
    I'll not give thee so much leisure as to pray.   45
ANTONIO O, I am gone. Thou hast ended a long suit
    In a minute.
BOSOLA   What art thou?
ANTONIO   A most wretched thing,

That only have thy benefit in death,
To appear myself.
    [*Enter Servant with a lantern*]
SERVANT   Where are you, sir?
ANTONIO Very near my home: – Bosola?
SERVANT   O, misfortune.   50
BOSOLA [*to Servant*] Smother thy pity, thou art dead
    else. – Antonio!
The man I would have saved 'bove mine own life!
We are merely the stars' tennis balls, struck and bandied
Which way please them. – O good Antonio,
I'll whisper one thing in thy dying ear   55
Shall make thy heart break quickly: thy fair Duchess
And two sweet children –
ANTONIO   Their very names
Kindle a little life in me.
BOSOLA   Are murdered!
ANTONIO Some men have wished to die
At the hearing of sad tidings: I am glad   60
That I shall do't in sadness; I would not now
Wish my wounds balmed, nor healed, for I have no use
To put my life to. In all our quest of greatness,
Like wanton boys whose pastime is their care,
We follow after bubbles, blown in th'air.   65
Pleasure of life, what is't? Only the good hours
Of an ague; merely a preparative to rest,
To endure vexation. I do not ask
The process of my death; only commend me
To Delio.   70
BOSOLA Break heart!
ANTONIO   And let my son fly the courts of princes.
    [*Antonio dies*]
BOSOLA Thou seem'st to have loved Antonio?
SERVANT   I brought him hither,

To have reconciled him to the Cardinal.
BOSOLA I do not ask thee that.
   Take him up, if thou tender thine own life,   75
   And bear him where the Lady Julia
   Was wont to lodge.
        [Servant picks up the corpse]
                  O, my fate moves swift!
   I have this Cardinal in the forge already,
   Now I'll bring him to th' hammer. O direful misprision!
   I will not imitate things glorious,   80
   No more than base: I'll be mine own example.
   [To Servant] On, on, and look thou represent, for silence,
   The thing thou bear'st.
      Exeunt [with the Servant carrying Antonio's body]

Act V Scene V

     [Enter] Cardinal, with a book
CARDINAL I am puzzled in a question about hell.
   He says, in hell there's one material fire,
   And yet it shall not burn all men alike.
   Lay him by. How tedious is a guilty conscience!
   When I look into the fishponds, in my garden,   5
   Methinks I see a thing armed with a rake
   That seems to strike at me.
     [Enter Bosola, and Servant with Antonio's body]
                  Now? art thou come?
   Thou look'st ghastly:
   There sits in thy face some great determination,
   Mixed with some fear.
BOSOLA   Thus it lightens into action: 10
   I am come to kill thee.

CARDINAL   Ha? Help! our guard!
BOSOLA Thou art deceived:
  They are out of thy howling.
CARDINAL Hold, and I will faithfully divide
  Revenues with thee.
BOSOLA   Thy prayers and proffers   15
  Are both unseasonable.
CARDINAL   Raise the watch!
  We are betrayed!
BOSOLA   I have confined your flight:
  I'll suffer your retreat to Julia's chamber,
  But no further.
CARDINAL   Help! We are betrayed!
      [*Enter above, Pescara, Malateste, Roderigo and
      Grisolan*]
MALATESTE   Listen.
CARDINAL My dukedom for rescue!
RODERIGO   Fie upon his counterfeiting!   20
MALATESTE Why, 'tis not the Cardinal.
RODERIGO   Yes, yes, 'tis he,
  But I'll see him hanged, ere I'll go down to him.
CARDINAL Here's a plot upon me; I am assaulted! I am
      lost,
  Unless some rescue!
GRISOLAN   He doth this pretty well;
  But it will not serve to laugh me out of mine honour.   25
CARDINAL The sword's at my throat!
RODERIGO   You would not bawl so loud then.
MALATESTE Come, come,
  Let's go to bed; he told us thus much aforehand.
PESCARA He wished you should not come at him; but
      believe't,
  The accent of the voice sounds not in jest.   30
  I'll down to him, howsoever, and with engines

Force ope the doors.
    [*Exit Pescara*]
RODERIGO   Let's follow him aloof,
  And note how the Cardinal will laugh at him.
    [*Exeunt all above*]
BOSOLA There's for you first,
    He kills the Servant
  'Cause you shall not unbarricade the door   35
  To let in rescue.
CARDINAL What cause hast thou to pursue my life?
BOSOLA   Look there.
CARDINAL Antonio?
BOSOLA   Slain by my hand unwittingly.
  Pray, and be sudden; when thou killed'st thy sister,
  Thou took'st from Justice her most equal balance,   40
  And left her naught but her sword.
CARDINAL   O, mercy!
BOSOLA Now it seems thy greatness was only outward,
  For thou fall'st faster of thyself than calamity
  Can drive thee. I'll not waste longer time: there!
    [*Stabs the Cardinal*]
CARDINAL Thou hast hurt me.
BOSOLA   Again!
    [*Stabs him again*]
CARDINAL   Shall I die like a leveret   45
  Without any resistance? Help, help, help!
  I am slain!
    [*Enter Ferdinand*]
FERDINAND   Th'alarum! Give me a fresh horse:
  Rally the vanguard, or the day is lost.
  [*Threatens the Cardinal*] Yield, yield! I give you the
    honour of arms,
  Shake my sword over you, will you yield?   50
CARDINAL Help me, I am your brother.

FERDINAND   The devil?
  My brother fight upon the adverse party?
  There flies your ransom.
          He wounds the Cardinal, and in the scuffle gives
          Bosola his death wound
CARDINAL   O Justice!
  I suffer now for what hath former been:
  Sorrow is held the eldest child of sin.   55
FERDINAND Now you're brave fellows. Caesar's fortune
  was harder than Pompey's: Caesar died in the arms
  of prosperity, Pompey at the feet of disgrace; you both
  died in the field. The pain's nothing; pain many times
  is taken away with the apprehension of greater, as the   60
  toothache with the sight of a barber that comes to
  pull it out: there's philosophy for you.
BOSOLA Now my revenge is perfect.
          He kills Ferdinand
                                  Sink, thou main cause
  Of my undoing! The last part of my life
  Hath done me best service.   65
FERDINAND Give me some wet hay, I am broken
          winded.
  I do account this world but a dog-kennel;
  I will vault credit, and affect high pleasures,
  Beyond death.
BOSOLA   He seems to come to himself,
  Now he's so near the bottom.   70
FERDINAND My sister! O my sister! There's the cause
          on't:
  Whether we fall by ambition, blood, or lust,
  Like diamonds, we are cut with our own dust.
          [*Ferdinand dies*]
CARDINAL Thou hast thy payment too.
BOSOLA Yes, I hold my weary soul in my teeth;   75

'Tis ready to part from me. I do glory
That thou, which stood'st like a huge pyramid
Begun upon a large and ample base,
Shalt end in a little point, a kind of nothing.
          [*Enter Pescara, Malateste, Roderigo, and Grisolan*]
PESCARA How now, my lord?
MALATESTE   O sad disaster!
RODERIGO   How comes this?   80
BOSOLA Revenge, for the Duchess of Malfi, murderèd
    By th'Aragonian brethren; for Antonio,
    Slain by this hand; for lustful Julia,
    Poisoned by this man; and lastly, for myself,
    That was an actor in the main of all   85
    Much 'gainst mine own good nature, yet i'th' end
    Neglected.
PESCARA   How now, my lord?
CARDINAL   Look to my brother:
    He gave us these large wounds, as we were struggling
    Here i'th' rushes: And now, I pray, let me
    Be laid by, and never thought of.   90
          [*The Cardinal dies*]
PESCARA How fatally, it seems, he did withstand
        His own rescue!
MALATESTE   Thou wretched thing of blood,
    How came Antonio by his death?
BOSOLA In a mist: I know not how;
    Such a mistake as I have often seen   95
    In a play. O, I am gone.
    We are only like dead walls, or vaulted graves,
    That, ruined, yields no echo. Fare you well.
    It may be pain, but no harm to me to die
    In so good a quarrel. O, this gloomy world!   100
    In what a shadow, or deep pit of darkness,
    Doth, womanish and fearful, mankind live!

Let worthy minds ne'er stagger in distrust
To suffer death, or shame for what is just:
Mine is another voyage.   105
    [*Bosola dies*]
PESCARA The noble Delio, as I came to th' palace,
  Told me of Antonio's being here, and showed me
  A pretty gentleman, his son and heir.
    [*Enter Delio, with Antonio's son*]
MALATESTE O sir, you come too late!
DELIO   I heard so, and
  Was armed for't ere I came. Let us make noble use   110
  Of this great ruin; and join all our force
  To establish this young, hopeful gentleman
  In's mother's right. These wretched eminent things
  Leave no more fame behind 'em than should one
  Fall in a frost, and leave his print in snow;   115
  As soon as the sun shines, it ever melts,
  Both form and matter. I have ever thought
  Nature doth nothing so great for great men,
  As when she's pleased to make them lords of truth:
  Integrity of life is fame's best friend,   120
  Which nobly, beyond death, shall crown the end.
    Exeunt

Notes

Technical terms used in these notes are defined in the Glossary, pages 229–233.

sd = stage direction

Title page

8–10 **divers... Presentment** Webster explains that he provided the players with a fuller text which they cut.

12–13 **Hora... mecum** from Horace's epistles, I.vi.67–8, loosely translatable to: 'If you know of a better play, let's hear it; if not, listen to mine.'

15–16 **John Waterson** a bookseller of the time.

Dedication

1 **George Harding** the thirteenth Baron Berkeley would have been a valuable patron for Webster.

Commendatory verses

1–23 **Thomas Middletonus** an important fellow dramatist, who praises Webster for the moving account of the Duchess's life and death.

19–21 'To Tragedy. As light springs from darkness at the stroke of the Thunderer,/ So does she [Tragedy] become life for famous poets (ruin for the bad).'

24–32 **Wil. Rowley** actor and another noted fellow playwright, who praises Webster for making the Duchess so eloquent.

33–40 **John Ford** another fellow dramatist who also later wrote about revenge within a family, in *'Tis Pity She's a Whore.*

Act I Scene I

Daylight, indoors: an initially busy, public scene which Webster closes down to two final trios on stage, with very different moods. All the central characters are introduced, behaving on stage exactly as they are described. Ferdinand employs Bosola to spy on his sister, joining his brother to warn the Duchess against remarriage. Nevertheless she fulfils her plan to marry Antonio, which Cariola sees as *madness*. By the end of the scene all key images are evident, and tragedy is inevitable.

23 **court-gall** Bosola resembles an ulcer on the face of the court.

25 **rails** mocks.

33 **enforce** urge.

38 **blackbirds... weather** although most birds fluff up their feathers to keep warm, melancholic Bosola only notices the black ones.

39 **dog-days** the 40 days from about 11 August when the dog star rises; the weather is hot, unhealthy and unusually still for sailors.

52–3 **crows... caterpillars** typifies the animal imagery used to describe the brothers and their court.

54 **panders** people who organize illicit sexual encounters, also anyone who engages in suspicious activities.

58 **Tantalus** he stole food from the gods for humans, and was punished in Hades by having to stand up to his neck in water with a fruit tree hanging over his head. Both moved out of his reach whenever he tried to either drink or eat.

73 **suborned** organized. The Cardinal organized the murder, and let Bosola take the blame.

74 **Gaston de Fois** mentioned by William Painter (see 'Webster's Sources', page 155) as winning a great victory at Ravenna. Webster changes the details.

84 **the presence** the Duchess's presence chamber where she greets visitors. The coffin will be her *last presence-chamber* in IV.ii.176.

89 **ring** this is carried off by the victor at jousting as he threads it on the top of his lance. The imagery of the ring is related to the

Duchess and to Antonio. There is a reference to the wedding
ring he will later have, and also to female sexual anatomy.

93 **Give him the jewel** Ferdinand immediately draws attention
back to himself.

94–5 **fall to action** Ferdinand mocks Antonio's achievements as
only sport, not real war. This shows Ferdinand's valour, but
also begins the sexual innuendos occurring frequently in
Ferdinand's words.

120–1 **put up** to stop; also another sexual innuendo.

122 **jennet** a small horse.

125 **Pliny** a Roman writer who believed that in Portugal some mares
were impregnated by the west wind, making their foals very fast.

126–7 **ballasted with quicksilver** loaded with quicksilver, or
mercury; suggests the speed of the jennet.

128 **reels from the tilt often** because of the speed of the boat, it
tilts and moves, suggesting the movement of the lance from the
ring in jousting.

145–6 **out of compass** without restraint.

152 **Grecian horse** the Trojan horse in which Greek soldiers hid
to capture Troy.

159 **come about** gone back into port.

169–71 **The spring… toads** the Cardinal's face is as unpleasant as a
stagnant pond where foul toads breed. Unpleasant animal
imagery is related to both brothers.

172 **Hercules** the mythical Hercules had to perform 12 great feats.

175–6 **primitive decency** refers to the pure and uncorrupted state
of the early Church.

190 **foul black cobweb to a spider** dark animal imagery related to
Ferdinand.

193 **shrewd** harmful.

198 **the devil** the Cardinal is directly linked with the diabolical.

201 **Cast in one figure** copied from the one original.
temper mixture, or temperament.

208 **galliard** lively dance.

211 **continence** self-control or restraint.

218 **play the wire-drawer** spin or draw out excessively.

229 **The provisorship of your horse** Bosola will be in charge of
the horses in the Duchess's stables. Elizabeth I made Leicester
her 'Master of the Horse'.

233 **leaguer**   military camp, probably engaged in a siege.

237 **intelligence**   secret information.

250 **cozens**   cheats.

257 **next**   nearest.

259–60 **such showr's... them**   a reference to the mythical Jupiter who seduced Danae by appearing in the form of a shower of gold.

271 **familiars**   demons who were attendants of witches; Ferdinand often refers to witches and witchcraft.

276 **angels**   gold coins depicting the archangel St Michael defeating the dragon.

289 **complimental**   fine behaviour suited to a gentleman.

294 **politic dormouse**   Ferdinand, at the Cardinal's suggestion, wants Bosola to behave as a wise mouse would in not being seen to be a spy.

295 **Feed in a lord's dish**   eat at a lord's table.

309 **luxurious**   unchaste, lecherous.

310 **livers**   the liver was considered to house the passions.

311 **Laban's**   a reference to Genesis 30:31–42. Jacob's and Laban's sheep were of mixed colours, as is an unhealthy liver.

314 **I'll never marry:**   the colon appeared in Quarto I, suggesting that the Cardinal interrupted her speech. This probably avoided the Duchess telling a direct lie.

326 **Vulcan's engine**   Vulcan made a net of fine bronze thread to catch his wife Venus in adultery with Mars.

335 **executed**   one of the words used which connotes death.

345 **chargeable**   costly.

348–9 **lamprey**   a type of fish. Again Ferdinand uses sexual innuendo, referring to a penis.

361 **winked**   perhaps the word suggests that the Duchess closed her eyes to wisdom or goodness when she made this rapid choice.

367 **ingenious**   true and reliable.

378 **husbands**   a steward husbands, or looks after, the house. The Duchess makes puns on this word as she promotes Antonio.

401 **In a couple**   wrapped in two sheets rather than the single 'winding' sheet around a dead body; one of several images of death in this scene. There is also a pun on *couple*, to have sex.

402 **Saint Winifred**   an early martyr who died for her virginity but who revived. The reference becomes ironic as the Duchess is pure, but enjoys sexual relations, which causes her death.

424 **dancing in this circle**   this has an overtone suggesting the rituals of witchcraft, and also there is a reference to the ring, in a repetition of the ring/sexual imagery.

443–5 **This darkning... off**   shopkeepers would dim their lights to disguise bad goods.

448 **progress through yourself**   look into yourself bit by bit, just as a prince travels through the country on a ceremonial journey.

453 **woo... woo**   there is a pun on the word 'woe'.

461 **You do tremble**   this suggests they are embracing and the Duchess thinks that Antonio trembles from fear, not passion.

476 *Quietus est*   words used literally to indicate that a debt is 'quit' or paid. This is another pun on death, as the release death brings is commonly compared to paying off a last debt.

480 **without this circumference**   outside this embrace; another image of the ring.

490 *Per verba de presenti*   'through words about the present'. This was a form of legally binding marriage which should not be consummated without a church ceremony.

491 **Gordian**   a knot in Greek myth which no one could untie until Alexander the Great simply cut through it with a sword. There is an ironic reference to a 'sword' of death.

493 **spheres**   in Ptolemaic astronomy, the spheres were thought to revolve around the earth making perfect music; another image of the ring.

494 **Quickening**   coming to life, in a pun on sex and pregnancy.

496–8 **palms... divided**   it was thought that palm trees could only reproduce if they were close together.

503–4 **church... echo this**   the Duchess recklessly dismisses Church laws.

505 **blind**   a reference to medieval theories of fate; Fortune was always personified as blind and impartial, so human fate was always unpredictable.

511 **Alexander and Lodovic**   two identical friends. One married the other's girlfriend so put a sword between them for chastity, to avoid betraying his friend.

Act II Scene I

Daylight, but the scene moves symbolically inwards to the chamber and darkness. After a light-hearted opening, Webster builds up tension. At first, Webster parodies the theme of ambition through Castruccio; after meditating on the condition of mankind, Bosola plans to entrap the pregnant Duchess by giving her apricots. As these induce labour, Antonio and the Duchess fear that their secrets will be revealed; the stress of secrecy begins to build up.

2	**courtier**	a judge or a lawyer who attends a law court.
5	**your night-cap expresses your ears**	the skullcap you wear pushes your ears outwards.
7	**strings of your band**	strings used to tie your ruff.
18	**roaring boys**	revellers or rioters.
24–5	**night-caps**	lawyers.
28	**face-physic**	face make-up.
30	**sloughs**	muddy holes in a road.
37–8	**careening... disembogue**	Bosola compares the Old Lady to a boat turned over for cleaning before it can be sent back to sea.
45–7	**dead pigeon... plague**	it was believed that the flesh of dead pigeons worked medicinally when applied to infected skin.
49	**footcloth**	richly embroidered drape hanging from the back of the horse to the floor; the quality indicated wealth.
50	**high-prized**	both highly sought after and expensive.
62	**ulcerous wolf**	a disease which eats the flesh surrounding a sore.
76	**loose-bodied gown**	in Jacobean England only older, married women wore these.
78	**apricots**	thought to be laxatives and also capable of inducing labour.
86	**tetter**	boil-like eruption of the skin.
105	**ascendant**	a point in the zodiac which is just rising above the eastern horizon; as this is related especially to the time of birth, it links to the birth of Antonio's son.
120	**litter**	an enclosed coach.
126	**lemon pills**	lemon peel.

128 **mother** pun as 'mother' relates to pregnancy, but also a form of hysteria which created swelling.

132 **bring up** promote.

137 **in colder countries than in France** an allusion to the English court.

138 **bare** bare-headed.

142 **to-year** this year.

146 **pare** peel.

156 **This grafting** a sexual pun.

157 **crab** crab-apple tree.

159 **bawd farthingales** hooped petticoats which hide the results of illicit sex, i.e. pregnancy.

Act II Scene II

Daylight: again a tense internal scene, relieved by the parody of the officers. To avoid discovery of the birth, Delio suggests that they declare the apricots poisoned, wrong-footing Bosola; Antonio adds the story of theft. A son is born. The idea of confinement in both senses of childbirth and entrapment becomes evident as the Duchess and Antonio are forced into more deceit.

6 **glass-house** a factory where glass is made.

16–21 **give entertainment... receive them** while some young women offer sex for love, some older women offer it for money. (See note to I.i.259–60 for Jupiter and Danae.)

22–5 **mathematics... centre** Bosola intends to find where all the lines meet in the centre; he intends to find out what has gone on, and 'centre' is a crude reference to the Duchess's anatomy, like the puns on 'ring'.

25–6 **your foster-daughters** the children you have delivered.

30 **posterns** back doors.

32 **Forobosco** originally a character in the play, he was later written out.

38 **Switzer** a Swiss mercenary soldier.

41 **pistol** the word was pronounced 'pizzle' colloquially, which means penis; the part clothed in the cod-piece.

51 **French plot** the French were considered lascivious, plotting to seduce ladies; it is ironic because Antonio is described as a Frenchman at the beginning of the play.

58 **cabinet** small private chamber.

82 **stumbling of a horse** an omen of death, as are events mentioned in lines 81–3.

84 **whole man in us** our masculine courage.

86 **lay this unto your breast** take this to your heart.

91 **set a figure for's nativity** cast a horoscope from his birth.

Act II Scene III

Darkness, and Webster's use of the pathetic fallacy (see Glossary) with a storm brewing, suggests the tension of this urgent, brief and very significant scene. Antonio, meeting Bosola in darkness, drops the horoscope; Bosola sends news to Rome.

1 sd **dark lantern** a lantern with shutters that could be closed to hide the light.

5 **wards** apartments.

6 **freeze** dry up.

20 **setting a figure** a pun for casting a horoscope, and to value.

22 **radical** an astrological term meaning 'fit to be judged'.

31 **A Spanish fig** a rude gesture equivalent to our V sign, but also echoes the apricots.

39 **scarce warm** image relating to snakes needing external sources of heat, and also to Bosola's recent promotion.

40 One or more of Bosola's lines may be missing.

55 **false friend** the dark lantern.

63 **human sign** signs of the zodiac depicting humans, i.e. Aquarius, Gemini, Virgo or Saggitarius.

64 **the eighth house** often indicating death.

65 **caetera non scrutantur** the rest of the horoscope has not been written; it is worth remembering this at the end of the play.

67 **bawd** pimp.

69 **cased up** locked up.

74 **posts** travels.

Act II Scene IV

Darkness seems appropriate for the dark deeds of the Cardinal. The love scene between Julia and the Cardinal in his rooms, a sharp contrast to I.i, reveals her wit and his cruelty. Delio still pursues Julia for himself; the news of the birth arrives.

4–5 **anchorite... devotion** Julia's witty pun on the Cardinal and their sexual relationship; an anchorite is an old hermit.
16 **that fantastic glass** the telescope.
26 **cuckold** a husband with an unfaithful wife.
28–30 **I have taken... fly at it** the Cardinal describes Julia as a sad, tame falcon that he plays with.
35 **fingering** a sexual pun on playing a musical instrument and sexual play.
39 **one in physic** someone who requires medical attention.
41 **to't** compared to it; an irony because as lightning moves fast, so do the Cardinal's whims.
54 **If he had had a good back** sexual innuendo suggesting that not only is he a poor horseman, he is impotent.
80–1 **Antonio... ambition now** a suggestion that Antonio was ambitious.

Act II Scene V

Daylight: a tense scene with the insistent rhythms of stichomythia (see Glossary) suggesting that things are nearly out of control. The Aragonian brothers discuss their sister; Ferdinand's uncontrolled behaviour alarms the Cardinal. His madness becomes evident in his violent language related to darkness, torture, hell and sexuality; his motives become increasingly complex. Webster ends the scene on an ominous note of threat.

1 **digged up a mandrake** doing this was reputed to drive a person mad; also the shape of the mandrake is phallic.

3 **loose i'th' hilts**   unchaste or unreliable.

9–11 **cunning... turn... conveyances... service**   Ferdinand's words are all related to female anatomy and sexual intercourse.

12 **Rhubarb**   a cure for bile and choleric humour (see Glossary).

13–14 **Here's... here 't**   Ferdinand probably places the revealing paper close to his heart.

24 **balsamum**   soothing balm.

25 **cupping-glass**   surgical glass used to create a vacuum for drawing blood.

33 **left side**   metaphorically the wrong, evil side.

34 **bark**   small boat.

38–41 **I see... sin**   the Cardinal talks in abstract terms, but Ferdinand is deeply and personally involved.

43 **quoit the sledge**   throw the hammer.

45 **carries coals**   a pun; to carry coals means to be willing to do dirty work.

privy lodgings   a sexual pun as *privy* relates to genitalia, and *lodge* relates to penetration.

68–72 **bodies/Burn't... match**   links sex, fire, hell and religion.

ventage   air hole.

82 **fix her in a general eclipse**   cast her into eternal, total darkness.

Act III Scene I

Webster's use of night-time again builds tension, and the indoor setting creates a sense of claustrophobia. Despite the cheerful opening, the audience remembers Ferdinand's previous threat, recalled as soon as he reappears on stage. Antonio reveals the birth of two more children. Ferdinand arrives to visit his sister, and his quietness is disturbing – more so when he deceives his sister; the audience's fears are confirmed when he asks Bosola for a copy of the key to her chamber.

14 **reversion of**   right to succeed to; also, property left after the bequests in a will have been distributed.

19–24 **Ferdinand... devil**   Ferdinand is biding his time, exactly as he said he would: is he really mad?

29 **The left-hand way**   illegally.
45 **How is't, worthy Antonio?**   the Duchess steers her brother away from trying to identify Antonio as her husband.
49 **Pasquil's paper bullets**   mocking cartoons displayed publicly.
57 **Hot-burning coulters**   ambiguous words which suggest either that the Duchess would tread on hot coals to prove her innocence, or that Ferdinand's mind is burning up.
70 **gulleries**   deceptions.
71 **mountebanks**   tricksters.
73 **will**   probably suggesting sexual desire.
75 **lenitive poisons**   probably the contemporary equivalent to modern date-rape drugs.

Act III Scene II

Darkness and the confinement of the chamber create a sense of entrapment in a complex scene. The happiness of I.i is recalled in our last glimpse of it until Ferdinand shockingly replaces Antonio, threatening his sister. The visit causes mistrust and upset – the Duchess suspects Antonio, and Antonio doubts Cariola; relationships are already under threat. Tension is at its height when Bosola discovers that Antonio is the father. Deceit is evident in the plan for Antonio's flight, and the Duchess's feigned pilgrimage. As in I.i, Cariola expresses the alarm which the audience also feels; the Duchess's downfall now seems inevitable.

 5 **with cap and knee**   go down on bended knee, cap in hand.
 7 **lord of misrule**   traditionally, a temporary appointment for a servant to reign over festivities at Christmas; ironically Antonio, a 'servant', has become a lord, but this will be temporary.
 9 **use**   a sexual double-entendre.
25–7 **Daphne… Syrinx… Anaxarete**   in Ovid's *Metamorphoses* these women were transformed for spurning their would-be lovers.

31 **olive, pomegranate, mulberry** fruitful, as opposed to the fruitless, frigid transformation of the virgin lovers referred to in lines 25–8.

41 **benight** puzzle.

45 **hard-favoured** ugly.

55 **divers** several.

59 **wax** grow.

60 **orris** powdered arrowroot.

68 **your gossips** your children's godparents.

73 **eclipse** linked to the theme of darkness opposed to light, and also to Ferdinand's lunacy.

87 **basilisk** a creature whose gaze killed everything it looked at.

106 **use to sound** the ability to articulate.

115 **hollow bullet** a cannonball filled with explosive.

141 **you have** there are.

145 **this** i.e. the pistol.

150 **warrantable** justifiable.

155 **rank gall** loathsomeness.

158 **'Tis Bosola** as in I.i, Cariola is a silent witness, this time to the Duchess's entrapment, and as before finally speaks to express disapproval.

169 **stood engaged with me** stood security for me.

177–8 **Our... wheels** a proverb which suggests that the Duchess needs to be wary.

181 *Magnanima menzogna* a quotation from the Italian writer Tasso. The Duchess plans to tell a lie.

191 **let him** leave him alone.

192 **done that** one of the Duchess's double-entendres to the officers.

216–17 **pig's head... Jew** Jews do not eat pork.

221 **black wool** considered to be a cure for deafness.

228 **chippings of the buttery** wood-shavings from the servery floor.

229 **gold chain** Antonio's chain of stewardship.

247 **Pluto** the Roman god of riches also came to be considered the god of the underworld, because gold, silver and precious stones are mined from the earth.

251 **he... scuttles** he travels quickly with large numbers.

263 **herald** someone who settles questions of precedence or records established pedigrees.

270 **Bermudes** these tropical islands were stormy, causing many shipwrecks.
287 **unbeneficed** penniless, without endowment.
302 **coats** coats of arms.
312 **league** a distance of five kilometres.
319 **Lucca... Spa** Lucca, near Pisa, was famous for its waters, and Spa for its springs.
330 **rests** remains.
335 Men who dutifully carry out mundane business affairs are praised.

Act III Scene III

Daylight in the Cardinal's rooms. After some parody of valour in which Malateste's behaviour is contrasted to Pescara's courage, the latter's shrewdness is shown in his comments on the cardinals falling out. Webster thus prepares the audience for his serious role at the end of the play. The tension is ratcheted up again as the Cardinal prepares to arm. Ferdinand is increasingly uncontrolled; descriptions link him to hell, and Pescara notes his *pangs of death*; fear for the Duchess grows.

1–5 **Emperor... Lannoy** in a battle of 1525, Spanish troops led by Pescara defeated the French, and Lannoy captured the French king, Francis I.
11 **muster-book** register of military personnel.
12 **voluntary** volunteer.
21 **by the book** according to theoretical rules.
27 **from taking** from being taken.
29 **pate** head.
30 **pot-gun** toy pop gun.
34 Merely to decorate the court on its progress (travelling visits).
35 **Bosola arrived!** prior to this, Pescara has not taken part in the spiteful discussion.
40 **goes to wrack** is destroyed.
48 **speculative** theorizing, but can also mean deceitful.
50 **salamander** lizard reputed to be able to live in fire.

70–1 **my young nephew... husband**   in the account of the
Duchess's story by William Painter (see 'Webster's Sources',
page 155), the Duchess renounces her title in favour of this
son; here, there is no other reference to him.

72 **honesty**   chastity.

Act III Scene IV

Daylight at the Shrine of Loreto, and the scene could be played
either indoors or outdoors. Webster portrays the arming in
dumb-show, a visual emblem of the irresistible power of Church
and state; the audience realizes that now the Duchess can resist
no longer. The pilgrims comment on injustice, although they do
not understand the Duchess's lack of conformity to social
convention.

8–23 During the correcting of the Quarto version, Webster wrote a
note disclaiming this 'ditty'; he either did not like it in his text,
or it was by another author.

41 **no matter... to't**   it doesn't matter who is pushing.

Act III Scene V

Daylight, outdoors, but the Duchess has no freedom as she is
banished. Antonio refuses to meet Ferdinand as invited; Bosola
scorns his breeding and his cowardice. Perhaps the audience
begins to sympathize with Bosola's view here.

5 **buntings**   sparrow-like birds.

19 **benefit**   gifts freely given.

29 **politic**   crafty, clever.
   equivocation   double-talk.

42 **league**   agreement.

48 **brothers**   brothers-in-law.

57 **conjure**   appeal earnestly to.

60 **bottom** the hold of a ship.

63 **in sunder** apart.

71 **eternal church** it seems that either the Duchess and Antonio have been married in church, or she considers herself married according to Church rites, so they will meet in heaven at the resurrection of souls.

74 **unkindly** with unnatural cruelty.

75 **cassia** cinnamon.

93 **laurel is all withered** the evergreen wreath shrivelled on the death of a king. Perhaps Antonio is her king who will die, or perhaps she refers to herself as a prince.

94–5 **Look, madam... toward us** Cariola's first words in the scene, echoing I.i; her silence, like that of the children, underlines their plight.

108 **Charon's boat** the ferryman, Charon, carried the souls of the dead over the River Styx to Hades, the underworld.

118 **counterfeit face** the vizard.

144 **some great hill** probably an echo of Psalm 121: 'I will lift up mine eyes unto the hills...'

Act IV Scene I

Darkness and claustrophobia create a sense of the Duchess's entrapment. Webster presents Bosola using the Duchess's register of goodness, obviously beginning to change. Echoing I.i and III.ii, Ferdinand offers the ring from the dead man's hand, then shows his sister the wax figures. Devilishly, he wants to *bring her to despair*, but a changed Bosola tries to help her avoid this. Bosola's role is complex; part villain, part the Christian, medieval figure of Good Counsel.

16–17 **I... heart** I will no longer try to understand her behaviour.

17 sd Unusually, the Duchess is unattended, so that the two men can trick her.

25 **gently** please.

29 Bosola remains hidden on stage to carry out the trickery.

50 **owed** owned.

55 sd **discovered**   revealed.

    traverse   curtain.

    the figures   although these are later described as wax, actors would have been used.

68 **lifeless trunk**   Antonio's body.

72 **Portia**   the wife of the Roman Brutus; Portia committed suicide by swallowing burning coals when she heard that Brutus had lost the epic battle of Philippi.

81 **broke upon the wheel**   breaking on the wheel was a medieval torture.

91 **vipers**   under stress, the Duchess may hallucinate, but references to *vipers* recall hell, and to *daggers* (line 90) recall the *poniard* of I.i.343 and stage directions at III.ii.68 and 72.

92 **long life**   the servant is mocking the Duchess.

107–8   Crowned martyrs became stars in the sky, but if the heavens stopped crowning them, the number of stars would decrease.

109 **howl them this**   ironic in view of Ferdinand's lycanthropy (see V.ii).

113 **curious**   skilled.

    quality   craft.

114 **Vincentio Lauriola**   probably an imaginary person.

120 **Next to her delicate skin**   Bosola tortures Ferdinand with this reference to his sister's body.

124 **courtesans**   prostitutes.

130 **full o'th' moon**   lunatics and werewolves (like Ferdinand) were believed to go mad at full moon.

135 **intelligence**   spying.

138 **Thy... thee**   pity isn't natural to you, so it doesn't suit you.

142 **Intemperate agues**   serious illnesses.

Act IV Scene II

Darkness, imprisonment and unbearably quiet solitude mark this scene up to the entry of the noisy madmen, in which the audience shares the Duchess's relief. The scene echoes I.i extensively, with Bosola replacing Antonio as the Duchess's support. However, whereas Antonio ministered to her physical needs, Bosola more significantly addresses her soul. After defeating self-pity, the Duchess still has pride, which Bosola helps her overcome, to gain humility through mortification and acceptance of death. The madmen, Bosola's second meditation and dirge have helped her to find perspective, and she dies certain of heaven. Ferdinand, 'dazzled' by his first real sight of his sister, denies Bosola his due, and seems bound for madness and hell. Possibly Bosola has received some grace from the Duchess, and embarks on his final transformation as her revenger.

8 **Discourse to**   discuss with.

12 **durance**   imprisonment.

34 Cariola remains silent for many lines after this, which stresses the Duchess's isolation.

35–6 **Fortune... tragedy**   the figure of Fortune is always depicted as blind, so impartial.

45 **secular priest**   a priest not attached to an order.

55 **in grain**   grain dealers were notoriously dishonest.

56 **hindered transportation**   losing money because exports were stopped.

57 **broker that's mad**   a man, although mad himself, who tried to resolve arguments between others.

60 **chained**   madmen were usually chained; here the Duchess is entrapped by her brothers.

86 **alum**   harsh laxative.

90–1 **woodcock**   a bird which is easily trapped, as is a fool.

93–4 The mad priest is probably a Puritan who hates the Authorized Version of the Bible.

96 **lay**   apply.

101 **glass**   a telescope or a magic mirror.

109 **caroche**   coach.

115 **milch-bats**   slightly curdled milk.

117–18 **throw... me**   give me up for lost.

118 **I... costive**   soap-makers suffered from diarrhoea, so to make them 'costive' (constipated) would have been a feat; soap was also used as a laxative.

129 **worm seed**   a herb for purging intestinal worms; perhaps a pun on 'semen'.

Notes

130 **mummy** a compound from dead bodies used as medicine; *green* could suggest either that the Duchess has not yet decayed, or is in an advanced state of decay.

170 **charnel** cemetery vault.

178 **common bellman** Webster's father had contributed to a fund to provide a man to ring a bell before executions to remind prisoners of their own deaths, and to make them repent. Bosola sees himself as providing this religious service.

182 **mortification** the state of stupor before death, and also the recognition of past sins.

214 **apoplexy** fit.

227–8 **strange... both ways** either voluntarily by suicide, or by murder.

241 **mandragora** a narcotic.

251 **come to my answer** be formally accused in court with the opportunity to plead.

260 **When!** get on with it!

261 **Your credit's saved** your reputation will be safe, as no one will know after your death.

262 **this** the Duchess.

267–9 **murder... bedews the heavens** from the biblical belief that murder victims cried out to God, and also that the earth refused to accept their blood, which would rise wailing to heaven.

270 **mine eyes dazzle** literally, smeared with tears.

298 **quicken** here sharpen, but also to come alive, as at conception.

329 **take much in a blood** run strongly in families.

342 **painted** Bosola thinks that his duty to Ferdinand is now only skin-deep.

349 **sensible** palpable.

353 **pity would destroy pity** either noise would bring Ferdinand, or Bosola doesn't want to disturb her peace.

360 **cords of life** sinews of the heart.

Act V Scene I

Outdoors; Delio is concerned about Antonio's naïve hope of reconciliation with the Cardinal. Julia receives the Citadel of Saint Benet, dishonourably seized, which noble Pescara refused to Delio. His explanation increases his worth in the eyes of the audience.

  6 **in cheat** in escheat, the property reverts to the lord of the manor.
13 **heretic** disbeliever.
14 **shape** accommodate.
19 **Benet** Benedict.
20 **demesnes** lands.
46 **strumpet** prostitute.

Act V Scene II

Outdoors, significantly in sunshine, this is a complex scene in which Webster prepares the way for the events of the following scenes. Ferdinand's lycanthropy (a psychiatric condition that involves the sufferer believing he has turned, or is turning, into a wolf) is apparent as his confinement to darkness and isolation is stressed. Is divine retribution at work? The Cardinal tries to employ a reformed Bosola to murder Antonio. In another echo of I.i, Julia is ironically murdered by kissing the poisoned bible. Webster presents Bosola imagining that he sees the ghost of the Duchess, so she stays firmly in the audience's mind, reminding us of the justice of Bosola's cause, and linking the scene to earlier acts.

  6 **lycanthropia** lycanthropy; Ferdinand claims he has turned into a wolf.
24 **nearer** more direct and forceful.
25 **Paracelsus** a Swiss physician interested in magic, alchemy and mythology.

53 **a sheep-biter**   a sneaking person, like a dog or wolf that bites sheep.

67 **cockatrice**   a basilisk (see note to III.ii.87), or a mythical cockerel with a serpent's tail.

76 **fetch a frisk**   cut a caper, do a dance.

81 **cullis**   hearty meat broth.

82–3 **anatomies… Hall**   skeletons in Barber-Surgeons Hall, London.

85 **tongue and belly**   body parts used as sacrifices to ancient gods, linked to the *flattery* and *lechery* of the same line.

111 **engagement**   battle.

114 **oft-dyed garment**   a garment of fading colours.

129 **style me**   set up for me.

139 **ways**   paths to follow and also methods to use.

141 **Jews**   money-lenders.

187 **familiar**   pun on a devil's assistant.

194 **purloins**   obtains dishonestly.

230 **consumption**   decay, disease.

249 **rack**   medieval torture machine on which people were stretched.

263 **adamant**   especially hard substance.

299–300 Why pretend while talking to me that you are a decent man or persuade me into your wicked plans by smooth talking.

336 **frost-nailed**   nails were driven into the soles of boots to prevent them from slipping on ice.

340 **dead**   unbroken.

Act V Scene III

Darkness, outdoors, but below the Cardinal's window: Webster changes mood with a Gothic interlude of moonlight, mystery, a ghost and a graveyard. This echo scene, recalling I.i, is a lyrical but ominous interlude amid violence. The audience is invited to contrast the love that was once shared between Antonio and the Duchess with the sad situation of the present. Webster also ensures that the audience remembers the Duchess, linking the scene to earlier acts.

6 **withal**   altogether.
45 **folded**   crumpled or overtaken by.

Act V Scene IV

Darkness, with a storm under way. This reminds the audience that the play's climax is approaching, and perhaps hell is becoming apparent on earth for the brothers. The Cardinal, plotting to remove Julia's body, ironically ensures his own death; Bosola mistakenly kills Antonio and all but loses his new-found hope of redemption.

3 **suffer**   allow.
10 **sensibly**   in his right senses.
19 **osier**   willow tree.
48–9 **That... myself**   what I have through your killing me is to be myself.
58 **Kindle**   revive.
61 **I shall do't in sadness**   Antonio realizes that with his misfortunes it is a mercy to die.
82–3 **represent... bear'st**   be as quiet as the body you carry.

Act V Scene V

Darkness until the final image of the sun relieves the gloom. The Cardinal, experiencing visions of hell, is killed by Ferdinand, who also kills Bosola. Both brothers have acknowledged the justice of this; is there further evidence of divine retribution? Perhaps there is some optimism about the future for the young heir nominated by Delio and Pescara; this remains uncertain.

2 **He**   the author of the book.
4 **Lay him by**   put it aside.
16 **Raise**   summon.
31 **engines**   tools.

35 **'Cause**   so that.

49 **honour of arms**   opportunity for honourable surrender.

52 **adverse party**   other side.

53 A dead man cannot be ransomed.

61 **barber**   barbers also acted as dentists.

68 **vault credit**   overlook disbelief; he is dying and hopes for better things to come.

73 As diamonds are cut by other diamonds, so man kills man like a wolf; as Ferdinand has killed his siblings, he is really wolf-like.

120–1 See Horace's Odes, i.22, which says that a good man innocent of sin is safe, wherever he may roam; linked to the proverbial saying that the end crowns all.

Interpretations

Webster's sources

As mentioned on page 10, Webster's drama is based loosely on an actual historical event, making it partly a history play. The widowed Duchess of Amalfi wed her chief steward, Antonio Bologna, and events unfolded broadly as in the play with the Duchess fleeing in 1510 to join Antonio. She was chased and then banished by her brothers, and later disappeared with her children, having been captured by their armed horsemen. This story was fictionalized by Matteo Bandello in the mid-sixteenth century; he perceived the Duchess's relationship with Antonio as a love-match, and added the characters of Delio, Silvio, and Daniele da Bozolo as the murderer.

A French writer, François de Belleforest, writing in 1565, defined the relationship as a tragedy. He was judgemental, regarding the Duchess as guilty of lust, and Antonio of social ambition. He added dialogue, and characters were developed further, with the Duke being choleric, and Antonio a mixture of strength and weakness. The most important source that Webster read was a translation of Belleforest's account by William Painter, *The Palace of Pleasure*, Vol 2, 1567, in which Antonio and the Duchess had some complexity of character, the maid was introduced and Ferdinand was described as choleric. There were two central concerns: the Duchess's social 'sin' in marrying Antonio, and the idea of the madness of love, which Webster further developed. He made many changes for dramatic effect including the manipulation of time and the creation of a sub-plot. He showed each character to be ambiguous and complex, and intensified dramatic confrontations.

When studying a seventeenth-century text it is important to have a foot in two camps; you should be aware of how Webster's contemporary audience might have viewed the play, and also explore what the text might offer to other periods including your own. An example of differing responses can be seen in the Duchess's choice of Antonio as her husband. The Jacobean audience would have some sympathy with her, but would also consider that she had infringed the rules of 'degree' or social order by marrying outside her class. Nowadays, this would not really matter; instead the Duchess's independence might be praised. The interpretation of any work of art does not rely solely on the author; every reader or spectator brings an individual reading which extends the author's original purposes. When new readings arise that are relevant to successive periods of history, a text may be is described as universal; such is the case with *The Duchess of Malfi*.

Always avoid generalizations during your study of this play: Webster does not work in black and white. For example, some commentators suggest that Webster has devised a scheme with the Duchess as the emotional pole of the play, and Bosola the intellectual pole. This categorization is unwise; the Duchess shares her brothers' strong-mindedness, evident at once in her rejection of their complaints (I.i.353–5) and in her firm control over Antonio (III.ii.161ff). On the other hand Bosola, while very intelligent, is also very emotional, as seen in his tears of pity (IV.ii.367). Similarly, some commentators claim that the Cardinal represents cold, intellectual force and Ferdinand fire and emotion. Yet the Cardinal foolishly falls victim to his own schemes, whereas Ferdinand is clear-sighted enough to see through the pretence of the doctor (V.ii.69–70), has a clear perception of the state of society (V.ii.83–5), and is aware of the cause of his downfall (V.v.71–3). 'Perhaps' is a key word to use when discussing *The Duchess of Malfi*.

Webster's worldview

There are many different areas of enquiry in *The Duchess of Malfi* which are presented in a strikingly unusual way. Instead of offering a developing argument, Webster restlessly moves a spotlight to illuminate individuals, couples, and groups. In this way he amplifies themes, presenting differing responses to situations side by side, rather than by forming any sort of synthesis or conclusion.

The themes of the play fall broadly into three groups – universal, social and personal – which are all inter-related.

Universal themes include the eternal question of what happens after death; and whether there is evidence of a scheme governing man's destiny, be it fate, fortune or the Christian promise of salvation, redemption, and possibly retribution. Through his imagery, Webster presents the conflict between the forces of good and evil at the beginning of I.i, with the Cardinal and Ferdinand linked to hell and the diabolical, the Duchess to heaven and virtue. The Duchess, through her virtue, seems to be assured of a life hereafter as she enters *heaven' gates* (IV.ii.238). At the moment of death other characters display a variety of attitudes; for example Julia, always pragmatic, has no certainty of an afterlife: *I go,/ I know not whither* (V.ii.290–1); the Cardinal wants to be *never thought of* (V.v.90); Bosola's conscience has finally brought him to repent of his sins: is there a hope of redemption for him? Webster is non-committal throughout, offering a variety of choices to the audience.

Social and personal themes are developed in tandem. Webster raises issues about the nature of government; he shows the dreadful effects on a society when the two leaders, the Cardinal and Ferdinand, indifferent to the lives of their people, are obsessed with their own dynastic power. Many characters comment on the general corruption; Antonio talks of the danger in Bosola's discontentment (I.i.82); even Ferdinand refers to the *pestilent air* in *princes' palaces* (III.i.50). Perhaps Webster questions whether it is possible to have an individual identity in this society. Consider what happens to the identities of Antonio, Bosola and the Duchess, for example. The Duchess wishes to pursue her own happiness in marriage, and establish a new order of society based on openness, family life and love, yet powerful forces oppose her.

The theme of confinement relates to this corruption; it is evident in the physical confinement of the Duchess in Act IV, but the theme emerges early in the play. Bosola, for example is trapped in his role; perhaps the same is true of Antonio; perhaps even comic characters like Castruccio are confined to a course of aping their superiors in order to make progress in life (see II.i).

Is 'preferment' or ambition the only way to survive and succeed? Antonio has no illusions: his reference to *a saucy and ambitious devil* (I.i.422) alerts the audience to the dangers of advancement in such a society. Has the system of secrecy practised by the brothers generated further secrecy, such as that of the Duchess's marriage? At her death she mentions all the *whispering* (IV.ii.229). Malfi seems to be similar to a modern fascist state denying individuality and personal freedom; some of Webster's contemporary audience may well have drawn parallels with court life in London.

Other themes expand the question of governing; has justice vanished, as Bosola suggests in his remark *The office of justice is perverted quite/ When one thief hangs another* (IV.ii.312–3)?

In this society only money and status matter, so most characters are not what they seem as they have to 'feign' for the sake of survival; appearance and reality diverge widely. By the end of the play Webster has presented so many conflicting aspects of all the major characters that it is impossible to assume that we can know any of them. The Church and religion also come under scrutiny; the Cardinal as representative of the Church is totally corrupt, with his illicit affairs, immoral behaviour and bribery; the Pope is criticized because he unjustly *seized into th' protection of the church/ The dukedom* (III.iv.32–3).

Webster also addresses some concerns over personal morality; questions about sexual liaisons and the remarriage of widows become evident, as well as an enquiry into the morality of revenge itself.

But perhaps the unifying theme spanning all concerns is that of madness, which touches all characters. The condition which

Antonio identifies, *Ambition, madam, is a great man's madness* (I.i.431), has become contagious; the madness of the power-hungry, obsessive brothers has convulsed their nation. There is madness in love, as Cariola says (I.i.517); Bosola, addressing the Old Lady (II.i.52ff), details the distorted madness of humankind; there is obsessive madness in the Cardinal's scheming, in which he entraps himself; and Ferdinand's unhealthy sexual obsession helps to drive him literally insane (V.ii). The madmen, in their song and dance (IV.ii.61ff) represent this society: unhealthy, ego-centric, competitive and cruel. The Duchess alone can view this detachedly as a spectacle and choose to withdraw; but it will bring death to all those who are drawn into it. The spree of killings in Act V therefore seems to be impelled by the very madness of society itself. Has it finally run its course?

Activity

Explore the aspects of government which Webster presents in this play.

Discussion

You might begin by looking at Antonio's speeches in I.i describing the French court, compared to those of the brothers. You might think about how people are forced into acceptance by the tactics of the Cardinal and Ferdinand: consider how and why both brothers have created a system of *miserable dependences* (I.i.56) leading, for example, to Bosola's despised career. Think about the combined pressure on the Duchess culminating in the arming of the Cardinal (III.iv): is any justice evident? Is there a just reason for the massacre of Act V, or any hope or even wish for change?

Characterization

Webster presents each character in *The Duchess of Malfi* from several varying points of view to create the complexity produced during the course of the play. As a result, most of the characters are ambiguous, appearing to change during the play both within themselves and in the estimation of the audience.

The Duchess

The Duchess represents purity and goodness in sharp contrast to her corrupt brothers. Webster immediately presents her virtue in Antonio's words: *...but in that look/ There speaketh so divine a continence/ As cuts off all lascivious and vain hope* (I.i.210–2). The register is beyond saintly: she could cure and *raise* a palsied man, an echo of Christ raising Lazarus to life; she has *virtue*; her *nights* are *in heaven*. Her first action is as gracious as Antonio's praise suggests: she submissively and generously grants Ferdinand's request for Bosola's employment (I.i.229–30). The audience is invited to admire the Duchess for her goodness; later her courage will also demand respect.

However, Webster also displays her flaws: she is strong-minded, wilful, sensual, at times deceitful, and proud of her social status. The Duchess is very much her brothers' sibling, sharing their strength of mind. She stands up to them on their tirade about remarriage (I.i.), and she privately dismisses their objections: *Shall this move me?.../ I'd make them my low footsteps* (I.i.353–5). In her wooing of Antonio she is bold and direct: *This is flesh, and blood, sir;/... Awake, awake, man* (I.i.464–6). The double-entendres of the wooing/marriage scene of I.i suggest her sensuality, and she is seen to be imperious in her marriage, even at intimate moments: *Must? You are a lord of misrule* (III.ii.7).

Her response to her brothers' warnings against remarriage is ambiguous. Her statement *I'll never marry:* is interrupted by the Cardinal, who interjects *So most widows say* (I.i.314), leaving the audience uncertain about what she was going to say. This scene is the only time in the play when the Cardinal directly addresses his sister. She commits some 'sins': she consummates her marriage to Antonio without the proper church ceremony: *What can the church force more?* (I.i.499); she tells *a noble lie* to protect her family (III.ii.181); dismissing Cariola's fears, the Duchess goes on a feigned pilgrimage: *Thou art a superstitious fool* (III.ii.323). However, it is worth remembering audience responses to this; wouldn't this act of pilgrimage be seen as a sensible, if desperate, way of preserving her family?

She is also very naïve in believing that Ferdinand sees her innocence: *O blessed comfort!/ This deadly air is purg'd* (III.i.55–6), and in accepting Bosola unquestioningly into her household, later revealing her husband's identity, *As I taste comfort in this friendly speech* (III.ii.303). Dramatic tension increases as the audience is aware of his motive; perhaps her own openness prevents her from seeing the bad in others.

It is possible that Webster's contemporary audience would infer some comparisons between the Duchess and their recently dead queen, Elizabeth I. Elizabeth had at first struggled to survive, isolated from her two half-siblings, Edward VI and 'Bloody' Mary I; she had to be independent and resourceful to retain her crown; there were fears of unequal matches to the Earls of Leicester or Essex. These clear echoes would have heightened the audience's esteem for the Duchess, but unlike her, Elizabeth I put her duty to her country first and did not marry.

During her torture, the Duchess, guided by Bosola, may be seen to progress through despair (IV.i.95–6), self-pity (IV.ii.13–14), and pride (IV.ii.128), to be deflated by Bosola's mocking words *Thou art a box of worm seed* (IV.ii.129), followed by resignation (IV.ii.168–70), and acceptance (IV.ii.173). She has scorned the belated 'wedding presents' of coffin, bell and cords sent by her brothers, she has rejected the corrupt society with its *whispering* (IV.ii.229). Finally, she embraces death; she is *well awake* (IV.ii.230) as she humbly kneels to pass through *heaven' gates* (IV.ii.238).

At this moment, Cariola's words are recalled: *Whether the spirit of greatness or of woman/ Reign most in her, I know not* (I.i.515–6). Demeaning her torturers through her integrity, her greatness shines through as a woman, a mother, a prince and as the representative of 'everyman', all humankind facing the moment of death. Perhaps Webster presents her as a Christian martyr, a universal emblem of all who suffer and die unjustly, and as the victor or mediator in a battle between the forces of good and evil represented by her brothers.

In Acts IV and V Webster shows the effects of her death on other characters, and finally the retribution for it. Ferdinand, for the first time, sees the truth about his sister and himself: *Cover her face: mine eyes dazzle* (IV.ii.270). Bosola seems to receive some of the Duchess's grace; has she helped him, with her *Mercy* (IV.ii.359), to repentance? Perhaps Webster suggests that despite her denial (III.ii.110–11), the Duchess instinctively seeks a new order in society based on openness, family life and love. He presents a clear contrast between her healthy and fertile marriage and the sterile sexuality of her corrupt brothers. Perhaps the nomination of her son as heir will cure the ills of Malfi. We do not know finally, but Webster leaves the audience with some hope.

Helen Mirren as the Duchess of Malfi at the
Royal Exchange Theatre, 1980

Cariola and Julia

Minor characters are also complex, and change in the estimation of the audience.

Cariola is wise and steadfast; she has the wisdom to see the dangers of the Duchess's choice, her *fearful madness* (I.i.517), but remains loyal throughout. In the manner of her death she is a foil to the Duchess as she struggles to evade strangulation. However, should this fear of death determine our judgement of Cariola? She is an ordinary mortal of fairly low rank; why should she not be afraid?

Julia has some representative value as she typifies the fate of women who try to live through men in this society. Like the Duchess, she is independent and seeks to make her own route through the world. Webster seems to enlist some sympathy for her as he presents her as attractive in her wittiness (II.iv.75–6); but she also seems increasingly brazen in her wooing of Bosola (V.ii.154–5), and in her petitioning for land from Pescara (V.i.26ff). She is a foil to the Duchess as her love again brings death, and in a way she is as steadfast as the Duchess at the moment of death (*I go,/ I know not whither* (V.ii.290–1); she faces death with no hopes or self-deception. Is she presented as corrupt or as yet another hapless person coping in a ruthless society by using her best assets to seek social preferment?

Perhaps collectively, the Duchess as wife and mother, Cariola the maidservant and Julia the courtesan suggest the limited choices available to women in the male-dominated society of Malfi, and possibly of London.

Ferdinand

Ferdinand, Duke of Calabria, is more complex than his brother; his motivation is elusive, perhaps even to himself: *Do not you ask the reason* (I.i.269, see also III.i.83). He is linked to the diabolical, to witchcraft, fire, storms, darkness and blood (see 'Imagery', page 181). His choleric temperament contrasts with the Cardinal's cold reserve. Webster mentions his sinister laughter in the first scene and throughout the play: *If he laugh heartily, it is to laugh/ All honesty out of fashion* (I.i.183–4); see also I.i.130–3 and III.iii.55–6. This laughter is presented as disturbing, divorced from its roots as a response to comedy. Cause and effect are not related in the dark, deranged mind of the powerful Duke.

There are obvious sexual innuendos in many of his speeches, shockingly when he speaks of the *lamprey* (I.i.348–9) to his sister. Such language might suggest incestuous feelings as he imagines her *in the shameful act of sin* (II.v.41). In the bedroom scene (III.ii), Ferdinand, having replaced Antonio, echoes I.i.343ff when he offers the Duchess a poniard for her suicide. The phallic symbolism might hint at Ferdinand as the would-be husband.

Perhaps Webster also suggests some homosexual tendencies when Ferdinand imagines his sister engaged in sex *Haply with some strong thighed bargeman* or *lovely squire* (II.v.42ff). The word *haply* is a pun, in one sense suggesting an encounter which the Duke might enjoy. Ferdinand claims it to be his motive that he is concerned for her *reputation* (III.ii.123ff), and later adds that he had hoped to gain *An infinite mass of treasure by her death* (IV.ii.291). Further motivation might be suggested through an analysis of the imagery he uses (see page 181).

Ferdinand properly sees his sister for the first time after her death: *Cover her face: mine eyes dazzle* (IV.ii.270). Failing to shift the blame to Bosola, caught perhaps by his conscience, he tries to strangle his own shadow (V.ii.40), and dies a madman. He has achieved revenge without satisfaction as he laments *My sister! O my sister! There's the cause on't* (V.v.71). In his death there is a sense of divine retribution, as Ferdinand has admitted earlier: *for I do think/ It is some sin in us heaven doth revenge/ By her* (II.v.65–7). Perhaps the brothers are crucial in affirming for the audience the theme of the divine scheme of salvation and punishment.

The Cardinal

The Cardinal, as in the sources, is left unnamed, perhaps partly because he might be seen as a 'type' figure of medieval morality representing the diabolical (see 'Imagery', page 181). He is introduced as devilishly evil (I.i.47–8), and like Ferdinand he is linked with hellfire (V.v.1–3), storm (III.iii.54) and serpents: *This fellow doth breed basilisks in's eyes* (V.ii.148). He appears to be the older, dominating brother as he manipulates Ferdinand into carrying out his plans: *I would not be seen in't* (I.i.237). He should have inherited the dukedom but has obviously, as in the historical source, passed the title over to his younger brother. His use of bribery and his illicit affairs suggest corruption within the Church (I.i.164–78), but Webster offers little insight into his feelings as the Cardinal becomes a soldier, switching roles with ease. The device of the arming presented in dumb-show (III.iv) contrasts with his sister's frail family in the following scene, and is a visual statement of his irresistible power.

The Cardinal has 'feigned' all his life as man of the Church and man of state, and ironically feigning brings about his death. Perhaps there is a touch of humanization when he thinks he sees *a thing armed with a rake* in his fishpond (V.v.6). His meditations about hell could be a prick of conscience. However, his tone is that of a curious scholar: *I am puzzled in a question about hell* (V.v.i).

Webster makes a wry point about this superficially powerful man through the manner of his death. Despite his assumed power he has no inner strength; he cannot fight for himself and dies *like a leveret* (V.v.45). Bosola points out the final irony that such a great man should *end in a little point, a kind of nothing* (V.v.79). His death, like Ferdinand's, might suggest a possibility of divine retribution: *O Justice!/ I suffer now for what hath former been* (V.v.53–4).

The Cardinal's ominous silences suggest a threat as potent as Ferdinand's psychotic outbursts; in the hostility of two such formidable enemies, Webster makes us believe even by the end of the first scene of the play that a tragic outcome for the Duchess is inevitable.

Daniel de Bosola

At the beginning of the play Webster presents Bosola as a
divided character. Ambiguously, Antonio immediately refers to
him as *the only court-gall* who *rails at those things which he wants*
(I.i.23ff); then later adds *I have heard/ He's very valiant. This foul
melancholy/ Will poison all his goodness* (I.i.76–8). Delio also reveals
that he is a *fantastical scholar* (III.iii.41). But Webster displays
Bosola's darker side; it is revealed that he had spent *seven years in
the galleys/ For a notorious murder* (I.i.71–2), and when he is denied
his reward by the Cardinal he becomes the tool of Ferdinand:
Whose throat must I cut? (I.i.261).

He is an effective spy, as the ingenious trick with the apricots
shows (II.i). But Webster complicates his presentation of Bosola
when he attacks the Old Lady for social pretence. Deliberately
distancing the audience by using a clearly artificial convention,
Webster reveals an intelligent and sensitive man as Bosola turns
into an instructor: *Observe my meditation now* (II.i.52). He is aware
of the true nature of most of mankind: *And though continually we
bear about us/ A rotten and dead body, we delight/ To hide it in rich
tissue* (II.i.64–6). This insight is crucial in preparing the audience
for the changes seen in Bosola in Acts IV and V, as he ministers
to the Duchess and becomes the scourge of society.

His pricks of conscience become irresistible when he is faced
with the Duchess's nobility of spirit, and he pleads with
Ferdinand to stop the cruelty (IV.i.117–8). In Act IV Scene I he
plays a crucial role as he replaces Antonio in caring for the
Duchess; his words *Come, be of comfort, I will save your life*
(IV.i.86) are prophetic as Bosola prepares her for death. His
remark *Look you, the stars shine still* (IV.i.100) are seen by some
commentators as evidence of indifference and cruelty, but he
could also be reminding the Duchess of the pointlessness of her
curses. He experiences increasing pity: *Now, by my life, I pity you*
(IV.i.88), and seems to be on the verge of reform.

Webster creates parallels between the wooing scene of Act I
and the death scene (see page 191). As Antonio takes on

responsibility for the Duchess's physical well-being, Bosola seems to care for her Christian soul. He helps her to a state of acceptance, completed with his dirge, and it could be argued that he leads her into achieving greatness.

Even before the Duchess's ordeal Bosola adopts her verbal register (IV.i.2ff), and after her death he seems to absorb some of her virtue. True, he has been rejected by Ferdinand and refused his reward, which immediately persuades Bosola to 'save' Antonio, but he had already been touched by the Duchess's grace. He acts as her avenger, although in an ironically disordered way as Antonio falls victim. Bosola's last words are enigmatic, leaving any judgement on him uncertain: *Mine is another voyage* (V.v.105). Does Webster imply that Bosola is going to a different place than the Duchess, that is, to hell? Or is he facing another *voyage*, another punishment in purgatory? Bosola acts virtuously in helping to save his Duchess's soul; does this goodness carry any weight in divine judgement? He goes on to commit murder, but for him the motive is justifiable: revenge. Is all revenge damnable? Bosola seems to feel despair: *All our good deeds, and bad, a perspective/ That shows us hell. That we cannot be suffered/ To do good when we have a mind to it!* (IV.ii.364–6). But perhaps the audience takes another view.

Webster shows Bosola's commitment, loyalty and wrong-headed but perhaps inevitable career as a tool and a villain given his low social standing. But we are also aware of his crucial support for the spiritual well-being of the Duchess. In view of his harsh self-knowledge, Bosola may be viewed as a tragic character who *would look up to heaven, but.../ The devil... stands in [his] light* (II.i.103–4).

Antonio Bologna

Antonio is presented at the start of the play like a chorus, commenting on the main characters and their actions. This role leads the audience to respect him immediately. Even the brothers praise him: Ferdinand calls him *the great master* of the Duchess's *household* (I.i.91), and the Cardinal states that his nature is *honest* (I.i.242); Antonio himself claims *I have long served virtue* (I.i.450).

As ever, Webster suggests some ambiguities. Antonio appears isolated in his *formal* French clothes (I.i.3) and his gold chain of office. Ironically this perception persists as he fails to cope with the entry into Aragonian society his marriage brings. Ferdinand is scornful of the jousting at which Antonio excels as it is not real battle; ironically Antonio will be incapable of battle with the brothers.

After describing the Duchess's virtues with great respect, he is naturally overcome and fearful in the wooing scene: *Ambition, madam, is a great man's madness* (I.i.431). His acceptance of her marriage proposal seems passive. From now on, Antonio seems to diminish in the audience's eyes. Shocked at the early onset of the Duchess's labour, he admits that he is *lost in amazement* (II.i.184) and he seems very much concerned for himself: *How I do play the fool with mine own danger!* (II.ii.74). Evidence of his fear and self-concern recur after this point, for example in II.ii.77 and III.i.18. His ineptness leads him to drop the horoscope (II.iii.54), and when Ferdinand stealthily takes his place in the Duchess's chamber (III.ii) Antonio arrives brandishing a pistol far too late. When all are abusing him, Webster curiously has the Second Officer cast doubts upon his manhood: *Some said he was an hermaphrodite, for he could not abide a woman* (III.ii.224–5). Later he accepts unquestioningly the Duchess's orders to flee with his son, leaving her helpless; at this point his kiss is *colder* than that of an *anchorite* (III.v.88–9), perhaps because he is thinking of himself: *I sound my danger* (III.v.92).

Despite the moving evidence in the echo scene (V.iii) of abiding love for his wife, he is seen to be naïve in hoping for peace with the Cardinal. His accidental death, and his comment that *We follow after bubbles* (V.iv.65), seem to sum up an unfortunate life. Perhaps Webster suggests the folly of ambition here, but is Antonio as ambitious as Delio might suggest (II.iv.80–1)? There is ambiguity; in the echo scene the reliable

Delio talks of his *virtue* (V.iii.51). Is Antonio a coward, an over-ambitious man, or is he a good man of middling rank who cannot survive in the vicious Aragonian society?

Delio and Pescara

Delio rises in the audience's esteem. He is clearly a good man of sound judgement, and Antonio trusts him absolutely: *Our noble friend, my most beloved Delio* (III.i.1). In the course of the play his status seems to grow as Antonio's declines. We see him nimble-witted in moments of crisis, as at the onset of the Duchess's labour, II.i.178–80. In Act V he cares for the hapless Antonio, aware of the futility of an appeal to the Cardinal's good nature: *I would not have you go to th' Cardinal's tonight:/ Do not* (V.iii.28–9). Delio has his flaws, as he has been one of Julia's *old suitors* (II.iv.46), but does Webster intend us to see anything more than the typical sins of an ordinary man?

Delio has an equivalent in the upper classes in Pescara, the noble commander who enters the play in the third act seemingly to represent wisdom and justice. He is shrewdly aware of the true behaviour of churchmen (III.iii.36), wise when he denies Delio's request for lands unjustly obtained from Antonio (V.i.40ff), and when he senses the Cardinal's danger: *The accent of the voice sounds not in jest* (V.v.30). These two noble men, Delio and Pescara, are suited to the important role of bringing hope for a new future when they nominate the heir.

Activity
What is your response to the character of the Duchess?

Discussion
Weigh up her strengths and her weaknesses. Look carefully at Webster's presentation of her torture and death in Act IV. How do you think Webster wants the audience to respond to her?

Structure, language and effects

Settings

Webster uses the settings of *The Duchess of Malfi* to reflect the movement of the drama. Settings are restricted, mostly indoors, including the Duchess's presence chamber and the Cardinal's rooms in Rome. Settings are seen to diminish, becoming increasingly claustrophobic, until the Duchess faces her *last presence-chamber* (IV.ii.176), the coffin. Several scenes are set outdoors, but there is no sense of relief from the oppressive atmosphere; there is perhaps an outside setting for the shrine at Loreto, but no sense of freedom as the dumb-show of the Cardinal's arming reveals the massive and irresistible power of the Church, now allied to the state. The succeeding outdoor scene ends in the Duchess's banishment; and the echo scene in the ruined abbey is ominous, warning of death and danger, overshadowed again by the impregnable walls of the Cardinal's palace.

To intensify the relationship of settings to dramatic movement, Webster uses a patterning of light and dark. Night scenes on a darkened stage are numerous: see II.iii, II.iv, III.i, III.ii, V.iv and V.v. The two scenes of Act IV take place on a darkened stage in prison. Webster increases the tension further by having a storm brewing in II.iii and actually happening in V.iv (see line 18).

He also varies the construction of scenes to provide contrasts and at times relief for the audience from suspense or tension. For example, the play opens with Antonio introducing the characters and develops into a public, crowded court scene where Webster variously centralizes individuals and groups. Bosola enters, and the focus moves to his dealings with Ferdinand; this episode yields to the confrontation between the brothers and the Duchess; then the scene closes down to focus on the private, with the intimate wooing scene between the Duchess and Antonio. Finally Cariola stands alone on stage directly addressing the audience about her fears.

Handling of time

During the original performances of *The Duchess of Malfi* at the Blackfriars Theatre there would have been musical intervals between the acts. To ensure continuity, Webster uses various characters, usually Antonio and Delio, to indicate that time has passed. Delio mentions this near the beginning of Act II, asking Antonio *And so long since married?* (II.i.79); Antonio introduces the idea addressing Delio at the beginning of Act III: *O, you have been a stranger long at court* (III.i.2). Ferdinand performs this service at the beginning of Act IV: *How doth our sister Duchess bear herself/ In her imprisonment?* and Antonio's question to Delio at the opening of Act V about *reconcilement* to the brothers shifts the action to another time and another place. These passing references suggest a time-scale, but also create a curiously non-temporal feel to the action: time and place do not seem to matter in this universal tragedy.

Structure

Critics of Webster's structure in *The Duchess of Malfi* suggest three weaknesses: the death of the heroine in Act IV instead of the usual Act V; a lack of clear structure; and Ferdinand's strange delay in implementing his enraged threats of II.v (see page 196).

Webster had practical problems in presenting the Duchess's death. In keeping with the conventions of revenge tragedy, Ferdinand, the Cardinal and Bosola all had to die. Antonio also had to die; throughout the play his worth has seemed to diminish, and he could not be the man to introduce the heir, or bring some hope for the future. Webster may have felt that to add at least four more deaths to that of the Duchess in the same act would have diluted the tragedy of her death, so another act was necessary. But he extends the functions of Act V far beyond this, as the audience is presented with the effects of the Duchess's death, which develop the themes of revenge and retribution, damnation and salvation.

Retribution begins immediately for Ferdinand, as is evident

in his exchange with Bosola: *I'll go hunt the badger by owl-light:/ 'Tis a deed of darkness,* he says, to which Bosola responds: *He's much distracted* (IV.ii.340–2). Ferdinand breaks down into madness; in imagistic terms, the devil has declared himself. His tortured madness extends over the fifth act, a just punishment for his treatment of his sister.

The Cardinal is a tougher character, seemingly more controlled in his murder of Julia (V.ii.277ff) and in his assumption of control over Bosola (V.ii.304). Several times Webster presents the Cardinal as a type of stage villain, for example in his soliloquy to the audience: *The reason why I would not suffer these...* (V.iv.22); this reminds the audience of his villainy and of the danger he poses to the reformed Bosola, who is fortunately too intelligent to be fooled. Act V is not an anti-climax, however, as the beneficial effects of the Duchess's grace are revealed; Webster also forges links by use of repetition as the Cardinal/Julia scene (V.ii) echoes I.i, III.ii, IV.i and IV.ii, in its themes of love, ambition and death.

A second charge against Webster's presentation of Act V is that it uses gratuitous violence and sensationalism (see 'Critical Views', page 219). But it seems that the playwright deliberately smashes the safety barrier of artificial convention. He shows what happens when control is lost: bloodshed, carnage, social and personal mayhem. Form and theme seem to be perfectly harmonized.

There seems to be a growing consensus among critics that Webster's central structural device is the use of repetition, although there is some dispute about where the central point of the play lies. David Gunby, for example (see 'Critical Views', page 221), suggests that the first part of *The Duchess of Malfi* ends at II.v, and that in the second half Acts III and IV, and to some extent Act V, are reworkings of the first two acts. There are clear echoes of I.i in III.i; in the earlier scene, Antonio had praised the Duchess's virtue (I.i.199); at the beginning of III.i he has to admit to Delio that she is commonly considered a *strumpet* (III.i.25-6). Earlier, the Duchess had praised Antonio as her *upright treasure*

(I.i.384); later she is forced to accuse him of dealing *so falsely... in's accounts* (III.ii.168). Webster reworks scenes in this way to present different views of the Duchess's decision to marry Antonio; it is left to the individual to draw conclusions.

Other commentators, such as Jacqueline Pearson (see 'Critical Views', page 221), believe that the central structure of the play rests on the repetition of the wooing scene of I.i throughout *The Duchess of Malfi*. This is evident at III.ii, IV.i, IV.ii, and at V.ii.154ff; in most cases there is a trio on stage. There are parallels between I.i and III.ii; in fact Webster revises our perceptions of the wooing scene three times. The latter scene begins with the same characters on stage as in I.i: the Duchess, Antonio and Cariola. All seem relaxed, sharing sexual double-entendres, for example at III.ii.18–20; it is initially a happy reflection of the wooing scene. However, Ferdinand stealthily replaces Antonio, ironically showing the passion of a lover which Antonio had lacked; the conversation is intimate but aggressive, with sexual overtones. Echoing I.i.343, Ferdinand offers his sister a poniard for suicide, which also recalls the Duchess's suggestion that she could sleep with *a naked sword* (I.i.512) between herself and her husband. This also echoes another offering, the love-gift of the wedding ring in I.i. The funerary imagery of I.i, *'Tis not the figure cut in alabaster...* (I.i.465), is repeated with Ferdinand's reference to the *massy sheet of lead* (III.ii.112) of the same tomb. This first part of the scene is concentric, with the central point being Ferdinand's visit, leaving the audience to compare the characters and their attitudes before and after this event. As a result the Duchess suspects Antonio of betrayal (III.ii.87–8), and Antonio similarly accuses Cariola (III.ii.144–5), replaying Ferdinand's gestures by threatening her with a pistol, and the departed Ferdinand with the poniard. Already bonds of love, trust and harmony are weakened, flight is inevitable, and the Duchess resolves to *sin* by telling a *noble lie* (III.ii.181).

In the second part of this scene, after Bosola's entrance (III.ii.161), Webster reworks the wooing scene and also the first part of this scene. The optimism and openness have disappeared.

Instead, the Duchess and Antonio present a 'play', accusing her husband of a crime he did not commit for the benefit of Bosola and of the officers. They are engaged in 'feigning'. Then, from line 231 onwards, the 'play' version of Antonio is revised, as Bosola praises him: *Sure/ He was too honest* (III.ii.246–7). It is left entirely to the audience to decide which version is accepted. The Duchess, confronted by an angered, unjust brother and by a deceitful agent, has stood by her principles of trust in love and family, but it is all far removed from the openness and happiness of the wooing scene.

The parallels between I.i and the two scenes of Act IV are more extensive (see page 191). The Duchess and Bosola are each presented as *galley-slaves* and there is in both scenes ritual, ceremony, kneeling, promises, physical contact, oaths, music and possibly dance. In both there are references to weapons, to the poniard/sword/dagger sequence, to rings, jewellery, madness, quietus, love, sex and death, and funerary imagery. Bosola replaces Antonio as the Duchess's carer, minister and then scourge in the most extensive reworking of the earlier scene in the play.

Activity

Analyse V.ii from line 104, the scene played by Julia, the Cardinal and Bosola, as a reworking of the wooing scene.

Discussion

Think about the similar pattern of promises and threats, the poniard/sword now a pistol, of jewels and of a love-gift. Consider Julia as a foil to the Duchess, comparing their attitudes to love, sex, life, death and eternity. Think about what this scene contributes to an understanding of the play as a whole.

Other critics such as Christina Luckyj (See 'Critical Views', page 221) believe that the pattern works in exactly the opposite direction: that IV.ii, which marks the ending of the first part of *The Duchess of Malfi*, is a point of focus, with all that goes before and after reflecting on this climactic scene. (She argues for a two-part structure with the second part, Act V, being the resolution.)

Despite their different claims about the mid-point of the play, many critics agree that the key to Webster's structure is his careful repetition and replays, leaving the audience free to select their own version of the 'truth'.

Continuity through juxtaposition

Webster frequently links acts and scenes to create a sense of seamless continuity in developing his ideas. Take, for example, the link between I.i and II.i; in the wooing scene Antonio twice refers to the dangers of ambition (I.i.423–4 and 431): *Ambition, madam, is a great man's madness.* Act II opens with the comic scene between Bosola and the foolish Castruccio, who says that to be an eminent courtier is *the very main of my ambition.* Webster economically achieves several things here: the audience is reminded how the previous act ended; one of the main themes of the play is carried forward in comic counterpoint, providing variety of tone; there is the suggestion of Bosola's wisdom; and the audience realizes that if such a fool as Castruccio seeks preferment, then society is rotten to the core.

There are also clear links between Ferdinand's dire threats about the Duchess, which end Act II, and Act III which begins with Antonio assuring Delio that his wife is *Right fortunately well.* Webster builds up tension resting on dramatic irony as the net begins to close on the Duchess and her family; a point is clearly made about the links between love and death, and the frailty of happiness in such a society.

Activity
Links between scenes may be exemplified by that between II.i and II.ii. Explore the effects of this juxtaposition.

Discussion
What do you think of Antonio's response to the crisis of the birth?

Consider Antonio's words: *I am lost in amazement, I know not what to think on't* (II.i.184–5). What might this suggest about Antonio, and about the Duchess's trust in him? Immediately after, in the first line of II.ii, Webster picks up Bosola's viewpoint: *So, so: there's no question...* Webster contrasts the responses of the two men to the same event, a central device of his, and draws the audience's attention to the differing characters of the two men. What do you think about Bosola here, and how might you compare the two men at this point in the play?

Throughout the play Webster works as a lawyer might, allowing the audience to consider evidence from many different perspectives through his use of repetition and multiple perspectives.

Language and effects

Webster also uses repetition as a central device in his use of language, as words and phrases recur throughout the play, accruing new meanings each time. Again, the effect is to increase perspectives on actions and situations.

There are many word chains including rings and jewellery, weaponry, the quietus, will, animals, birds, horse-leeches and other insects, horse-dung, painting and paintings, eclipses, geometry, glass-houses, hair, anchorites, panders, cassia, diseases, poison, witchcraft, blood, sex, ruins and echoes. Central thematic concerns are also amplified in language linked to madness, love and death; noise, whispering and silence; storms, light and darkness; virtue, goodness, angels and heaven; evil, devils and hell.

Activity

Consider the different meanings of the word blood, what it means to various characters, and how it introduces certain themes.

Discussion

To the Cardinal it is *The royal blood of Aragon and Castile* (II.v.22), but he also refers to the Duchess's *high blood* ambiguously (I.i.309), perhaps also suggesting passion. Ferdinand refers to the Duchess's *rank blood* (III.i.78), which is a reminder to the audience that they literally share the same blood as they are twins, but he perceives hers to have been tainted. Another reference to *blood* is more straightforward, when Malateste calls Bosola *Thou wretched thing of blood* (V.v.92).

It might be useful to explore the word *will*, as verb and noun, in the same way as the word *blood*, perhaps beginning with the Duchess's abbreviated *I'll never marry:* (I.i.314).

Variety of language

Webster uses many different types of language to create specific effects. Puns create ambiguity, for example in Bosola's words to Julia: *Let us grow most amorously familiar* (V.ii.187). Webster plays with the meaning of *familiar* as a witch's accomplice; Julia responds to a sexual meaning, while Bosola wants to get close in order to use her. In the world of Malfi there is no common agreement about what words mean. Many puns focus on the words *will/wilful*, *service* and *blood*. Double-entendres appear frequently, notably in the sexual innuendos of Ferdinand's language, which helps to define his lustful, disturbed character. But they are also prominent, for example, in the exchanges between the Duchess and Antonio (see I.i.512–3, III.ii.18–20) which reveal their intimacy.

Overall, Webster works by blending poetry with prose, at times using verse to indicate social status; by including song and dance (the madmen and the dirge); by careful sequencing, as in I.i where the formality and public speech of the Cardinal's and Ferdinand's combined warnings to the Duchess are followed by the more intimate language of the wooing scene; by replacing dramatic language with powerful visual emblems, such as the dumb-show of the Cardinal's arming; by the use of rhetoric, as in the fables and sayings or *sententiae*; and by the use of imagery (see page 181 below).

Activity

Analyse the passage II.i.118–132, exploring Webster's skills as a dramatist in creating tension here.

Discussion

This extract is a typical example of Webster's skills as a dramatist. The situation is tense; the Duchess, Antonio and Bosola all have secrets to keep. Immediately before, we have learned of Bosola's *pretty* plan to entrap the Duchess with the apricots; he is waiting to play his hand. The Duchess and Antonio are trying to keep their secret, although she is nine months pregnant. In other words, each of the trio has a double perspective on the situation, creating suspense for the audience; who is going to crack?

The verse is wonderfully controlled; the pauses and broken rhythms created by Webster's use of insistent punctuation and short sentences suggest the breathlessness of a heavily pregnant woman. The alliterative sequence of 's' throughout also suggests short breaths, but in contrast to these soft sounds there is a sequence of hard 'd' consonants which suggest a certain imperiousness of manner, with emphasis falling on the repeated *Duchess*. The Duchess's irritability shows in her remarks to the Old Lady, which are brusque commands and complaints.

In conversation with Antonio she is initially intimate in discussing her body, but by contrast her address of Bosola is formal, addressing him as *sir*, almost distancing herself from him. Is she nervous in his presence? The short sentences and rapid changes of subject suggest a lack of concentration. Webster makes a point of Bosola's stagey aside: is it to remind us that at this stage he is the arch-villain? Even at this uncomfortable moment, the Duchess is seen as a royal prince; she issues instructions, and refers to her rank by mentioning *the presence* chamber. On the other hand, her formal courtesy to Bosola, who is the servant in charge of her horses, reminds the audience of her more democratic views of society. She ignores his low status in a way which Ferdinand would never dream of.

Webster uses the word *mother* as a pun, on the one hand to refer to her pregnancy, and perhaps to remind us that the Duchess is about to take on a new role. The other meaning is 'hysteria', which simultaneously suggests her state of mind. Her adventurous marriage is presented as fruitful, in contrast to the sterility of her brothers. Antonio plays a typically minor role with a single-word response; there is no doubt at this stage who are the dominant members of the trio.

Webster advances important themes here; as well as the richness of the Duchess's marriage, the audience is aware that all three are acting parts: they are not what they seem, which simply underlines the usual state of affairs in Malfi. There is some ambiguity in Bosola's phrase *I fear too much*; it may be a sarcastic comment on the pregnancy, but possibly Bosola reflects on the dreadful role he has to play as intelligencer. It is a crucial moment in the play, a brief pause before the 'tempest' begins and the Duchess and Antonio's relationship is revealed to her brothers.

Distancing or alienation

Webster's use of distancing or alienation creates pauses and allows the audience to stand back and reflect on the situation on stage. There are three ways of achieving this: by the use of *sententiae* and fables, through the dirge and through theatrical references.

Like many other writers, Webster compiled a commonplace book, entering any sayings, snatches of poems and quotations from other writers which he might use himself; this was not considered plagiarism, however. There are many such *sententiae* throughout *The Duchess of Malfi*, which often occur at critical points in the play; see Appendix, page 234. For example, at the end of III.i Ferdinand ends his discussion with Bosola by saying: *That friend a great man's ruin strongly checks, / Who rails into his belief all his defects* (III.i.92–3). This is an excellent example of Webster's use of irony; already the audience knows that Ferdinand will not be criticized (I.i.130), so it is clear that he is entirely without self-knowledge. This spells out the dangers for Bosola in working for someone so unstable. Bosola was introduced as *railing* in these terms (I.i.23), he is the *court-gall*, and ironically he will purge Ferdinand of all his faults through revenge and retribution.

Ferdinand's saying also creates a pause in proceedings here; earlier in the scene the Duchess believed that he had forgiven her (III.i.55), but now it is obvious that Ferdinand is out for revenge. The audience is given time to digest the situation on stage, and the generalizing *sententiae* extend the debate to allow the audience to form more general and balanced conclusions.

Twice during the play Webster distances the audience by using the convention of fables. There is a fable about reputation at III.ii.120ff, and one about a salmon and a dog-fish at III.v.125ff. Both are presented at critical times, and create a pause in the action to allow dramatic tension to subside a little before the next crisis.

The dirge (IV.ii.183–200) is most strikingly a moment when action is suspended and the audience is invited not simply to think about what is happening, but to join in as a congregation might in this prayer for one about to die. It is ceremonial, ritualistic, and universalizes the moment, as all in the audience will share this experience. From now on, except for the sad domestic moment when the Duchess thinks about her children (IV.ii.209–11), until her death the action is solemn, the language elevated.

Finally, and perhaps most daringly, Webster uses theatrical references that remind the audience they are watching a play; see III.ii.295–300, IV.i.84–5, IV.ii.7–8, IV.ii.35–6, IV.ii.294–6, and the device of the echo in V.iii.

Activity

Perhaps the use of the alienation technique is most striking at the end of the play when Bosola, having killed Antonio in error, admits to *Such a mistake as I have often seen / In a play* (V.v.95–6). What effects does Webster achieve here?

Discussion

Think about your response to Bosola, and also the effect of alienation on the audience. Are you still able to suspend disbelief? If not, what are you led into thinking about? Perhaps there are considerations of causes and effects, perhaps about Malfi, or fate, or Bosola's character?

Imagery

Webster uses imagery schematically and cumulatively to expand the perspectives from which the audience understands the drama. His method may be seen clearly in the treatment of certain key imagery related to Ferdinand, the Cardinal and the Duchess: hell and the diabolical, witchcraft, fire, storm, and darkness, contrasted with heavenly light.

Webster uses imagery to develop the character and motivation of Ferdinand, with references to hell and the diabolical the most extensive. At the beginning of the play Webster uses Bosola to 'place' Ferdinand for the audience: *Thus the devil/ Candies all sins o'er* (I.i.287–8). Antonio later supports this link: *The devil, that rules i'th' air, stands in your light* (II.i.104). There are many such references throughout the play, for example I.i.198, III.ii.251, III.v.40, and IV.i.39. Ferdinand himself admits he is bound for hell (V.ii.43–4).

The Cardinal likewise is immediately linked to the diabolical: *...this great fellow were able to possess the greatest devil, and make him worse* (I.i.47–8); when he calls to his brother for help: *Help me, I am your brother...* Ferdinand identifies him as such: *The devil?* (V.v.51). His concern over *a question about hell* with its *one material fire* (V.v.1–2) perhaps suggests his spiritual home and final destination.

Ferdinand often refers to witchcraft, which was always linked in the Jacobean mind with the diabolical, generally when he is concerned with his sister (see I.i.321–3 and III.ii.141–2), and notably in his conversation with Bosola: *The witchcraft lies in her rank blood* (III.i.78). The Cardinal also links Ferdinand with witchcraft (II.v.49–51). Ferdinand attaches a sexual force to the word, but the audience is constantly reminded of his links with the diabolical, particularly when he tortures the Duchess with paraphernalia typical of witchcraft: the dead man's hand with its ring, and the wax figures. See also the Duchess's own account of herself as a wax figure stuck with pins (IV.i.63–4). Bosola suggests that witchcraft has contagiously spread to society in II.i.42–4 and III.i.63–4.

In keeping with his humour, Ferdinand is fiery, and images of fire abound; yet again, there is a link to the diabolical. Examples are II.v.24–6, III.i.56–7 and III.ii.116. Pescara's words are significant: *A very salamander lives in's eye,/ To mock the eager violence of fire* (III.iii.50–51), as this lizard was said to live in fire. Near his death the doctor brings Ferdinand a salamander's skin to protect him from the sun, and Ferdinand has *cruel sore eyes* (V.ii.64–7). He is being scorched by his own fire, perhaps the flames of hell.

The Cardinal too is linked with fire, in Pescara's words about great men who *carry fire in their tails* (III.iii.39–40) and in his own words to Bosola: *Throw to the devil/ Thy melancholy: The fire burns well* (V.ii.309–10).

Imagery of the diabolical is linked to that of the storm in Malateste's description of the effect on Ferdinand's chamber: *'Twas nothing but pure kindness in the devil/ To rock his own child* (V.iv.20–1). Was it just the tempest that shook his room? Echoes of *Dr Faustus* suggest otherwise, as this also happens immediately before Faustus is taken by devils to hell.

There are many references to storms, such as I.i.482–3, II.v.16–17, III.i.21–2, III.ii.162, and III.v.25–6. The Cardinal is also linked to storms; as he prepares to do battle, *he lifts up's nose, like a foul porpoise before a storm* (III.iii.54). The verbal imagery is made concrete by literal storms that occur during the course of the play.

Connected to the diabolical imagery, images of darkness attend Ferdinand, becoming increasingly physically evident on stage as the play progresses. Ferdinand curses Antonio with darkness (*Let not the sun/ Shine on him, till he's dead* (III.ii.103–4) and also the Duchess, whom he will visit *i'th' night ...neither torch nor taper/ Shine in your chamber* (IV.i.24–6). Seeing his dead sister he recognizes his true ambience: *I'll go hunt the badger by owl-*

light:/ 'Tis a deed of darkness (IV.ii.340–1). These words are enacted in his lycanthropy (V.ii.7–21). Other images suggest how darkness spreads, for example I.i.329–30 and I.i.443.

Webster meticulously interweaves images traditionally related to a universal perception of hell: references to hell itself, the devil, fire, storm and darkness all suggest at the deepest level that the brothers have created hell on earth in Malfi. This seems clear in the Duchess's imprisonment when Bosola tells her that she *must live*. She replies: *That's the greatest torture souls feel in hell,/ In hell: that they must live, and cannot die* (IV.i.70–71). Webster's use of repetition makes the point clear: hell is the here and the now, created by the brothers.

Ferdinand's anguished cry *Cover her face: mine eyes dazzle* (IV.ii.270) marks a triumph of light over dark; but he is from now on a creature of the night. This is supported by the incident in the last act when he asks Malateste to protect him against his own shadow: *Stay it, let it not haunt me*. Malateste of course cannot help, because *the sun shine[s]* (V.ii.37–9). The shadow which he attempts to throttle is caused by heavenly light, which perhaps reveals Ferdinand's inner blackness. By now it is clear to all on stage and in the audience that he is the centre of darkness. Strangling, whispering, evil deeds to be *done i'th'dark* (V.iv.36); in his tortured recapitulation of events, has Ferdinand achieved some self-knowledge?

The Cardinal similarly has been linked to the devil, to storms, to hell and also to darkness. He and his brother are the same, as Bosola notes: *You have a pair of hearts are hollow graves,/ Rotten, and rotting others* (IV.ii.325–6).

Just as Webster presents Ferdinand creating hell on earth for his sister, he graphically places the Cardinal as about to enter the jaws of hell: *When I look into the fishponds, in my garden,/ Methinks I see a thing armed with a rake/ That seems to strike at me* (V.v.5–7). This suggests a picture of the devils at the jaws of hell raking sinners in; it is a medieval convention with which the Jacobean audience would be familiar. Ferdinand finally sees him not as his brother, but the devil (V.v.51).

At this point, some of Webster's purposes in creating this extensive scheme of imagery become clear as the brothers' deeper motivations are revealed. They are creatures of hell set to wage war on goodness. Many images throughout the play suggest their effects on society at large, for example II.ii.25–8, II.iii.52–3, and III.v.24–5. But does the devil win? Have Ferdinand and the Cardinal drawn society as a whole into hell? Webster schematically contrasts diabolical images with those of light centred on the Duchess, as Antonio explains how she *lights the time to come* (I.i.221).

The Duchess is linked to light and to heaven, and she uses a sacred register, as in the wooing and marriage scene: *Bless, heaven, this sacred Gordian* (I.i.491); she feels *blessed comfort* (III.i.55); she compares herself to *a holy relic* (III.ii.140); she shares Antonio's belief that *Heaven hath a hand* (III.v.62) in their situation; she accepts the penance of *heaven's scourge-stick* (III.v.81) in a dialogue where the word *heaven* is used three times; and she questions Bosola: *What devil art thou, that counterfeits heaven's thunder?* (III.v.100). Finally, Webster makes her destination after death clear when she addresses the executioner:

> . . . pull down heaven upon me.
> Yet stay; heaven' gates are not so highly arched
> As princes' palaces; they that enter there
> Must go on their knees. (IV.ii.237–40)

Humble and holy, she is the antidote to the brothers' evil, although the imagery of heaven and light is not as pervasive as that of the diabolical.

The struggle between good and evil may be seen in terms of the image of the eclipse of the Duchess's light. Ferdinand is determined to *fix her in a general eclipse* (II.v.82); he ironically asks her *What hideous thing/ Is it that doth eclipse* virtue (III.ii.72–73). Ferdinand's aversion to light and the sun was noted above, and this culminates in Delio's speech at the end of the play:

> These wretched eminent things
> Leave no more fame behind 'em than should one
> Fall in a frost, and leave his print in snow;
> As soon as the sun shines, it ever melts,
> Both form and matter.   (V.v.113–7)

There is a clear suggestion that heavenly light has triumphed over the dark forces of evil.

Webster uses imagery to reveal character on three levels:
- naturalistically, character traits such as hot temper and anger, coolness and cunning, virtue and grace
- psychologically, revealing a character's motivation, at times hidden even from himself
- thematically, at a level of meaning below the surface of the play.

Imagery helps to establish mood, to reveal truths below the surface, to summarize situations and to foreshadow things to come. Aural interpretations extend the visual images presented on stage. All of the imagery of the play works cumulatively, and many categories are evident, including imagery of poison, blood, disease, painting, laughter, status, ambition, politics, service, madness, fortune, jewellery, money and value, and preferment.

Activity
Explore the imagery of the ring, so intimately connected to the Duchess.

Discussion
This is a recurring image which accumulates several meanings to suggest various aspects of love, marriage and society. Each time it is used the context differs, modifying the audience's response. You might begin with the following examples:
- Antonio's winning of the ring at jousting and Ferdinand's crude revision of it (I.i.94)
- the Duchess's link with grace as she heals Antonio's eye with her ring (I.i.416–7).

185

Perhaps there are links here between the royal ring of a prince, love, sex and marriage. In the wooing scene Antonio negatively refers to the devil dancing in the circle (I.i.423–4), an impression that the Duchess corrects. The ring becomes the *circumference* of marital harmony (I.i.480).

Negative associations of the ring accrue through the brothers; the Cardinal wrenches the ring from the Duchess at the Loreto shrine (III.iv.36–9), and it reappears, as a distorted symbol of Ferdinand's feelings, on the dead man's hand (IV.i.44–7). Finally, on its last appearance the ring has become the executioner's noose, an ambiguous image of both repression and release.

Write notes exploring what Webster suggests through this imagery about love, sex and marriage, society and power, confinement, life and death. The whole process of the drama is contained in this sequence of imagery.

Literary interpretations

The morality play

Some of Webster's audience would have known of morality plays. These were medieval allegorical plays in which human qualities were personified and acted out on stage in a conflict between goodness and evil. Other audience members would have seen Christopher Marlowe's *Dr Faustus*, where the morality play forms part of the structure. The Good and Bad Angels (allegorizing goodness/hope and evil/despair, respectively) appear on stage to persuade Faustus towards different courses of action. Old Man (representing the medieval Good Counsel) tries to persuade Faustus to repent, and Mephistopheles is a terrifying presence who succeeds in tempting Faustus to despair and damnation.

The first stage of looking at this interpretation would draw on some of the analysis of imagery related to the central characters (see 'Imagery', page 181), where Webster is seen to present below the surface of the text a conflict between the forces of good and evil. It could be demonstrated that Ferdinand and the Cardinal may be seen as devilish, working for the forces of evil to destroy the virtue of the Duchess and Antonio; the Duchess may represent heavenly light in the moral conflict that Webster presents in *The Duchess of Malfi*.

It would be helpful to consider how Webster adds further details which might suggest that there are echoes of the biblical Fall of Man from Eden. At times the Duchess views Bosola as the devil's agent: *What devil art thou, that counterfeits heaven's thunder?* (III.v.100), and there are clear echoes of this in three scenes of the play:

- II.i, with resonances of the fall from Eden
- III.ii, with the presentation of a morality tableau on stage (the Duchess, Cariola and Bosola)
- IV.ii, where Bosola switches roles and sides to become a character similar to Good Counsel, and Cariola has overtones of the Good Angel.

Acting as Ferdinand's spy, Bosola needs to entrap the Duchess into admitting her pregnancy. Webster makes the moment when Bosola conceives his plan significant by soliloquizing Bosola's thoughts about her: *I have a trick may chance discover it,/ A pretty one; I have bought some apricots,/ The first our spring yields* (II.i.77–8). Bosola is presented in his direct address to the audience as a stage villain, full of self-satisfaction with his own scheming, calling his plan *pretty*. Symbolically, Bosola goes on to enact the role of the serpent in Eden by offering the Duchess, as Eve, apricots to eat (instead of the biblical apple). Having tasted the fruit, the Duchess is immediately entrapped, forced into using the deceit and 'feigning' of her oppressors. For example, the good Delio is compelled to suggest lies on her behalf: *Give out that Bosola hath poisoned her/ With these apricots* (II.i.178–9). Her age of innocence with Antonio is over, and she is forced to equivocate in reporting a robbery, and enter into direct conflict with her brothers.

Webster adds further detail from the typical morality play by presenting a tableau at the end of III.ii; the Duchess, flanked on stage by Bosola and Cariola, listens to advice about a *feignèd* pilgrimage. Representing the Bad Angel, who acts for the devil, Bosola suggests that she undertakes the pilgrimage, falsely promising her *a princely progress, retaining/ Your usual train about you* (III.ii.315–6). The Duchess, seduced, accepts: *Sir, your direction/ Shall lead me by the hand* (III.ii.316–7). Cariola, perhaps representing the Good Angel, objects, saying *I do not like this jesting with religion* (III.ii.321), but is brushed aside: *Thou art a superstitious fool* (III.ii.323). This is another significant stage in her loss of 'Paradise'; the audience suspect that she is irreversibly doomed.

Later, with supreme irony, Webster has Ferdinand, one of the arch-demons, make a clear reference to the Fall of Man: *O horror!/ That not the fear of him which binds the devils/ Can prescribe man obedience* (IV.ii.320–2).

The overlay of the morality structure is complicated when Bosola switches allegiances to work for the side of good, but the Duchess still has to face temptation presented by her devilish brothers. Webster makes Ferdinand's aim explicit in answer to Bosola's query about his purposes: *To bring her to despair* (IV.i.116); diabolically, he wants to see her soul damned in hell as despair is a mortal sin. However, unlike Faustus who surrenders to this, with Bosola's ministrations she resists: *O fie! Despair? Remember/ You are a Christian* (IV.i.74–5). Cariola, in an echo of the role of the Good Angel, tries to strengthen her: *Yes, but you shall live/ To shake this durance off* (IV.ii.11–12).

Bosola, in a reworking of the role of Good Counsel, helps her through her stages of self-pity (*thy sickness is insensible*, IV.ii.124–5), then through pride (*Thou art a box of worm seed, at best*, IV.ii.129), to acceptance (*Let me know fully therefore the effect/ Of this thy dismal preparation*, IV.ii.168–9); and finally to humility and acceptance of death: *Pull, and pull strongly, for your able strength/ Must pull down heaven upon me* (IV.ii.236–7). Cariola, the Good Angel, has been proved right: the Duchess will achieve eternal life in heaven. Perhaps some cautious optimism might be evident here, as goodness is seen to be rewarded.

Although some critics suggest that Webster offers no moral vision, this reading disproves such a charge, and shows that Webster offers a traditionally Christian view of morality, but is not moralistic; instead, he offers alternatives, leaving the individual to decide on outcomes.

Providence or fortune

While the Christian belief in a redemptive plan for humankind suggests a reading of history which is providential – meaning that God has provided for our salvation – Webster refers to other views that rest entirely on chance, offering no such reassurance. Antonio and the Duchess both refer to *Fortune*, traditionally presented as a blind-folded goddess arbitrarily dealing out triumph or disaster; references to the wheel of fortune connote the medieval belief that people would rise only to fall again as the wheel turned. Bosola also refers to an external force controlling human destiny as *the stars*; Webster raises the issue of whether we can control our own destinies, and therefore take responsibility for our own actions.

Activity

We are merely the stars' tennis balls, struck and banded/ Which way please them (V.iv.53–4). Is this the case, or is there evidence of a providential scheme in *The Duchess of Malfi*?

Discussion

Webster might well suggest through Bosola's words in Act IV that there is some form of divine justice: *Other sins only speak; murder shrieks out./ The element of water moistens the earth,/ But blood flies upwards, and bedews the heavens* (IV.ii.267–9). There are other comments that seem to support a belief in Christian scheme of salvation, such as Antonio's words *Since we must part/ Heaven hath a hand in't* (III.v.61–2), and the Duchess's words in the same scene: *And* yet, *O Heaven, thy heavy hand is in't* (III.v.78). She adds: *nought made me e'er/ Go right but heaven's scourge-stick* (III.v.80–1).

Webster changes the pace of action in III.v when the Duchess, now overcome by force and bereft of Antonio and their elder son, recounts the fable of the dog-fish and the salmon (III.v.124–144). This could be seen as an echo of the gospels, where the image of a basket of fishes recurs, suggesting Christ's 'harvesting' of Christian souls into heaven. Perhaps Webster uses the parable to suggest that a person's true value is seen only at death, when through the Last Judgement virtuous souls are selected for salvation. Her words may suggest a spiritual scheme of eternal life.

Set against this Webster has some repetition about a belief in fortune, for example Antonio's hopeful words at his marriage, *That Fortune may not know an accident* (I.i.500), and the Duchess's later bitter reference to *Fortune's wheel* (III.v.96). However, these references are not schematized in the play, perhaps merely a theatrical convention that a Jacobean audience might expect.

In contrast, the idea of divine justice is systematically presented in the words of the brothers. Early in the play, Ferdinand says that *It is some sin in us heaven doth revenge/ By her* (II.v.66–7), and on his death the Cardinal admits: *O Justice!/ I suffer now for what hath former been* (V.v.53–54).

It would be worth using some of the evidence of the imagery to complete this investigation, and compare the way characters' behaviour is set against the outcomes of *The Duchess of Malfi*. Webster offers no answers, but you will be equipped to draw your own conclusions.

The roles and significance of Antonio and Bosola

At the start of the play there seems little similarity between Antonio and Bosola; Webster invites respect for Antonio in his role as chorus, offering sound judgements about the differences between the courts of France and Malfi. He is distinguished in his French clothing and somewhat apart from the comings and goings on stage. The rulers respect him; to Ferdinand he is *the great master* of his sister's *household* (I.i.91–2); the Cardinal admits to his *honest* nature (I.i.242). On the other hand, Bosola is described as a *court-gall* (I.i.23), and is seen to be begging unsuccessfully for reward for murder from the Cardinal (I.i.29ff), although Antonio describes him as *very valiant* (I.i.77). He is a mercenary who has achieved no success in life.

However, there are similarities between the two men. Both have embarked on a path of self-determination; Antonio has achieved respect and bureaucratic success as steward, seemingly contented with his limited role. In contrast, despite his studies, Bosola has not been rewarded similarly; he is forced to go into the service of ruthless rulers although one has *slighted* him (I.i.238). His moral worth is apparent when he initially rejects the gold offered (I.i.275–8), but he is without options, and is therefore forced to accept the role of spy for Ferdinand: *I am your creature* (I.i.299). Ironically by the end of I.i both men are in different ways in the Duchess's service.

There is constant tension between the men, as when Antonio mocks Bosola for his behaviour, suggesting that he is *puffed up with your preferment* (II.i.94); Bosola in turn mocks Antonio's new role: *O sir, you are lord of the ascendant, chief man with the Duchess* (II.i.105–6). Shortly afterwards further distinctions between the men appear. Antonio is *lost in amazement* in the panic of the first child's arrival (II.i.184), while Bosola at the same time seizes his opportunity with dexterity (II.ii.1–3). This marks the start of what might be seen as a cross-over in status; as described earlier (see page 168), Antonio's worth seems to diminish from now on, while Bosola steadily improves in standing in the audience's esteem.

The comparisons between the two men may be seen clearly in a comparison of the wooing and marriage scene of I.i and the torture and death scenes of IV.i and IV.ii. Both Bosola and the Duchess are presented as 'galley-slaves', Bosola at the start of the play and the Duchess in her words to Cariola: *I am acquainted with sad misery, / As the tanned galley-slave is with his oar* (IV.ii.27–8); this creates a ground for some sympathy between them. A bond slowly grows, with the Duchess's words to Bosola, *Let me be a little merry* (IV.ii.156), clearly recalling her words to Antonio,

When were we so merry? (III.ii.53). Her light-hearted comment in the same scene that when she goes grey she will have her courtiers *Powder their hair with orris* (III.ii.60) is echoed in the dirge (IV.ii.195). In the same scene Antonio admits that his *rule is only in the night* (III.ii.8); here Bosola has evident power over the Duchess in the darkness of the imprisonment scenes as she faces her dark night of the soul. A pattern seems to emerge which suggests that while Antonio was for a time her physical protector and comforter, albeit with limited success, Bosola takes over this role to become spiritual minister, responsible for guiding her through the stages before death to ensure that she reaches heaven. He has, it would seem, far more success than Antonio.

Webster establishes a clear pattern of parallels to link the two significant episodes. The Duchess had jested that she would place a *naked sword* (I.i.512) in their bed; the sword echoes the poniard shown to her earlier in the same scene (I.i.343), which Ferdinand gives her in III.ii; in IV.i it is echoed in the Duchess's words *I am full of daggers* (IV.i.90). The poniard has found its mark.

There are two elements connected to the ring with which the Duchess 'cures' Antonio's bloodshot eye (I.i.416); the first is the continued link with the ring imagery. In the wooing scene it becomes a circle, circumference and sphere; it re-appears as the ring on the dead man's hand (IV.i.44), an accurate visual emblem of her marriage and its effects; then finally, as the circular noose which is placed around her neck, as if she is entrapped by her own gift. The second element is the matter of the sore eye; the Duchess makes Antonio's eye better; she has the opposite effect on Bosola, as he experiences for the first time *tears* of *manly sorrow* (IV.ii.367–9).

The gift of the ring as a love-token is completed with the belated wedding gift from the brothers of coffin, cords and bell. In the wooing scene the Duchess was all too aware of her status: *us that are born great* (I.i.452), and throughout the scene and indeed the play, she is dominant. However, this is reversed in the death scenes by Bosola's skilled ministrations; her haughty *I am*

Duchess of Malfi still (IV.ii.147) is contextualized and deflated in Bosola's brusque reply: *That makes thy sleeps so broken*; she has to achieve humility.

Complementing the verbal echoes with body language, Webster repeats some of the earlier gestures; Antonio kneels until the Duchess raises him (I.i.430); later the Duchess herself kneels (IV.ii.240). Bosola had prepared her for this gesture in a reversal of Antonio's passive role. The ceremonial and ritualized feeling of the wooing scene is replicated in IV.i and IV. ii, but whereas the Church was considered unnecessary in the wedding scene (I.i.499), and rituals were profane rather than sacred, *That we may imitate the loving palms* (I.i.496), there is religious ceremony here with the purgation, mortification, the wearing of the crucifix, and the ritual chanting of the dirge (IV.ii.178). However, the Duchess invokes *heaven* to *bless* her marriage; as she dies she invokes heaven to open the gates to receive her (IV.ii.238). The oaths of love sworn earlier reappear as the Duchess's final statement of faith.

Musical images harmonize the wedding scene *like the spheres* (I.i.493); Webster inverts this later into the hideous parody of the madmen's song. Similarly the rhythms of the *loving palms*, a form of dance, are hideously parodied in their dance. But the madmen also recall Antonio's words: *Ambition, madam, is a great man's madness* (I.i.431); these madmen, representing the so-called professionals of society, seem to prove that view correct. In fact, despite the elevation of the human spirit earlier, by this stage of the play Bosola's assessment of humankind seems to be more accurate (IV.ii.129). Cariola had feared her mistress's *madness* (I.i.517); she has been proved correct.

Even in the wedding scene there are many images of death which undercut the surface joy; there is the funerary image, for example: *the figure cut in alabaster/ Kneels at my husband's tomb* (I.i.465–6); there are images of death as she seals Antonio's quietus (I.i.475), having remade her will (I.i.388). There is a joking reference to the *winding sheet* (I.i.401); this becomes her shroud in IV.ii. Concealment figures in both episodes; the wedding has to be kept secret from her relatives, a claustrophobia which will kill the marriage. In the death scenes, concealment is essential. But as with the attempted concealment of the marriage, it is not possible to keep the secret: *murder shrieks out* (IV.ii.267).

Whereas the Duchess has physical contact with Antonio when she wishes to *shroud my blushes in your bosom* (I.i.513), Bosola also has significant contact with her at the end of IV.ii. She stirs, and thinking she may still be alive Bosola touches her; although he cannot call for help, it is quite likely that in the theatre he would be seen trying to help her breathe, perhaps with the kiss of life (IV.ii.350–1).

In the wooing scene the Duchess urges Antonio to acceptance: *Awake, awake, man* (I.i.466); this is reversed in her death scene as she accepts death: *now I am well awake* (IV.ii.230); and after her death Bosola has a similar experience: *now that I wake* (IV.ii.331). Antonio does awake, but ironically through marriage gains torment and death.

The concept of death in IV.i and IV.ii has been inverted to represent a triumph through the promise of spiritual life for the Duchess, and a hope of redemption for Bosola in the Duchess's last word to him, *Mercy*. Bosola has helped her to save her soul and seems to achieve far more than Antonio ever could; he goes even further when he tries to protect his rival. There could be a final ironic similarity when both men die. Antonio dies apparently defeated, bitter about ambition and *the courts of princes* (V.iv.71). Bosola faces yet *another voyage* (V.v.105).

Perhaps the similarities and differences between the two men could be summed up in the ambiguity of the word *virtue*: originally Antonio had great virtue in the moral sense, while Bosola deliberately suppressed his until influenced by the grace of the Duchess. However, Bosola has virtue in the other sense of the word, inner strength; this allows him to display great commitment and persistence. This seems to be the very quality which fails Antonio when he is forced to tangle with the corrupt politics of Ferdinand and his brother.

The sense of menace

When looking at this issue it will be helpful to think about the following: characters, continuity, language and imagery, settings and theatrical effects. At the beginning of *The Duchess of Malfi*, it is generally assumed that the Duchess is about 19 years old, fairly recently widowed. As a widow the Duchess is in a strong situation; unlike unmarried girls who were ruled by their parents, or married women who were entirely subject to their husbands, widows had an independent status. They inherited their husbands' property and titles (although the Duchess is herself entitled to the dukedom, which may be passed on to her son when he is of age), and they were subject to nobody. Possibly the brothers see her as self-willed and want to protect the family interests, so they try to intimidate her into agreeing not to remarry.

The Cardinal reminds her of the importance of *honour* (I.i.308). Ferdinand's motives are unclear, but he threatens his sister with his father's poniard (I.i.343–4). Together, they create a sense of menace at the start of the play. The Duchess will not be bullied; *Shall this move me?* (I.i.353). The audience realizes that the Duchess has been making her own plans for marriage in direct conflict with those of her brothers. This typifies relationships in Malfi; there is no clear communication even between family members. Conflict is inevitable.

At the start of the play Webster presents the Cardinal and Ferdinand as powerful, tyrannical and corrupt (see pages 163–165); the images of disease and corruption (I.i.15, 47–8, 50ff) are justified in their immediate actions. Webster makes some sharp distinctions between the siblings; having concluded that the Cardinal, like his brother, is linked to the devil (I.i.197–8), Antonio immediately makes it clear that the Duchess is of a *different temper* (I.i.201). She graciously accepts Bosola into her household (I.i.229–30), so she has already been entrapped. Although she has Antonio beside her she seems powerless against two such ruthless, corrupt men and by the end of I.i a tragic outcome is inevitable.

Webster's skill in sequencing is significant in building up a sense of menace; at the start of II.i, firstly there is the comedy of Castruccio's obviously futile ambitions, then suddenly the tone changes to savagery in Bosola's attack on the Old Lady. In Bosola's scathing summary of humankind, Webster prepares the audience for the dirty work ahead in entrapping the Duchess. The act ends with Ferdinand's threat that he will *fix her in a general eclipse*. From now on the plot rests on the game of cat and mouse between the Duchess and her brothers, with a continual narrowing of her choices.

Continuity matters here; Webster plays with the audience again as Ferdinand's fevered threat seems to dissolve in a time gap of three years. But the threat is still ringing in the audience's ears when Ferdinand visits his sister in III.i; Antonio immediately senses danger from Ferdinand (III.i.19–24). Ferdinand tries more trickery when he surprisingly suggests a marriage for his sister, and then deceives her into believing that she is safe: *This deadly air is purg'd* (III.i.56). However, in the following line Ferdinand returns to his theme of revenge, and Webster develops the plot with the request for a false key.

Dramatic irony increases as the audience witnesses the last scene of happiness between the Duchess and Antonio. Ferdinand's entry is a stroke of theatrical brilliance as his sister continues with her excruciatingly relevant chatter, unaware of the change; things could not be worse. Reduced to suspecting even Antonio (III.ii.87–8), the Duchess seems to recognize that she is truly *undone* (III.ii.111), and is forced to flee.

There may possibly be a biblical echo of Mary, Joseph and Jesus in their *feignèd pilgrimage* (III.ii.322), and perhaps more so on their banishment, III.v.

Webster's dramatic language heightens a sense of menace at critical times, as in his references to Ferdinand's laughter. For example in III.iii.55–6, Delio completes Pescara's line in an example of stichomythia that rattles words out like cannon balls; the stressed word *deadly*, with alliterative 'd', points up the sense of menace. In the same exchange Delio adds: *In such a deformèd silence, witches whisper/ Their charms* (III.iii.59–60). The sibilance ('s') and aspirants ('w/wh') are soft; *deformèd* evokes the underlying corruption. The idea of 'whispering' picks up the motif which the Duchess refers to in her dying moments (IV.ii.229): the sinister secrecy with which the brothers work. Ferdinand is always linked to witches and witchcraft.

The increasingly dark settings help create the sense of fear (see page 170). The settings complement the increasing danger of the Duchess, and the relentless cruelty of her brothers. Storms also create a sense of disturbance at II.iii and V.iv, implying that the entire universe is disordered.

Webster also uses theatrical effects such as Antonio's dropping of the horoscope (II.iii), and the dumb-show in III.iv creates a totally different effect, doing more than language could to suggest the tremendous might of the Cardinal as Church and state join. The echo scene works lyrically to break up the violent sequence of Act V; there is a sense of secrecy, uncertainty and confusion; perhaps it helps prepare the audience for the issues that will arise from the ending of the play.

In the imprisonment scenes, stage effects are central. The deliberate theatricality of the dead man's hand and the waxworks distance the audience from a shadowy spectacle of horror, a Theatre of Blood in which the Duchess is forced to join with the entry of the madmen masquers in a ritualized, ceremonial presentation of purgation, preparation, and acceptance of death.

Crucially, in Act V the spirit of the Duchess hangs over all of the action. To Bosola she seems to appear as a form of support: *Still methinks the Duchess/ Haunts me; there, there* (V.ii.347–8). In the echo scene she seems to impart a warning to Antonio: *and on the sudden, a clear light/ Presented me a face folded in sorrow* (V.iii.44–5). The reference to sorrow is disturbing; is she aware of Antonio's impending death? A sense of uncertainty is created. The source of menace is brilliantly reversed as the spirit of the Duchess haunts and torments the evil-doers. Her torturers cannot forget their acts, and die with this knowledge. Ferdinand cries *My sister! O my sister! There's the cause on't* (V.v.71), and the Cardinal *I suffer now for what hath former been* (V.v.54).

Abuse of power

Webster offers damning evidence about the tyrannical rule of Duke Ferdinand and his brother the Cardinal; using Antonio as chorus, their faults are presented at the start of the play. The French court is offered as an example of good rule with the image of the *common fountain* issuing *Pure silver drops* (I.i.12–13). The opposite, it is implied, occurs within Ferdinand's dukedom where the *head* is poisoned and *Death, and diseases through the whole land spread* (I.i.15). Bosola links the Cardinal to the devil (I.i.46–8), and goes on to describe the methods used. The brothers create *miserable dependencies* (I.i.56), and establish a system of *flattering panders* (I.i.53–4). Having established character through imagery, Webster shows how the brothers' actions and words fulfil these profiles.

Already the Cardinal has been revealed as corrupt in his dealings with Bosola; having *suborned* murder (I.i.73), he slights his agent by refusing payment.

Ferdinand arrives with a flourish to award the jousting prize; but he is dismissive of sport in favour of war: *When shall we leave this sportive action, and fall to action indeed?* (I.i.94–5). His language is ambiguous, and during the course of the play it becomes evident that aggression may have replaced sexuality for the Duke; he is *most perverse, and turbulent* (I.i.181). Both are seen as dishonourable men; the Cardinal works for the opposite of good, strewing bribes in his path, while Ferdinand laughs *All honesty out of fashion* (I.i.184). The Cardinal appears to be Machiavellian (see Glossary), a cunning politician adept at strategies to maintain his power; having rejected Bosola's expectations of due payment, he persuades Ferdinand to employ him as a spy in the Duchess's household, although he himself *would not be seen in't* (I.i.237).

Ferdinand differs from his brother – his laughter (see pages

163–164) indicates mental instability, and he is a bully to his courtiers: *Methinks you that are courtiers should be my touchwood, take fire, when I give fire* (I.i.130–2). This captures the world of the courtier precisely and concisely; all are prescribed a life of flattery, fawning and imitation of the Duke. In this way Ferdinand establishes a system of absolute power, backed up with the Cardinal's religious and military might.

J.W. Lever (see 'Critical Views', page 221) broke from the line of traditional thought which considered *The Duchess of Malfi* in Christian terms as a play with a moral premise. Instead, influenced by the theories of new historicism, he offered a political reading of the play; the suffering of individuals was not necessary, but was inflicted because of abuse of power by the rulers.

He also suggested that Webster offers some indirect criticism of the reign and personal behaviour of his king, James I. This king was on the one hand scholarly, involved in the production of the King James Bible, and until the end of the first parliament in 1610, worked with the government on many areas of reform. After that, however, between 1610 and 1621, only one parliament was called, in 1614, and he adhered to his belief in the divine right of kings, according to which only the king could make laws. He was an absolute ruler, just as Webster suggests of Ferdinand and the Cardinal.

James I's personal behaviour was open to criticism; he was bisexual, with a wife and children and also gay lovers whom he promoted to positions of power. The first of these was Robert Carr, created Earl of Somerset for his 'services' in 1611. George Villiers, likewise, became Earl of Buckingham, and was an arrogant, troublesome mischief-maker. Known to be lavish in personal gifts, the king must have contributed to the national debt, which had reached £600,000 by 1608. His solution was to make a mockery of the honours system by selling baronetcies. In 1611 a title cost £1095; in 1622 the system had become so corrupt that the selling price dropped to £220. It is unsurprising that there was unrest among the people, evident in various plots of 1603, 1605 and the peasant revolt of 1607.

Webster reflects some of these issues in *The Duchess of Malfi*; the Duchess, a young widow with an ancestral title, could have attracted a wealthy second husband to increase the worth of the royal house. Perhaps the brothers hoped to arrange her second marriage, as they had probably arranged her first. The Cardinal wants a marriage with *honour* (I.i.308) for the Duchess, which would enrich rather than taint *The royal blood of Aragon and Castile* (II.v.22). This could be the reason why Ferdinand proposes *The great Count Malateste* as a match (III.i.41). Ferdinand had hoped to gain *An infinite mass of treasure by her death* (IV.ii.291). The brothers were greedy and ambitious, but the Duchess was not ruled by such considerations.

Evidence of corruption recurs throughout the play. As in the England of his time, Webster makes it clear that wars are fought for enrichment. Just as their soldiers and courtiers petition them for land and treasure, so the rulers' desire to aggrandize themselves makes them *spoil a whole province, and batter down goodly cities with the cannon* (II.i.116–7). Even the Pope is seen to countenance territorial ambition by seizing the Duchess's *dukedom* (III.iv.31–33). Similarly Antonio's property and land are seized; Julia gains *The Citadel of Saint Bennet* (V.i.30). Honours are being bought and sold, not always for cash, but certainly for being a 'favourite'. Webster parodies this theme when Bosola instructs Castruccio on how to be an *eminent courtier* (II.i.1–2); obviously manners make the man (II.i.5–10), but to know how to judge unjustly is paramount: *if you smile upon a prisoner, hang him, but if you frown upon him and threaten him, let him be sure to 'scape the gallows* (II.i.11–13). Personal caprice rules in this system based on the ruler's absolute power, and there is no rule of justice, as we see in the concerted attack on the Duchess. Bosola summarizes the brothers' effects on their state as follows: *You have a pair of hearts are hollow graves,/ Rotten, and rotting others* (IV.ii.325–6). Tyranny has corrupted all.

With a Machiavellian Cardinal and a mad duke there is no opportunity for individualism. Bosola, a sort of Machiavelli himself for the sake of survival, is allowed no degree of self-worth, despite all his efforts as a scholar. Ferdinand instructs him, and he must obey: *Do not you ask the reason* (I.i.269), *Do not ask then* (III.i.83). All that is offered to Bosola is gold in the first instance, nothing but a pardon in the second; the clear-sighted servant knows that such payments would *take me to hell* (I.i.278). His survival depends on his stoicism, courage and perseverance, but he is degraded morally and socially. In Malfi there is no commonality, no normative code of behaviour because the rulers act capriciously and tyrannically.

Finally Webster shows that such absolute power is destructive, even to the holders of that power, the Cardinal and the Duke. In contrast, the Duchess has a different philosophy; believing in individual merit rather than rank, she marries Antonio and the outcome is in many senses fruitful, empowering and a contrast to the sterility of her brothers' lives. Webster presents a stark choice between madness and the rule of sweet reason, between death and life. As Delio says at the end of the play: *Nature doth nothing so great for great men,/ As when she's pleased to make them lords of truth* (V.v.118–9).

The beginnings of social change in Malfi

Critics such as Frank Whigham (see 'Critical Views', page 220), have suggested that Jacobean society might be seen as a period of social change, indicated by a new social and sexual mobility. Problems for individuals were to arise from the new social status of 'employee'. Jacobean society, reflected in Malfi, was one where honours could be bought and sold, so ancestry was of less social significance and individuals could rise through the ranks of society. As London was a centre of economic growth, the new wealth changed traditional class types; boundaries which had existed for years between the middle and upper classes were being challenged by the rise of the bourgeoisie.

It could therefore be argued that Webster mirrors the social and cultural life of London in his play. The Elizabethan acceptance of the 'Great Chain of Being' which claimed that social strata, having been established by God, were eternal and unchangeable, was beginning to fade. Once a king sold honours, he could no longer be seen as the representative of God, because he had usurped God's powers. In the 'chain', aristocrats would be at the top and poor 'employees' like Bosola near the bottom. Webster presents in Ferdinand an embattled representative of the older way of life, an almost feudal aristocrat who can see his world disintegrating in front of him; interestingly, such a reading will generate sympathy for the troubled Duke. The Duchess has the spirit of the new, is ready for change, and promotes people through merit rather than birth. Antonio is a 'new man', rising through his own merit, while Bosola is an example of the unfortunate group who are intelligent, sensitive and educated but are unable to find an appropriate role in society. Webster thus presents a patriarchal society on the brink of change.

Ferdinand, as absolute ruler, is an isolated man, impossible to know, and Webster shows how he plays the role of tyrant in a theatrical way, living an artificial life-style, stuck fast in the manners and ways of the past. Perhaps this suggests the self-importance of the Duke; perhaps Webster is revealing the unbridgeable gap between sister and brother. Above all, his strangeness makes Ferdinand unknowable and inaccessible.

To ensure that their bloodline and wealth survive, aristocrats rely on suitable marriages; so when the Duchess marries out of her class she is socially *going into a wilderness* without a *clew* or *guide* (I.i.371–3). She is breaking new ground. Ferdinand loses the opportunity for enrichment through marriage, but the Duchess refuses to be offered as a commodity to someone like Count Malateste, *a mere stick of sugar-candy* (III.i.42); instead she vows to marry for Ferdinand's *honour* (III.i.44). The word *honour* is an indicator of the gap between the principles of the Duchess and those of her brothers; their uses of the word are very different. She believes in moral values of the kind that she sees in her steward, Antonio. However, in their confrontation earlier, the Cardinal has made the brothers' interpretation clear: *honour* is linked to the *high blood* of the nobility (I.i.308–9).

Thus it is that Ferdinand sees his sister's marriage as a contamination of the family's blood, and since he is her twin, directly of his own blood. When he is telling his brother about her conduct, he says he would like to *Root up her goodly forests, blast her meads,/ And lay her general territory as waste/ As she hath done her honours* (II.v.19–21). She is described in territorial terms, her worth simply an extension of his family's lands; no human values are evident. The Cardinal's response is similar, considering only their lineage; he too talks in terms of contamination: *Shall our blood... Be thus attainted?* (II.v.21–3). Ferdinand has a solution to this; he will use *fire,/ The smarting cupping-glass, for that's the mean/ To purge infected blood, such blood as hers* (II.v.24–6).

Class-consciousness underlies his response as he imagines his sister's lover as a bargeman, a woodsman, or a young household servant (II.v.42–5); later he describes Antonio as *A slave, that only smelled of ink and counters,/ And ne'er in's life looked like a gentleman* (III.iii.73–4). Perhaps the central problem for Ferdinand is that he cannot respond to the ancestral family need for marriage and procreation to secure the dynasty; his life is sterile in every way. Unable personally to secure his lineage, with a brother removed by his profession as Cardinal from the 'duty' of procreation, both men look to the Duchess to fulfil this task. Instead, however, she has acted in the opposite way with a marriage that threatens the existence of feudal aristocrats like the Aragonian brothers. In his confrontation with the Duchess in III.ii, Ferdinand's language is filled with sexual images such as *enjoy, lust, lecher* (III.ii.98–100), images of darkness, and of natural and social disorder (III.ii.102–9). The only marriage Ferdinand could recognize would be an arranged marriage; all else contravenes his social and family rules. In this shocking encounter the Duke verbally assaults his sister; with stage business centred on the phallic poniard, he may well symbolically rape her. He has certainly robbed the Duchess of all hope of a reconciliation; seeing his intransigence, she has no option but to flee to safety.

Although the Duchess denies that she has tried to establish

Any new world, or custom (III.ii.111), in Ferdinand's eyes she has broken with the past; probably the audience, along with Cariola, will think so as well. Whereas Ferdinand defines himself in relation to his dynasty, she has sought self-definition through love and fertility; Webster makes sure that the audience appreciates her life-giving role as mother.

Confronting her in prison, Ferdinand emphasizes the isolation she must now face as no *friend* will be able to *aid* her (IV.i.49–51); ironically this will mirror his own later situation. In punishing the Duchess as a criminal in the first two scenes of Act IV, he is absurdly trying to protect his family interests. As revealed by his anguished words *Damn her! That body of hers,/ While that my blood ran pure in't, was more worth/ Than that which thou wouldst comfort, called a soul* (IV.i.121–3), she has contaminated his blood as well as her own. Ritual purgation by torture and death is the only way to correct this. Of course, he is not involved in this directly; that would be to reveal too much of himself. Instead Bosola acts as his agent, while presumably Ferdinand watches in secret. But on her death, perhaps seeing himself in his sister, he gains no triumph: *What was the meanness of her match to me?* (IV.ii.288). Ferdinand faces a problem which he cannot resolve; after the Duchess's death he is totally alone, excluded from any comfort. He increasingly withdraws, and tries to strangle his own shadow. Webster perhaps reveals some of the truth about his situation when Malateste asks: *Why doth your lordship love this solitariness?* Ferdinand's reply is telling: *Eagles commonly fly alone* (V.ii.30–1); his family line is now extinguished, and he is in a social group of just one.

While Ferdinand perhaps fights a rearguard action to protect his archaic heritage rights, new men are rising amid the breakdown of social boundaries evident in both London and Malfi. Antonio is the self-made man who has achieved his ambition by being recognized by the Duchess. But class-consciousness is powerful even in Antonio's mind, and he immediately creates his own hierarchy, mocking Bosola: *Saucy slave! I'll pull thee up by the roots* (II.iii.36). Bosola, equally intelligent but less fortunate in his patron, is also quick to resort to sneers about class; when Antonio refuses to comply with Ferdinand's invitation, Bosola retorts: *This proclaims your breeding* (III.v.52). Perhaps in his conversation designed to discover the identity of the Duchess's husband, Bosola speaks at least partial truth in saying: *Can this ambitious age/ Have so much goodness in't, as to prefer/ A man merely for worth...?* (III.ii.280–2). This is the ideal, but it would seem that Malfi is not yet ready for this.

New thinking about the play which has developed in the past 30 years shows the influence of the theories of Karl Marx and Bertold Brecht; they believed that the absolute power of rulers as individuals or a body necessarily led to social injustice for those at the lower end of the social structure. To Marx, social relationships were determined by economics, and employees were regarded by those above them in the hierarchy simply as a means of generating wealth. Seen in this light, Bosola is particularly vulnerable as an employee of the corrupt Duke. His work dehumanizes him; to compensate for this, Bosola takes pleasure in the ingenuity of his mind in a bid to ennoble his sordid enterprises. He describes the trick with the apricots as *pretty* (II.i.78), but he is full of self-loathing (*O, this base quality/ Of intelligencer!*, III.ii.331–2), and he weeps on the Duchess's death (IV.ii.367). Ferdinand has not appreciated Bosola's dedication, his *sweet and golden dream* (IV.ii.330) of being rewarded for his skill and loyalty. He has been entrapped in the despised role imposed upon him. At this stage, society does not work at any level; perhaps with the old aristocracy finished, and with the Duchess's son as ruler, merit will begin to be rewarded.

Feminist interpretations

The Duchess, seen by some commentators as subversive and innovative, is much discussed in feminist criticism, such as that of Mary Beth Rose, Kathleen McLuskie and Theodora A. Jankowski (see 'Critical Views', page 220). The brothers see that she is potentially dangerous to their interests if they cannot control her desire for remarriage; in fact, her situation is explosive as a young widow and an independent and intelligent woman. She is also a prince, responsible for the well-being of her subjects and a fellow ruler with her brothers. Webster shows two types of rule in the opening act; there is the corrupt rule of the brothers, set against the spiritual presence of the ideal ruler, the King of France; the Duchess is framed against these alternatives. The varied and perhaps competing aspects of her personality are made clear at the start of the play; she is introduced as *the right noble duchess* (I.i.199), then shown in a heated discussion with her brothers, and finally tender but determined in her wooing of Antonio. In other words, she is caught up in the conflicting aspects of her life, as prince amid the demands of the body politic, and as woman, amid the demands of the body sexual and maternal.

The Duchess will not conform to the social norm and she may be seen as an innovator, who *lights the time to come* (I.i.221), seeking personal development through a loving marriage with a virtuous partner rather than in a dynastic match confirming social status. She elevates natural law as superior to the social law represented through her brothers, so she uses ceremony rather than ecclesiastical confirmation to validate her marriage. The Duchess therefore internalizes the idea of self-worth into a private realm far removed from the public arena, and as such it is inaccessible to her brothers. She blows away social stereotypes, taking the masculine role in wooing: *The misery of us that are born great:/ We are forced to woo* (I.i.452–3); there is no gender distinction here. She is direct in her sexuality: *and like a widow/ I use but half a blush in't* (I.i.469–70); and as the audience learns, *She's an excellent/ Feeder of pedigrees* (III.i.5–6) – her fruitful marriage may be taken as fulfilling the divine purposes of matrimony.

Her marriage is unconventional in a patriarchal society, but so is Antonio's response. She rules her dukedom by day, an implication that she is not negligent, and as Antonio admits: *Indeed, my rule is only in the night* (III.ii.8); he recognizes and accepts the nature of their contract. This leads to a sympathetic view of Antonio, in contrast to all the criticism of his 'weakness'; he accepts subservience to his wife as ruler by choice, in a marriage which proves his worth. Their sexuality is a cause for pleasure and openness, and Antonio takes charge of this area in what seems a well-balanced marriage. The Duchess is seen to be a normal healthy woman with her resentment of greying hair (III.ii.59) and of getting fat when pregnant (I.ii.118), and in the fact that she produces three children.

On the other hand, the Duchess may be seen as profane in her parody of church ceremony: *What can the church force more?* (I.i.499), and when she orders Antonio to *Kneel* (I.i.486) for the marriage ritual. She prays *Bless, heaven, this sacred Gordian* (I.i.491), but it is not made clear that any church ceremony follows. Is she guilty of *hubris*, in trying to usurp the role of God through his Church? Or is the simple explanation that she knows her brothers and their views too well to be able to act openly?

A second criticism of the Duchess may be that she ignores her subjects as she manoeuvres to achieve safety with Antonio. Antonio acknowledges that *The common rabble do directly say/ She is a strumpet* (III.i.25–6). In contrast to this, the pilgrims suggest some sympathy:

> who would have thought
> So great a lady would have matched herself
> Unto so mean a person? Yet the Cardinal
> Bears himself much too cruel.   (III.iv.24–7)

There is no sign of changed attitudes about the social order here. She may be accused of some dishonesty when she assures Ferdinand that she had no wish to establish *Any new world, or custom* (III.ii.111); but on the other hand, she has acted to avoid confrontation, apparently believing at first that *time will easily/ Scatter the tempest* (I.i.482–3).

However, she has caused a shift in cultural values as her transgression of class rules by marriage marks the beginning of new social norms. The movement of the drama follows a clash in values between the representatives of the old order, Ferdinand and the Cardinal, and the Duchess with her new order which seems to be supported by Antonio, Delio and Pescara, and later, significantly, by Bosola. Perhaps the greatest difference between the sister and her brothers is that the Duchess's behaviour is ennobling and empowering; Ferdinand and the Cardinal ruin and destroy those within their power.

Throughout the play she resists the vicious attacks made by her brothers or through their agency. In the confrontations of III.ii and IV.i with Ferdinand she stands by her values of love and marriage: *You violate a sacrament o'th' church* (IV.i.39). The two incidents which clearly reveal her values are in her discussion with Bosola in III.ii and the final scenes of her torture and death. In the first, Webster complicates matters by having Bosola point up her values: *That some preferment in the world can yet/ Arise from merit* (III.ii.289–90); Bosola is also used to suggest her role as prophet and leader in his reference to the poorer *virgins of your land* who can hope for better marriages because of her example. She is therefore proposed as a role model. But why is Bosola the spokesman for this view? Perhaps because the audience respects his judgement; perhaps because his words suggest his own yearnings; perhaps also because the Duchess is not objective enough to assess the effects of her actions, and Antonio has declined too much in our esteem for such a noble role.

The scenes of her torture and death make the Duchess's values extremely clear as she shows her nobility and integrity (see page 161). She finally triumphs in the full complexity of her character; as prince: *I am Duchess of Malfi still* (IV.ii.147); as a woman: *I would fain put off my last woman's fault* (IV.ii.232); most pitifully as a mother, when she requests for her *little boy/ Some syrup for his cold* and that someone cares for her girl (IV.ii.209–11). Her language is colloquial and informal as she pleads for her children to be looked after. Finally, she is seen as a wife, asking for Antonio (IV.ii.356). She has become one of the great tragic heroines, and Webster makes sure she is viewed in this light.

Finally, there is a distinction to be made between her

personal role as wife and mother seeking self-fulfilment through marriage, and her social role as prophet and martyr – the representative of a new set of values who must not be simplified or made over-familiar by being given an informal, personal name. She is always the Duchess, a symbol of the end of one era, and the beginning of another.

The ending of the play

You will make your own judgements by carefully assessing the implications of the end of the play. In the discussion of 'Imagery' (page 184), a positive ending was offered in which the sun, representing the Duchess's heavenly light, is seen to triumph over the darkness of the brothers. Virtue banishes evil. However, it is uncertain whether the victory can last; the images of sun, snow and frost suggest natural cycles. Is the success ephemeral, as subject to change as the seasons, just as human beings themselves are subject to change?

The dramatic situation leaves a young child to hold centre stage amid a pile of bodies. How strong are the representatives of goodness, in the forms of Delio and Pescara? Critics debate the significance of Webster's reference to the Duchess's son by her first marriage, when Ferdinand instructs Bosola: *Write to the Duke of Malfi, my young nephew/ She had by her first husband, and acquaint him/ With's mother's honesty* (III.iii.70–2). What is the audience to make of this? Some commentators suggest that it is an error on Webster's part that he forgot to remove; others that it is a deliberate suggestion of further dynastic conflict. Is the rule of the young son secure, or will the cycle seen in the play start all over again? Ferdinand refers to the first son as *Duke* and as *my nephew*. Does Webster suggest that the bloodline might resurrect itself and challenge the Duchess's new order?

William Empson (see 'Critical Views', page 220), suggests, playfully or not, that this is not a difficulty. Because the title belongs to the Duchess's family, the line passes through her; on her death the town council, of which Delio and Pescara would have been notable members, are free to nominate her successor. Other commentators claim that this idea flies in the face of primogeniture, the unbreakable rule of inheritance which determines the succession of noble families, and which prescribes that the first male child has to be heir.

There is also the matter of the child's horoscope in II.iii.56ff, which forecasts a *short life* and a *violent death*; what do you make of this? Remember *caetera non scrutantur* (II.iii.65); we have not seen the whole horoscope. Perhaps the drops of Antonio's blood might suggest that he will be the sacrifice instead of his son, after a short marriage? Is it intended to undermine any sense of security at the end of the play? Perhaps this question is irrelevant, for Webster has simply planted a doubt in the audience's mind. At best, all that can be claimed is that at the end of the play there is a genuine wish for reform, and conditions have been laid down to achieve this. Perhaps all will end happily, but who can be sure? In Webster's world of checks and balances there are few certainties.

Activity

Some critics claim that Webster is more interested in presenting sin and damnation than virtue and redemption. How do you respond to this idea?

Discussion

Overall, Webster probably does give more stage time to the presentation of sin and damnation, because the sight of wicked characters committing evil deeds makes drama more exciting than that of good characters being happy! The progress of the play follows the Duchess as she responds to and tries to escape from the wicked plans of her devilish brothers, up to the point where, cornered, she turns and faces them, overcoming her tormentors. At this point, IV.i and IV.ii, the presentation of goodness and virtue itself becomes very dramatic; the scenes of goodness triumphing over evil form the spiritual heart of the play.

However, it should be remembered that Webster has compassion even for the villains, who become victims in the end. In successful productions some sympathy should be created for Ferdinand in his intense suffering; and as we have seen, in dynastic terms there may be some limited justifications for his behaviour. Perhaps Ferdinand truly does not know his own motives (I.i.269 and III.i.83). The Cardinal is shocked at his brother's madness: *Are you stark mad?* (II.v.68); the Duke seems to have no control over his emotions, saying to his sister *I will never see thee more* (III.ii.142), yet forced to return. In his lycanthropy Ferdinand is pitiful, digging up graves, carrying human limbs on his shoulder, wearing a hair shirt (V.ii.8ff). He is well past any form of penitence. Is it really meant to be a comic moment when Webster presents the image of Ferdinand driving six snails to Moscow (V.ii.49–53)? Perhaps Webster suggests compassionately that everyone has a need for grace, and that the mere wish for change which marks the end of the play suggests that its effects may have been felt – a little.

What do you consider to be the most dramatic moments in the play? Is there any evidence that Webster shows bias towards certain characters? Do you think that the logic of the play suggests that we are all damned, or is there any presentation of a redemptive scheme?

Theatrical interpretations

The Duchess of Malfi is seldom out of production, and when you see a performance of the play you will understand why this is; it is riveting on stage, moving and terrifying. But remember that when you watch a production of the play you are seeing an interpretation made by the director, which will have some sort of bias. There may be cuts, with some scenes lost. These often include the entire Cardinal/Julia subplot; the dumb-show of the Cardinal's arming, III.iv; exchanges between Bosola and Castruccio at the beginning of II.i.; exchanges between the officers in II.ii.34ff; and exchanges between the courtiers at the beginning of III.iii.

Even the smallest cuts affect the overall reading of the play. The subplot matters in many ways: Julia is a complex foil to the Duchess, illuminating the question of female independence, resourcefulness and courage, as well as contrasting in moral status. The Cardinal's cruelty and immorality is made evident, and crucially he oversteps himself here with Bosola, bringing about his own death. Bosola is shown in a favourable light.

Activity

Consider the effects on a performance of the play of losing the dumb-show in Act III Scene iv.

Discussion

You might think about what Webster suggests about the power of Church and state, and the situation of the Duchess. Also consider the effects of the pilgrims' comments; what might they suggest about injustice (III.iv.28–39)? In front of the shrine the Cardinal tears his sister's ring from her finger (III.iv.36–7); what might Webster suggest here? When does the ring next appear, and what does this suggest? How does this image link situations together?

The conversation between Bosola and the old man Castruccio comically underlines the themes of flattery and ambition in the old man's desire to be *an eminent courtier* (II.i.1–2). It directly follows on from the previous scene, with Antonio's concerns about ambition.

After the supposed robbery of II.i, the officers act as chorus figures offering another perspective on Antonio; the audience will recall that he was indeed in appearance and manner a French nobleman at the start of the play (I.i.3). There is again a comic counterpoising, a reduction to grotesque terms of the relationship between Antonio and the Duchess. Similarly the conversation between the courtiers in III.iii, up to the arrival of Bosola in line 35, has a choric function. Malateste's bad character is revealed, a reminder that Ferdinand was willing to sacrifice his sister to this coward. Importantly, Webster gives us an opportunity to hear more of Pescara's good qualities, as a prelude to his crucial role in presenting the heir at the end of the play.

With the exception of the dumb-show, all these extracts help provide the comic element in the tragicomedy genre of *The Duchess of Malfi* as they parody the serious issues revealed through more 'noble' characters. To cut them creates an imbalance in the genre of the play; the satirical elements are reduced to Bosola's railing and black humour, and possibly the excess of slaughter in Act V.

There have been many notable productions and performances of this great play establishing a coherent reading of character and text. Actors often begin rehearsals with improvisations to help them get inside a character's head; it might be helpful to try out such an exercise yourself as you will probably gain some insight into the motivations of the various characters.

The Duchess (Imogen Stubbs) in the West Yorkshire Playhouse production 2006

Antonio (James Albrecht) in the West Yorkshire Playhouse production 2006

Activity

Try a short improvisation exercise based on the childhood of the Duchess and her brothers. Perhaps work in small groups, with three people acting out a short scene. Devise a script based on the characteristics you have seen during the play. Here is an example of a scenario you could use.

The children are in their playroom, the little Duchess and her twin Ferdinand are about three or four years old, the little Cardinal about five or six. One of the royal household brings in a new pet, a puppy, which she passes to the Duchess, who walks back to her brothers cuddling and kissing the puppy. All want it, of course. Write a short scene between five and ten minutes long showing what might happen next, based on the characteristics you have observed in the play.

Discussion

What will you decide about group dynamics? How do you think strategies will develop? Will the twins side with each other? Or might the boys? Will the future Cardinal win out by his cunning? Who will give up the struggle first? You will look afresh at the characters after this role-play, and you will realize how interpretations of a character may be adjusted, and why no two readings are ever the same.

Notable productions

The variety of readings of the Duchess herself suggests the ambiguity, versatility and universality of Webster's character. Settings for productions have included Nazi Germany, and Italy under both fascist and Mafia rule.

1850 At Sadler's Well's, Samuel Phelps directed *The Duchess of Malfi*, with the play adapted by R.H. Horne.

1852 At Opera Comique, William Poel directed the play very much along the lines of the Phelps/Horne production which simplified Bosola, made the Duchess a simple, faithful martyr, rewrote many parts of the text and made much of the tortures and horrors of the fourth and fifth acts.

1945 At the Haymarket Theatre, Dame Peggy Ashcroft played the Duchess, John Gielgud took the role of Ferdinand, while Cecil Trouncer stole the show as Bosola. Just as the play opened, the horrors of the Nazi concentration camps at Belsen and Buchenwald were revealed to a horrified world; so the play, with Bosola's cynical views on mankind, was extremely relevant to the times.

1946 In New York, Elizabeth Bergner played the Duchess. This over-the-top production failed, unsurprisingly, as slaughtered children fell out of a big cupboard, and Bosola, played by the black actor Canada Lee, invited laughter with the pink make-up imposed on him.

1960 At Aldwych; the Royal Shakespeare Company reprised the 1945 production with Patrick Wymark as Bosola; some critics felt that Peggy Ashcroft was a little too genteel, and Wymark did not communicate the full range of suffering and intelligence of the part.

1964 27 April, ITV Granada presented an adaptation of the play by Kingsley Amis, set on a Caribbean island, with racism between the rich white landowners and the native black population replacing the code of honour.

1967 At the Pitlochry Festival, Scotland, Brian Shelton directed a play in the style of Brechtian alienation. The dumb-show was powerful, the dance of the madmen highly choreographed. The non-realistic performance distanced the audience, making for a thoughtful response.

1971 At Stratford, for the Royal Shakespeare Company, Judi Dench was praised for her psychologically convincing and moving performance.

1972 A BBC production directed by James McTaggart starred Eileen Atkins; you might be able to borrow a recording of this production from a library.

1980 At the Royal Exchange Theatre, Helen Mirren played the Duchess, Bob Hoskins was Bosola, and Mike Gwilym was a mad and cruel Ferdinand. In an attempt at realism the dumb-show was cut, weakening the balance of the play; Hoskins was a strong cockney rebel, but did not reflect the intellectual and emotional qualities of Bosola. Helen Mirren displayed great sexuality so that the audience felt like voyeurs, rather as Ferdinand himself might have done in Acts III and IV.

1985 The National Theatre offered a cutting-edge production, led by Sir Ian McKellen. Perhaps Eleanor Bron missed the vulnerability of the Duchess; this ironic production, dressing the heir as a miniature Ferdinand, gave a cyclical reading of the text.

1989 The Royal Shakespeare Company's production cast Harriet Walter as the Duchess, and she did radiate both sexuality and grandeur, although perhaps she was too perfect.

1999 The Cheek-by-Jowl company, directed by Declan Donellan, set the play in a decadent Italy ruled by the dictator Mussolini, on a darkened stage surrounded by a chessboard set, which suggested Webster's carefully controlled structure and the constant battle of wits portrayed on stage. Anastasia Hille portrayed a tough, chain-smoking Duchess, like her brothers tainted by her noble upbringing. She was not saintly, but fiery, sexy and imperious.

2006 At the West Yorkshire Playhouse, Imogen Stubbs created a vulnerable and affectionate Duchess. Director Philip Franks, designer Leslie Travers and lighting designer Charles Balfour cleverly staged the imprisonment scenes; the quartered backdrop revealed Ferdinand as a silent observer to the tortures. A bath was visible and the red coals of a stove glowed on the darkened stage: the presence of water as well as fire suggested the purification process happening on stage.

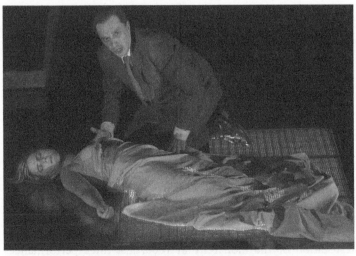

The Duchess (Imogen Stubbs) and Bosola (Sebastian Harcombe) in the West Yorkshire Playhouse production 2006

The Cardinal (Guy Williams) and Julia (Melanie Jessop) in the West Yorkshire Playhouse production 2006

Critical views

Although Webster's contemporary Henry Fitzjeffrey dubbed him 'crabbed Websterio' (*Notes from Blackfriars, Satyres and Satyricall Epigrams*, 1617), evidence suggests that this is unjust. He was known to be meticulous and slow in his writing, but must have maintained cordial relations with his fellow writers in Philip Henslowe's group to have collaborated for so long. Also the warm Commendatory Verses for *The Duchess of Malfi*, written by talented dramatists Middleton, Rowley and Ford, suggest respect.

The Duchess of Malfi remained popular until the closing of the theatres under the Commonwealth of 1649. After the restoration of the monarchy in 1660, just three performances were noted, but in 1691 the play was performed with the best actors of the period. After this the play faded from view.

In 1735 Lewis Theobald published a play, *The Fatal Secret*, which was a re-writing of *The Duchess of Malfi* suited to the eighteenth century's demand for order and symmetry. The resultant parody was bad; Bosola, for example, became wholly virtuous and did not actually kill the Duchess. In Samuel Phelps's production of 1850 the contexts of Webster's play were trimmed down to become merely court life; the madmen's noises became the Duchess's screams; but worst of all, the poetry was omitted. However, this production returned the play to the critical forum; writers such as Algernon Swinburne, Rupert Brooke, Charles Lamb and T.S. Eliot appreciated the sublime poetry and the Shakespeare-like mix of Webster's styles. In contrast, other critics such as William Archer disapproved because there was no 'rational' structure, and George Bernard Shaw dismissed Webster as the 'Tussaud laureate', a reference to the 'chamber of horrors' in the first two scenes of Act IV. Charles Kingsley thought the play was 'licentious' and undermined Victorian moral principles.

The Duchess of Malfi gained a dreadful relevance after the First World War with the horrors of Passchendaele and the Somme which, in revealing the evils that human beings could inflict on one another, shook the Victorian moral and cultural inheritance. Critics such as J.A. Symonds, Vernon Lee and F.L. Lucas, noting this relevance, viewed the drama as a history play. Further grim immediacy was reinforced after the Second World War when the Holocaust was revealed to the world.

With the writings of T.S. Eliot and David Cecil, the landscape of the play came to be seen as the internal landscape of the human mind, and the writings of Sigmund Freud and Karl Marx changed perceptions of the play for ever.

T.S. Eliot's early essays, between 1924 and 1932, presented Webster as a great genius of literature and drama, but believing that the structure was in 'chaos', Eliot called Webster's art 'impure' with its mix of conventions and styles. M.C. Bradbrook, with her *Themes and Conventions of Elizabethan Drama* (1935, reprinted up to 1969), developed the debate.

Although the views seem dated now because of the conventionally Christian reading in which the Duchess is presented as a penitent sinner finally redeemed into salvation, this was another important milestone in re-acclaiming the greatness of Webster, who is now generally considered to be second only to Shakespeare as a dramatist of this period.

There are several anthologies containing important essays, which will interest a student new to the works of Webster (see also 'Further Reading', pages 227–228). *John Webster* (eds. G.K. and S.K. Hunter) features important contributions from Inga-Stina Ekeblad on the significance of the masque of madmen in IV.ii; Hereward T. Price's study of the imagery; G.K. Hunter's study of Italy as moral landscape; and William Empson's important piece on Webster, which is also reprinted in *William Empson: Essays in Renaissance Literature*, ed. John Haffenden. Similarly, *John Webster* (ed. Brian Morris) has notable essays such as Elizabeth Brennan's on the reception of the play and genre, Roger Warren's assessment of theatricality and stage effects, I.E. Ewbank's essay on perspective and realism, and J.R. Mulryne's study of genre.

These essays offer a range of topics, and you will notice the different contexts of post-1980 criticism, which consider issues such as gender and sexuality, Marxist and Freudian readings, and interesting studies of the text as a political drama. These are evident in *The Duchess of Malfi* edited by Dympna Callaghan, New Casebooks, 2000. Topics hitherto ignored by critics are discussed here, such as the consideration of women in general Jacobean culture; there is Theodora A. Jankowski's study of the Duchess as woman/sovereign in her marriage; Kathleen McLuskie's essay on drama and sexual politics; and Mary Beth Rose's ideas on the 'heroics of marriage'. Notably, Callaghan includes Frank Whigham's important essay (see page 201).

There are many critical books which will interest students. For those interested in biography, there is M.C. Bradbrook's *John Webster: Citizen and Dramatist*; for readers interested in feminist issues there is Lisa Jardine's *Still Harping on Daughters: Women and Drama in the Age of Shakespeare*; Christopher Ricks's contribution to *English Drama to 1710* compares Webster to Shakespeare in an incisive essay. Travis Bogard's *The Tragic Satire of John Webster* offers a modern take on morality, and Kate Aughton's *Webster: The Tragedies* is a helpful book at the right level for new students, with some excellent examples of language analysis. David Gunby's *Introductions* to the Cambridge edition are very valuable and wide-ranging considerations of issues related to the text, theatre and sources.

For readers interested in genre, there are two useful books: one by Lee Bliss, *The World's Perspective: John Webster and the Jacobean Drama*, and Christina Luckyj's important book *A Winter's Snake: Dramatic Form in the Tragedies of John Webster*, in which she argues for the centrality to the play of repetition in a concentric structure as part of the Gothic multiplicity of the text. Structure is also considered in Ralph Berry's *The Art of John Webster*, Jacqueline Pearson's *Tragedy and Tragicomedy in the Plays of John Webster*, T.S. Eliot's *Essays on Elizabethan Drama*, and Charles Forker's important four-volume text, *The Skull Beneath the Skin: The Achievement of John Webster*, in which he looks at the plays as studies of chaos and lost identity, issues which lie at the heart of tragedy.

Finally, there are texts in which the writers concern themselves with the political, historical and social context, such as Dana Goldberg's important study of the Jacobean rise of individualism and social order, *Between Worlds: A Study of the Plays of John Webster*, and J.W. Lever's *The Tragedy of State: A Study of Jacobean Drama*, which is ideal for students.

Essay Questions

1 Read the following poem, then answer the question below:

> Webster was much possessed by death
> And saw the skull beneath the skin;
> And breastless creatures under ground
> Leaned backward with a lipless grin.
>
> Daffodil bulbs instead of balls
> Stared from the sockets of the eyes!
> He knew that thought clings round dead limbs
> Tightening its lusts and luxuries.

(T.S. Eliot, *Whispers of Immortality*, from *Poems*, 1919)

What points do you think T.S. Eliot is making here? How do you think these ideas relate to *The Duchess of Malfi*?

2 Compare and contrast the motivation of Ferdinand and the Cardinal.

3 'He is more sinned against than sinning.' How do you respond to this comment about Bosola?

4 Explore the function of imagery in *The Duchess of Malfi*.

5 How does the Julia/Cardinal subplot help to develop Webster's ideas?

6 Consider the significance of the following words in *The Duchess of Malfi*: 'politic', 'service' and 'preferment'.

7 Do you think that the Duchess is a revolutionary, or does she simply want the best of two worlds?

8 Explore the ways in which Webster uses Antonio to present the theme of ambition.

9 Explore the ways in which Webster presents the theme of confinement in *The Duchess of Malfi*. What is its significance in the play?

10 Do you think that Bosola's 'foul melancholy' has poisoned his 'goodness'? How do you respond to Bosola at the end of the play?

11 Discuss Webster's stagecraft in *The Duchess of Malfi*.

12 'The violence of the action suggests the moral corruption of society in *The Duchess of Malfi*.' How far do you agree with this comment?

13 Consider the effects of the Duchess's death in *The Duchess of Malfi*.

14 Analyse Antonio's role, and the ways in which he is presented in *The Duchess of Malfi*.

15 Consider the ways in which Webster distances the audience in *The Duchess of Malfi*, and analyse the effects of this distancing.

16 Explore the ways in which Webster creates suspense and tension in *The Duchess of Malfi*.

17 Explore the significance of images of poison, disease and painting in *The Duchess of Malfi*.

18 How does Webster avoid anti-climax in his presentation of the last act of the play?

19 Explore the ways in which Webster presents Ferdinand, the Cardinal and Bosola as revengers. Then go on to consider what Webster has to say about revenge.

20 Why is *The Duchess of Malfi* still relevant and popular today?

21 Consider the ways in which Webster presents the difficulties faced by the Duchess in her choice of husband.

22 What does Webster have to say about religion, and how does he present these views?

23 How far do you think Webster is interested in social change, and how does he present these ideas?

24 By close analysis of two scenes from *The Duchess of Malfi*, explore the ways in which Webster creates tension.

25 With close analysis of two or three speeches from *The Duchess of Malfi*, explore the language effects Webster creates.

26 Would it be accurate to claim that while Antonio forfeits the audience's respect, Bosola gains it?

27 How does Webster create the idea of war, and what are its effects in *The Duchess of Malfi*?

28 To what extent might *The Duchess of Malfi* be seen as a satire on contemporary London society? Go on to consider how Webster presents these ideas.

29 How does Act III Scene ii relate to the rest of *The Duchess of Malfi*?

30 'A great political drama.' How far do you agree with this reading of *The Duchess of Malfi*?

Chronology

Webster's life

c. 1550   John Webster senior born.

1571   John Webster senior made Freeman of Merchant Taylors Company.

1578/9   John Webster born.

1602   Webster receives an advance from Philip Henslowe as part of a group of writers.

1604   Webster revises John Marston's *The Malcontent* for the King's Men.

1604/5   Webster works with Thomas Dekker on *Westward Ho* and *Northward Ho.*

1606   Webster marries Sara Peniall, aged 17, and seven months pregnant.

1612   *The White Devil* performed unsuccessfully at the Red Bull.

1614   *The Duchess of Malfi* acted successfully at the Blackfriars and the Globe by the King's Men.

1615   Webster claims his right of entry to the Merchant Taylors Company.

1618   Orazio Businio, the Venetian envoy, notes the hostility of *The Duchess of Malfi* to the Catholic Church.

      Webster writes *The Devil's Law-Case*, performed by the Queen's Men at the Cockpit.

1623   *The Duchess of Malfi* and *The Devil's Law-Case* published in quarto.

1624   Webster writes the pageant *Monuments of Honour* for the Merchant Taylors Company.

c. 1634   Webster dies aged about 56.

Historical, literary and social events

1547	Henry VIII dies; accession of Edward VI.
1553	Edward VI dies; accession of Mary I.
1558	Mary I dies; accession of Elizabeth I.
1564	Christopher Marlowe, William Shakespeare born.
1572	Thomas Dekker, Ben Jonson born.
1575	Thomas Heywood, John Marston, Cyril Tourneur born.
1576	'The Theatre' built, the first in London.
1579	John Fletcher born.
1580	Thomas Middleton born.
1586	John Ford born.
1587	Thomas Kyd's *The Spanish Tragedy* acted.
1588	Spanish Armada defeated.
1588/9	Marlowe's *Dr Faustus* probably acted.
1603	Elizabeth I dies; accession of James I (James VI of Scotland).
	Shakespeare's *Hamlet* acted; Raleigh/Cobham rebellion.
1604	Marston's *The Malcontent* acted.
1605	The Gunpowder Plot.
1606	Tourneur's *The Revenger's Tragedy* acted.
1611	The Authorized Version of the Bible (King James Bible) published.
1621	Middleton's *Women Beware Women* acted.
1622	Middleton's *The Changeling* acted.
1625	James I dies; accession of Charles I.
c.1634	Webster dies; Ford's *Tis Pity She's a Whore* acted.
1642	Civil war; the closing of the theatres.
1649	Charles I executed; Commonwealth.
1660	Restoration of Charles II; theatres reopened.
1665	The Great Plague.
1666	The Great Fire of London.

Further Reading

Biography

Muriel C. Bradbrook, *John Webster, Citizen and Dramatist* (Weidenfeld and Nicholson, 1980; Columbia University Press, 1980)

Philip Henslowe, *Diary*, eds. R.A. Foakes and R.J. Rickett (Cambridge University Press, 1968)

Critical books

Kate Aughton, *Webster: The Tragedies* (Palgrave, 2001)

Catherine Belsey, *The Subject of Tragedy: Identity and Difference in Renaissance Drama* (Methuen, 1985)

Ralph Berry, *The Art of John Webster* (Clarendon Press, 1972)

Lee Bliss, *The World's Perspective: John Webster and the Jacobean Drama* (Harvester Press, 1989)

Travis Bogard, *The Tragic Satire of John Webster* (University of California Press, 1955)

Dympna Callaghan (ed.), *The Duchess of Malfi* (New Casebooks, Palgrave Macmillan, 2000)

T.S. Eliot, *Essays on Elizabethan Drama* (Haskell House, 1964)

Charles Forker, *The Skull Beneath the Skin: The Achievement of John Webster* (Southern Illinois University Press, 1986)

Dena Goldberg, *Between Worlds: A Study of the Plays of John Webster* (Wilfrid Laurier University Press, 1987)

David Gunby, David Carnegie and Anthony Hammond (eds.), *Introductions to The Duchess of Malfi, The Works of John Webster,* Vol. 1 (Cambridge University Press, 1995)

John Haffenden (ed.), *William Empson: Essays in Renaissance Literature,* Vol. 2: *The Drama* (Cambridge University Press, 1994)

Lisa Jardine, *Still Harping on Daughters: Women and Drama in the Age of Shakespeare* (Harvester Wheatsheaf, 1983)

G.K. and S.K. Hunter, *John Webster* (Penguin Critical Anthologies, 1969)

J.W. Lever, *The Tragedy of State: A Study of Jacobean Drama* (New York, 1987)

Christina Luckyj, *A Winter's Snake: Dramatic Form in the Tragedies of John Webster* (University of Georgia Press, 1989)

Brian Morris (ed.), *John Webster* (Mermaid Critical Commentaries, 1972)

Jacqueline Pearson, *Tragedy and Tragicomedy in the Plays of John Webster* (Barnes and Noble, 1980)

Christopher Ricks (ed.), *English Drama to 1710, Sphere History of Literature in the English Language*, Vol. 3 (Cresset Press, 1971)

Mary Beth Rose, *The Expense of Spirit: Love and Sexuality in English Renaissance Drama* (Cornell University Press, 1988)

Video

The Duchess of Malfi, BBC production directed by James McTaggart, with Eileen Atkinson, 1972

Websites

For further critical perspectives on performances and productions go to the websites of individual theatres or actors.

Glossary

alienation an effect achieved by preventing the audience from suspending their disbelief, and instead making them think about the issues presented on stage, as in the case of Ferdinand's fable on reputation

allegory an extended metaphor, usually a description or a narrative which works simultaneously on two levels; for example, the Duchess is tortured in a prison, but this becomes a vision of hell

alliteration a sequence of words which begin with the same consonant, as in Ferdinand's words at III.ii.71–3, with the repeated 'd' sound

ambiguity a condition where there are two or more meanings to words or ideas, as in the ending of *The Duchess of Malfi*, where it is uncertain whether there is a hopeful ending

anaphora the deliberate repetition of words, as in the Duchess's repetition of *mad*, IV.ii.24–6

antithesis a contrast of ideas or characters, as in the comparison between the Duchess and her brothers

aphorism the concise expression of a generally accepted truth, as in the *sententiae* (see *sententiae*)

archetype the prototype or original model, for example Ferdinand is the archetype of the tyrant

assonance a similarity or identity between the stressed vowels of two or more words, for example, the repetition of the 'e' sound in Antonio's words at I.i.493–4

aural something which has or presents the quality of being heard, as in the poetry of Webster's play which creates linked impressions in the audience's minds, for example in Antonio's descriptions of the main characters (I.i)

bathos a movement from the sublime to the ridiculous, as in the satire on Malateste at battle in III.iii.9ff

Bertold Brecht a German playwright and poet (1898–1956) who rejected the need for realism or sustained structure in his plays, which were anti-capitalist in theme

caesura a break between words in a metrical measure, used to create effects, as in the Duchess's words at II.i.118–19

colloquialism the use of everyday language, as in Ferdinand's 'Farewell, lusty widow' (I.i.352)

conceit   a far-fetched comparison in which the reader is made to admit likeness between two things while always being aware of the oddness of the comparison, for example in the comparison of a room in a palace to hell (IV.i and IV.ii)

concentric   sharing a centre; relates to the structure of the play, as some critics believe that all of the meanings are generated from one central point, either the wooing scene of I.i or the death scene of IV.ii

dirge   a song sung at a funeral, as Bosola's dirge to the Duchess in IV.ii

distancing   see *alienation*

dramatic irony   an effect created when a reader or an audience is aware of a situation when the character in the poem/drama, by contrast, is not; this effect is evident in III.ii with Ferdinand's visit

dumb-show   a scene without words, such as the scene depicting the Cardinal arming, which is carried out in mime

enjambment   a line or stanza in poetry which runs on to the next without a break in sense or punctuation, as in many of the long speeches in the play

fable   a short story, often with animals or personified human qualities, which conveys a moral, as in Ferdinand's fable of reputation, III.ii.120; see *parable*

Fall of Man   the Christian doctrine according to which mankind lost the joys of Paradise through the original sin of pride, which led to disobedience

fascism   a form of government which becomes a dictatorship, as in Ferdinand's dukedom

feminist criticism   a school of criticism which aims to view things from a female perspective, and discusses the rights of women

genre   the type or form of literature, as in the tragic genre of *The Duchess of Malfi*

Gothic   a type of literature developed at the end of the eighteenth century, typified by Mary Shelley's *Frankenstein*, in which there are supernatural events, terror, darkness, often a medieval setting, suspense, and a female victim; compare the echo scene (V.iii)

Great Chain of Being   an Elizabethan theory of the universe which proposed that there was a divinely ordered, fixed scheme in which every person had an appointed place; this accords with Ferdinand's ideas about his own status

Greek tragedy written about 480–420 BC by writers such as
  Sophocles and Aeschylus, which sought to present man's
  relationship with the gods. Aristotle later deduced certain laws of
  drama, confirming that through pride mortals would always face
  catastrophe, and that therefore the human condition was tragic.
  Seneca developed these ideas, which were very influential on
  Jacobean dramatists such as Webster

history play a genre of drama based on historical facts; Webster's
  play was loosely based on events in Italy

hubris the 'sin' of pride, such as that which some commentators
  believe that the Duchess has to overcome in IV.ii

humours a medieval theory according to which a person's nature was
  determined by a balance between the four elements in his or her
  make-up, or 'cardinal humours': blood (a 'sanguine' nature is
  courageous, hopeful and amorous), which is related to earth, as is
  the Duchess; choler (hot temper), related to fire, as is Ferdinand;
  phlegm (coolness), related to ice, as is the Cardinal; and
  melancholy (linked to depression), related to water, as is Bosola

iambic pentameter a line with five stresses in which the pattern is an
  unstressed syllable followed by a stressed syllable; there are many
  possible variations of this system, as used in the poetry of
  Webster

imagery the use of figurative language in literature, such as similes
  and metaphors, which appeals to the readers' senses or intelligence
  and extends the significance of a word; evident in the descriptive
  language of Antonio and Bosola in I.i

irony an effect achieved when words or actions carry a meaning
  apparently opposite from that intended (see also *dramatic irony*)

Jacobean drama written during the reign of James I; the Latinized
  version of his name is *Jacobus*

lyrical having the feeling of a song or musical interlude, usually
  emotional; as in the echo scene (V.iii), which is removed from the
  horrors of Act V

Machiavellian related to the ideas of Nicola Machiavelli (1469–
  1527), an Italian ruler and politician who advocated the use of
  ruthlessness to gain and hold power. A Machiavellian person will
  lie, scheme and even murder for gain or to achieve political power,
  as Ferdinand, the Cardinal and Bosola do

Marxism theories which follow the doctrines of Karl Marx

(1818–1883), in which there is a belief that social change is driven by conflict between the classes, between the 'haves' and the 'have-nots'

metaphor a literary image in which one thing is seen to take on the characteristics of another, as when Antonio says of Bosola's melancholy that it will *poison* his goodness (I.i.78)

metre the rhythm of poetry which arises from the pattern of stresses, such as Webster's use of *iambic pentameter*

morality play a medieval play in which allegorical presentations of human qualities were presented on stage

motif a recurring and important idea in a piece of literature, such as Ferdinand's constant references to sex

natural law laws which govern the world of nature as opposed to the social laws of the world of man; the Duchess appears to adhere to natural law

new historicism a theory of criticism which recasts literature from the perspective of the history of the time in which it was written

parable a story with a spiritual or moral force, such as the fable of the salmon and the dog-fish (III.v.125–141) ; see *fable*

pathetic fallacy a device whereby an author attributes human emotions to non-human things; here, the use of nature to endorse a mood, as the storm which brews at II.iii, echoing the tensions building up, and the storm of V.iv, as the brothers perhaps prepare to enter hell

patriarchy a male-dominated society as is the world of Malfi

providential scheme a belief that human destiny has been pre-ordained by a benevolent Christian God, perhaps demonstrated when the Duchess kneels down to enter heaven

purgation making someone or something spiritually pure and clean, as do the Duchess's trials before her death

redemption the belief that Christ died on the cross to redeem mankind from original sin, so that people could achieve salvation

register words and expressions appropriate to specific circumstances, or a specific person, such as Ferdinand's constant sexual innuendos

restoration comedy a genre of comedy popular after the restoration of the monarchy (1660), much of which was concerned with frivolous situations and bawdy comedy, although moral purposes were claimed for the plays

resurrection the belief that Christ, after lying in the tomb for three days, was brought back to life in the flesh; Christians believe that their souls will be resurrected on Judgement Day

revenge play a Jacobean genre of drama centred on revenge, which began with Thomas Kyd's *The Spanish Tragedy* (1587)

sacrament an action ordained by Christ for Christians to follow in order to gain grace and achieve a place in heaven

satire a literary work in which the aim is to teach or correct by means of ridicule, as in Webster's use of Castruccio (II.i) to parody the ambition of the courtiers

secular non-religious, as in a political reading of *The Duchess of Malfi*

Seneca a Roman writer who influenced Jacobean playwrights, see *Greek tragedy*

sententiae moral sayings intended to convey a lesson; used throughout *The Duchess of Malfi* in the two-line tag near or at the end of certain long speeches, such as the Duchess's at the end of Act III (see Appendix, page 234)

stichomythia a device from Greek drama in which the speech of two or more characters is in alternating lines and often shares a line; this creates an effect of speed or urgency, as in the brothers' tirade against the Duchess in I.i

suspension of disbelief when watching a play in performance, the audience accepts the conventions of the theatre without quibbling about 'realism', and enters into the 'experience' presented by the actors on stage

symbolism attaching clear significance to a scene or thing; the dumb-show of the Cardinal's arming (III.iv) takes its validity as a symbol from the surrounding stage context – the threat of the combined power of Church and state against the Duchess

wit in literature, a clever and unusual way of expressing something, such as Julia's replies to Delio (II.iv.75–6)

Appendix

Sententiae

Webster inserts *sententiae* or moral sayings several times during *The Duchess of Malfi*. Sometimes they are used to indicate the end of a scene or of an act (the Jacobean theatres, of course, did not have curtains as the stage was an open apron). They are also used at other key points, including twice on the death of a character. The *sententiae* would help remind the audience that the play was not merely for entertainment; there were also moral purposes.

Examples are listed below.

II.iii.77–8: at the end of the scene

II.iv.82–3: at the end of a scene

III.i.92–3: at the end of a scene

III.ii.335: at the end of a scene

III.v.141 and 144 at the end of a scene/act

IV.i.110: to mark the Duchess's exit

IV.ii.149–50: to mark the end of the Duchess's phase of pride

V.v.55: as the Cardinal nears death

V.v.72–3: on Ferdinand's death

V.v.120–1: at the end of the play